"Troncoso is a master storyteller; he weaves the threads of events in a way that sometimes surprises but always engages. Readers' hearts will be touched by episodes of loss, tragedy, and love; his characters witness and reflect on much sorrow and happiness."—*Multicultural Review*

"Each (story) is an organic whole, full of characters who have lives as complete as the reader's. . . . Enthusiastically recommended."—*Booklist*

"Troncoso really shines when he writes about El Paso and the life of Mexican Americans there. He has the gift for writing from his heart outward into his reader's heart."—*Bloomsbury Review*

"What the reader will encounter is Troncoso's ability to magnify the small gestures and events of life that are packed with meaning but go unspoken because language to describe them is elusive. Fortunately, Troncoso finds the precise words to describe these events and crafts them with great care."—*Austin Chronicle*

"Troncoso has a creative passion to raise ordinary, everyday, transitory human life to its holy ground: to transform it into literature."
—*El Paso Times*

"He is capable of finding wonder and warmth and tragedy in the simplest of lives."—*Albuquerque Journal*

"A collection of memorable and historically rooted and philosophically provocative stories from that part of our state where culture continues to evolve both bright and dark—while providing us the newest stars on our literary horizons."—*Texas Observer*

"Troncoso's wistful, endearingly romantic tales vividly dramatize the inherent richness of even subsistence-level lives. He's a respecter of persons, and in turn his characters earn your affection and respect."
—*Kirkus Reviews*

T0163480

Camino del Sol

A Latina and Latino

Literary Series

The Last Tortilla

& Other Stories

SERGIO TRONCOSO

With an Introduction by Ilan Stavans

The University of Arizona Press   Tucson

The University of Arizona Press

© 1999 Sergio Troncoso

11   10   09   08   07   06   8   7   6   5   4   3

Library of Congress Cataloging-in-Publication Data

Troncoso, Sergio, 1961–

The last tortilla and other stories / Sergio Troncoso.

p.   cm.— (Camino del sol)

ISBN-13: 978-0-8165-1960-6 (acid-free, archival-quality paper)

— ISBN-10: 0-8165-1960-9

ISBN-13: 978-0-8165-1961-3 (pbk. : acid-free, archival-quality

paper) — ISBN-10: 0-8165-1961-7

1. El Paso (Texas)—Social life and customs—Fiction. 2. New
York (N.Y.)—Social life and customs—Fiction. 3. Mexican
Americans—Texas—El Paso—Fiction. I. Title. II. Series.

PS3570.R5876L37 1999   98-58155

813'.54—DC21

Publication of this book is made possible in part by the proceeds
of a permanent endowment created with the assistance of a
Challenge Grant from the National Endowment for the Humani-
ties, a federal agency.

Para Papá y Mamá

Contents

Introduction

Ilan Stavans

"You don't think the artist as near the center of things as the ordinary man, do you?" the opinionated G. K. Chesterton, who wrote detective stories and also biographies of Dickens, Browning, and Robert Louis Stevenson, was asked during an interview in 1912. To which he replied: "No, I don't. Most people consider the joys and sorrows of the working-man chaotic and comic—only fit for a music-hall sketch. To me his emotions seem more permanent, less sophisticated than those of the artist."

More permanent, less sophisticated . . . but only after the artist makes something out of them. Life, after all, is inconsequential until meaning is extracted from it; and the artist's duty is to always be in the hunt for that meaning. This, I acknowledge with pleasure, is what Sergio Troncoso does so fittingly and unglamourously in *The Last Tortilla and Other Stories:* he makes art out of ordinariness; he finds meaning in meaninglessness.

His style has the same breezy, light-handed quality one finds in Grace Paley and Raymond Carver: it is straightforward, unobtrusive, and, more important even, unexcessive. He is obviously allergic to that nefarious trend perfected by the ethnic writer that makes literature a servant of ideology. "No artist desires to prove anything," Oscar Wilde once rightly said. Troncoso doesn't hide anger behind words. His are not angry tales about segregation and social discomfort, saturated with sex, drugs, and incoherent slang. Instead, his El Paso, Texas, the theater where his dramas for the most part take place, is a "normal" town, one where Mexicans eat, sleep, fall in love, and undergo epiphanies just like everyone else.

The fact that they are Mexican is but an accident of destiny. Their odyssey is not a lesson on the uses of suffering. They are common middle-class people, unremarkable, people caught at some turning point in their lives.

All this makes Troncoso a traditionalist. He is constantly obsessed with plot. I say this without a hint of regret. Plot is no doubt the great casualty in postmodern literature. The lessons of Borges, Nabokov, and Calvino have been misunderstood to the point that novels are shaped today as mere sequences of unrelated episodes; and impressionistic snapshots, delivered in the most primitive of forms, are applauded as stories. But the unrepentant Troncoso belongs to the secret club of believers who won't give up: he knows from Chekhov—to whom Paley and Carver owe so much—that good literature, the literature that lasts, is neither about verbal pyrotechnics nor about the author as superstar; it is, and shall always be, about the everlasting themes of humankind: unworthiness, love, friendship, betrayal, and forgiveness.

Troncoso, in short, is an American writer of the oddest kind: he tells the truth. He is as near the center of things as artists are allowed to be.

She asked me if I liked them. And what
could I say? They were *wonderful.* Her
breasts were round and white and everything you'd expect from a beautiful woman.
I couldn't believe she *asked* me, as if I could
have thought otherwise. I'd never been with
someone like her before. I was terrified. But
she seemed shy and even unsure about
herself. I didn't understand that at all. What
did she see in *me?* She had of course looked
at herself. Everyone I knew had looked at
her. I heard all the comments about her,
wishful comments. But with me she was
just playful and tentative. I kissed her,
looked out the window of my mother's
Buick Regal. She pressed against me and
unzipped her skirt. *She* unzipped her skirt

Angie Luna

and laughed. My God! Did anyone do this in a car anymore? Next to an office park in the middle of the night? Only in El Paso. Jesus. It was very warm holding her. I loved holding her hips. She was soft in all the right places. Her perfume was all over me hours after I got back home. I couldn't stop thinking about her. And when we were driving back to Juárez, to the place she shared with her sisters, speeding down the Border Freeway through a gauntlet of amber lights, she was joking and her hair was all over her face and she was smothering me with kisses and I thought I was going to explode again, but I kept the Buick between the lines. Angie Luna was something out of a Revlon ad. A remarkable woman. But why did she choose me?

She told me, after we were relaxing in the back seat, that she had had sex only once before. Only once. She told me that an older man, a semi-boyfriend, had forced her to do it with him, pushed her down, taken off her clothes. She said she didn't mind too much. She said she sort of wanted to. She wanted the experience with an older man. She wanted to be ready for when she got married. Now she wasn't sure she would ever get married. Now *she* was the older one, but she didn't really act that way. She was shy, I tell you. I didn't know why, but I got angry. Maybe the East Coast did that to you. I told her not to let a man do that to her again. Ever. It wasn't as if I had been trying to score PC points to "nail" her, as they said so crudely in Amherst. We were already completely naked, both of us quite happy. I told her it was terrible what he had done to her, I told her as vehemently as I could. She was way too shy for her own good. She became embarrassed, and I backed off. I told her it really wasn't her fault. But I also told her that anybody who did that to her was a fucking macho bastard. Was I going out of my mind? Mr. Goody Goody. Where did *that* come from? That's what a college education did to you.

When I took Angie back to her house just over the Free Bridge, off 16 de Septiembre, I noticed that the streets were quiet and empty and shiny from the rain that had fallen earlier. Whenever I had gone to Juárez as a kid, with my parents for dinner, I had thought Mexico was such a crowded country. Always packed and busy. A lot of sun and too much traffic. I almost never went to Juárez at night, and I had never been to Juárez at three in the morning. There was no one around. Angie said I could meet her sisters next week. They'd already be asleep by now. Three sisters alone in Mexico. Probably all gorgeous. At the Popular, she had told me that her older sister had left Chihuahua City for la frontera about five years ago. The reason? Rocío wanted to get away from her father, who wanted her to be a nice little girl and marry one of his friends. Shit. Can you believe that? That sister left, got a green card, found a job in El Paso as a secretary with the help of a woman she met at Cielo Vista Mall. Rocío then offered to put up Angie and Marisela if they also wanted to come to Juárez, but told them they'd need to get jobs. And they did. What a life! The three sisters had all pitched in for a down payment and had just bought this little house, in a clean neighborhood. And they were still saving money. Their goals were to become American citizens, buy a house in El Paso, and learn good English. My Spanish was perfect, Angie said, except that sometimes I would screw up the counter-factual with weird concoctions. She said my parents had done a good job teaching me about my heritage. I wasn't a gringo yet, she said. She hadn't met my parents. I wasn't sure what my mother would think of Angie. Or maybe I was.

I saw Angie at the Popular on Monday again, after I had finished putting out the cotton briefs for boys, all colors, size 6 through 20. I had already dumped all the designer jeans out, for the back-to-school sales. Joe was off my back. He was somewhere in the back room yelling to a supplier who had brought in the wrong stuff.

Angie Luna

That's what you get when you don't plan your summer job: a frenetic boss who's under pressure himself and vents it on the stock boys. At least I had met Angie Luna there. That made the entire summer. In two weeks I'd go back to Massachusetts. She was coming down the escalator, from the mezzanine bookstore and music shop where she worked one of the cash registers. God, she was a vision! She was wearing a tight black dress down to her knees so it wouldn't look like too much. But still, it was enough. She had Marilyn Monroe's body, with short, jet black hair. As she rode down the escalator, she leaned slightly back on one foot, the fabric pressed against her thighs. I almost fainted.

She didn't kiss me, and I guess I didn't expect to kiss her, not in front of all the idiots in the store. It might even be a good idea just to be seen as "friends," and that's what we did. She asked me if I wanted to have dinner at her place next Saturday night, and I said that I did. I don't care what anyone else says: women in their thirties can look *great*. I was having trouble breathing. She had on her confident look, the one she pushed like a shield against all the stares from the old men in the shoe department and the hungry male managers and assistant managers. The other stock boys just winked at her and asked her out brazenly and tried to get real close to her, but she didn't bite. Up to this day, I still don't know why she asked *me* out. Maybe to her I was an oddity. Born in El Paso, but on my way out. Just as soon as I finished my B.A. in economics. As we walked to the perfume counter of Estée Lauder, she said that she wanted to see me before Saturday. I was going back to school in two weeks, right? I said that I was. She said she wanted to get to know me better, to talk about what I was studying and how it was to live up there alone, without your family. I said that maybe we could see a movie, have dinner, spend a few hours just hanging out. She liked the idea. Before she turned around and went up the escalator, she asked me if I was coming home for Christmas, and I said that I was. She smiled and winked at me and marched up the escalator. Did she know how *fantastic* she looked just walking like that? She was really way too sweet for her own good.

"Ese Victor, did you plug her, man?" the voice of Carlos Morales hissed from behind me. I turned around. The fat bastard was wearing a dirty white T-shirt, his coiffed hair almost to his shoulders.

"What?" I said. I wanted only to get away from him, so I started walking quickly toward a dumpster in a corner filled with boxes of belts, dress shirts, polo shirts, and socks. He'd run back to the employees' lounge as soon as I started unloading this shit.

"You know, man. No te hagas pendejo." He plunged his hips forward and swung his arms back in a motion more vulgar than I can ever describe, all the while grinning stupidly.

"Shut the fuck up, man. What are you talking about?"

"You went out, didn't you? I heard about it already. From Cindy in Women's Wear."

"Yeah, so what? It's none of your business."

"'It's none of your business,'" he repeated in an exaggerated, snotty whine. "What a *man* you are!"

"Shut up, cabrón. You better get your ass to work. Guess who's coming down the aisle." Joe was whizzing by the dress shirts, and he didn't look too happy. Just as Carlos was stacking four cardboard boxes up to his chest, Joe almost slid to a stop right in front of him. He didn't say a word, but wiggled his finger in the fat boy's face, and Carlos waddled after him. He glanced back at me, raised his arms in bewilderment, and pretended not to know what the hell he had done wrong this time. Damn. The whole store knew about us now. I was glad I was only going to be there for a few more days. Doña Leticia Jiménez, the soft-hearted battle-ax who really ran the whole

Angie Luna

place from her perch in Women's Lingerie—42 years of selling panties!—rushed by me as I emptied the dumpster and gave me a thumbs-up and grinned. Shit.

By Wednesday I had already dreamed of Angie Luna twice. Once on Monday, in that black dress, on the escalator. And again the next night. A more complicated dream. We were in Central Park, in the Ramble. Doing it. I hadn't ever been to Central Park! I once read about it in a magazine, however. This woman was really getting inside my head. I told my mother I was going out with some friends, and she just kissed me on the forehead and told me not to drive too fast. She said she was going to send me back to school with a box full of flautas, some cookies, and a brick of Muenster cheese and tortillas, for making quesadillas. Did I have any requests for food? They might be going shopping later. I said that I didn't. As I was cruising down the Border Freeway toward the downtown bridges, I remembered how I had never really gone to Juárez in high school, not by myself. I always heard, mostly from my parents, how you could get pulled over by a Mexican cop who'd just want a mordida. And if you didn't have enough money or didn't play it savvy enough, if you made him feel like the asshole that he was, then you might wind up in a Mexican jail and no one would know where you were for a while. Maybe you'd escape only after you tasted your own blood. So I never went alone. That is, until now. And it wasn't that bad. I'd never been stopped at all. Sure, the traffic up the bridge was a mess during rush hour or a weekend night, but you'd sit and wait until you got there, that was all. I knew where to turn, I started recognizing the main streets, Avenida Juárez, 16 de Septiembre, Avenida Lerdo. I had even been on Avenida Reforma with Angie one day, the big boulevard that takes you south, outside the city, deeper into Mexico. We went to visit one of her friends who lived in a neighborhood where all the houses were freshly painted and neat but the streets were dusty, unpaved, full of swamplike puddles big enough to swallow a pickup. I wondered if my parents had always warned me about Juárez, their own hometown, because they really thought it was dangerous, or because they thought I couldn't hack it outside of gringolandia. I knew what to do on these streets.

When I finally got to Angie's house, it was just getting dark. The desert sun was just a faint crown of orange and yellow lights peeking out from the mountains. Angie had told me to be there by eight o'clock, and I was early. If I had waited any longer at home, my little brother might have taken off with the car. Anyway, maybe I could hang around and see what her house was like. I didn't mind. Angie answered the door, wearing an apron and looking like a voluptuous version of Ozzie's Harriet. An apron over a sharp party dress. She said she was glad that I was early, gave me a real wet kiss right on the mouth, and told me her older sister would be back in a second. Rocío had gone to the grocery store. Angie told me to relax and asked me if I wanted a beer, and I said yes. She said she was angry with her little sister, who had promised to be there to meet me but had then taken off with her boyfriend and probably wouldn't be back until late. Her little sister, Angie said, was a problem. A couple of months ago, Marisela had stopped going to nursing school. Now she had quit her job and was looking for a new one, and her novio would take her out dancing and drinking every week until the wee hours of the morning. Marisela did nothing around the house, and the two older sisters were having trouble controlling her, getting her on the right track.

Angie told me, as she was putting away a bucket and bottles of cleaning fluids, that they were planning a big get-together for Saturday. Could I still come? Sure I would. A couple of their friends would be over for dinner, including Rocío's boyfriend. After dinner they'd sit around and have a few beers and Cuba libres and maybe play the guitar and sing a round of old and new Mexican songs. One of the guys coming was an excellent poet at the Universidad de

Angie Luna

Juárez, and he might read some of his poetry. I never did any of that stuff at the Amherst parties I went to, except the drinking of course, so I was a little nervous about being out of place. A Chicano americanizado. But Angie had always made me feel right at home, so I quickly forgot about my fears.

"Oye, Victor," she whispered in my ear, catching me by surprise from behind as I strolled around the living room, "eres un amor," she said sweetly, kissing my earlobe. I shivered.

"Angie. What if I got a room for Saturday night after dinner?" I said, having thought about this now for hours, my shoulders and back still sore from pressing against the Buick's door handles.

"Perfecto. ¿En donde?"

"Maybe Motel 8 or the Holiday Inn. Something nice."

"Muy bien. You know, I'm going to miss you so much."

"Me too. I can see you en navidad, right?"

"Sí. Ay, mi rey, why do you have to go study in Massachusetts? Te vas a poner triste allá tan solo," she said, stroking back my hair so gently.

"Entonces dame algo para soñar en ti," I said coyly, finding everything I wanted in her dark brown eyes.

"¡Ay, diablo!" she said and kissed me so softly, her lips lingering over mine and opening up into a chasm and taking me completely in. I couldn't believe what I felt. I took a step back to kiss her hand, but it was really to calm down so I wouldn't be completely horny the entire evening. Jesus, she was incredible.

As we were about to walk out the door, Rocío stepped inside and said hello and asked what movie we were seeing. I said we weren't sure yet. She asked me if I was coming to the Saturday night reunión, and I said that I was. I didn't think I was too articulate, in fact I thought I was stammering. If Angie was voluptuous, Rocío was downright elegant. Like an Isabella Rossellini: reserved, confident, playful. When Angie and I finally got into the Buick, I kept thinking that in a weird way I could understand why they had had so many problems growing up, with their father and his friends and whoever else had tried to dominate them. These sisters were resplendent in a rough and unforgiving world. But I didn't get the sense, from that first and very brief meeting, that Rocío was shy like Angie. The older sister seemed capable of being tough and even competitive. I now knew where Angie had gotten her own confident look, the one she plastered on her face like a mask when she was at the Popular. What would have happened to the two other sisters without an older sibling like Rocío? In the cowboy country of Chihuahua City? Maybe El Paso wasn't that different from Chihuahua. Maybe here they just screwed you in English instead of Spanish. At least the sisters seemed in good shape now. At least here their father wasn't breathing down their necks.

We drove to the State Line, an expensive restaurant, at least for El Paso, which served steak and ribs and even barbacoa. Nothing here for a celery-chomping Yankee. I didn't mind blowing a big chunk of my paycheck on Angie; I really loved being with her. After last Saturday night, I felt as if the summer had been more than just a terrible blur of time passing away, and it had taken just her touch to do it. We got a cozy booth overlooking the lights of I-10. The young waitress brought us water and our menus. I didn't know if I could just reach out and hold Angie's hand. While I was thinking about it and pretending to look at my menu, she scooted over to my side and kissed me on the cheek. Maybe she could read my mind. That thought seemed frightening to me, and even more exciting than her holding me tightly in the back seat of the Buick. Finally the waitress came over and took our orders: barbecued baby-back ribs and a Corona for me, and a Texas T-bone and a Dos Equis for her. There were only a few couples generously scattered around the restaurant. Once in a while you could hear boisterous and arrogant laughter from a group of businessmen in a faraway corner, some of them struggling to understand the Spanish of the big Mexican client they'd been entertaining for the day. I took her hand and kissed it and thought about why I had been born when I was, and not ten years earlier, and why the hell I was up in bucolic New England studying how to calculate the present value of projected cash flows and the like. The beer had just the right cold sting slipping down my throat, and I knew then I didn't want to be anywhere else in the world.

Angie told me that she had just been promoted to "Assistant Manager" of her small department in the mezzanine, so I made an impromptu toast to her success, which made her eyes become even brighter and more loyal. I was really happy for her. She deserved every good thing she got. She said the new position meant more work and just a few extra dollars at the end of the week, but maybe she could eventually move up even higher. She said she was a little apprehensive about some of the things she would have to know in her new position. She was afraid the other cashiers would be jealous of her promotion and would jump on her mistakes when and if she made them. Up to this point, the manager in charge had been supportive and had told her she deserved a shot because she had worked so hard, without ever being absent. But she did have to master certain skills. I asked Angie what these things were. She said the most difficult one was something called "inventory accounting," something she had never had in school in Chihuahua. I laughed. She glared at me. For the first time, I knew she wasn't just sweet and shy but also proud. I told her I wasn't laughing at her.

"Entonces, what are laughing at?" she asked, still serious and stealing a pair of ribs from my plate.

"I just finished my second course in accounting. Got an A minus. I'll help you with inventory accounting if you want me to."

She smiled hard at me, in a friendly sort of way but still prideful. "Well," she snorted, "as long as you teach me so that I can get an A because I don't want any A minus." This Angie girl was something else.

So instead of going to the movies, we drove east on I-10 to the UTEP library, which I knew was open until midnight. She had never been there before. I told her anyone could just walk right in, find a comfortable sofa overlooking the atrium, and read or relax. I showed her where she could get snacks, where the newspaper room was, and where she could make copies of whatever book she wanted. I found old editions of the accounting books I had used at Amherst and took her to the bank of conference rooms with chalkboards on the third floor. It was hard enough getting through the basics of debit and credit and assets equals liabilities plus equity without having the titillation of Angie's turquoise dress rubbing back and forth over her thighs every time she crossed her legs. I kept my focus, however. She seemed mysteriously captivated by the provisions for uncollectible accounts and merchandise returned. She asked whether these things might vary by store because she knew from experience that many customers would buy a load of goods on credit but list fake addresses. Others would routinely return half of what they had bought the previous week. I said that the company probably had a rough idea of what these percentages were, and she could tell them if these numbers didn't really apply to the Popular downtown.

After a couple of hours, we drove back to Juárez. I promised to help her a couple more times so that she would be ready to get the specific information she needed for her new assignments. When I pulled the Buick up to the front of her house, she slid closer to me, to the middle of the front seat, and kissed me and stroked my neck and chest until I told her I was going to rip her clothes off if she didn't get out of the car. Before she opened the door and stopped tormenting me, she whispered in my ear that I shouldn't forget the room for Saturday night. I could hear her black pumps clicking on the sidewalk as she walked to the front door, each click opening up and pinning back my heart to the wall of a blissful hunger.

The next day I finally got my airline tickets in the mail, and it suddenly dawned on me that I would be leaving next week. I had already told Joe that this would be my last week, and he had grunted a thank you and told me to come back if I ever needed a summer job. Sure I would, I said, thinking that if I ever needed another mindless stint of time I might instead opt for a temporary lobotomy if there was such a thing. I didn't bother to say goodbye to anyone at the Popular except Doña Leticia and the rest of the "girls" in Women's Lingerie, none of whom was younger than fifty. I had always liked their raucous free-for-all and the fact that these ladies could talk enough trash to make me blush and then turn on a dime and face a waiting customer with the most serious of faces. Angie Luna I didn't need to say goodbye to because I would be seeing her on Saturday. I'd also see her a couple more times next week so that she could get a good sense of accounting, or at least enough for her to find, on her own, the answers to any questions that might come up. It occurred to me that I was teaching accounting to Marilyn Monroe's Mexican double and that somehow I should feel stupid about that. But I could never figure out where exactly the stupidity was in that situation. My mother, in another of her prolonged goodbyes, was already hugging me and kissing me whenever I walked through the house, imploring me to write and telling me not to walk alone at night in Amherst and to make my reservations for Christmas with enough time to spare. My father didn't say much except to point out that he was glad I had worked all summer and saved money for school. He said they, too, would add to the pot before I left. I thanked him.

On Saturday morning I got up early and told my mother I was going over to Grandma's to say goodbye in case I didn't get a chance next week. I had breakfast with my abuelitos, who were always early risers, and then drove my grandfather to his favorite store, the Western Auto on Paisano Street. I think he was looking for a new lawn mower bag. He told me he'd walk back the ten or so blocks because his legs were getting stiff from lack of exercise. As soon as I returned to their house, my grandmother said she needed a ride to El Centro, a community center for senior citizens. She said they were in the middle of a food drive. As soon as I dropped her off, I knew I was free for an hour or two before I'd have to pick her up. I went back to their house and dialed a couple of hotels and motels on I-10, the ones I had driven by many times before. I had never really done this before, yet I didn't think it would be a big deal, and it wasn't. Last year I had gotten a credit card from the tons of solicitations I always got in the mail at Amherst, a Visa with no annual fee ever. I got room rates, checkout times, and finally settled on the Holiday Inn next to the airport because it was convenient and probably nice. It wasn't the cheapest one, but I thought it would be worth it to be comfortable with Angie. I told the reservations desk that I was visiting relatives from out of town, made a one-day reservation for a junior suite, and told them I'd be arriving late today, probably around ten o'clock. No problem. Angie and I would spend part of the night there, I would drive her home whenever she was ready to go, and early on Sunday I would go back to the Holiday Inn and check out. Simple. As soon as I clicked the receiver down, I felt a great elation come over me, like a gust of the desert wind that sweeps through Transmountain Road. I couldn't wait.

I finally took off in the early evening, after renewing my lease of the Buick with my mother. Be careful, she said, don't get too crazy with your friends. She didn't know I was going to my first Mexican party. The whole scenario made me a little nervous. All of a sudden I thought I'd forgotten my Spanish. I didn't know if they would just hang around, drink some beers, or dance. What music would young

Mexicans dance to? I didn't know if I'd feel too young among Rocío's friends or if they'd think I was just a quasi-gringo invading their territory. I wasn't a real Mexican, and I wasn't an American either. At least not at Amherst where everyone just assumed I was the expert on the best place for Mexican food. I was more like a shadow playing both sides of the game. I didn't mind. I knew Angie would be there and we would have a good time. When I arrived at Angie's house, Rocío answered the door, kissed both of my cheeks, and introduced me to a few people who were already sitting on the couch and on the floor. The other women kissed me on the cheeks too—I thought this kissing was terrific, for its immediate friendliness and sophistication—and one of the guys handed me a beer and scooted over so I'd have a good spot on the couch. Angie came in, I stood up, and she planted a big one right on my lips and sat next to me, her hand curled around mine. I was in a semi-state of shock, smiling stupidly in the face of this unabashed, almost bohemian warmth.

It was unlike any party I had ever been to. The first thing that struck me was that this crowd was slightly older than me, in their thirties. A few were at the university, as instructors, others worked in Juárez, only one other person worked in El Paso besides Angie and Rocío. Only Marisela and her boyfriend—she, by the way, was just as beautiful as her sisters, if only a little runty—were close to my age. Since I was 6′3″, I didn't really stand out, at least I hoped I didn't, and no one even bothered to ask how old I was. After the initial flurry of kisses, I felt immediately comfortable being there. The other thing I liked was that they mostly sat around smoking and talked about politics and ideas, about the differences in American and Mexican cultures, about sexual politics and the differences between men and women, and even about sex itself, in an affectionate and open way, not in raunchy terms meant to shock or brag. Sure, I didn't like the smoking part, but even this seemed different than at Amherst. You weren't a pariah if you did it, and if you didn't smoke you didn't have that look of utter disgust. You just accepted it as being a part of this group of friends. There was also none of the paranoia of being checked out or the strange hope of checking someone else out. Just about everyone was part of a couple. This seemed the most natural thing in the world. It wasn't a room full of lonelies.

Someone brought in a tray full of little tostadas topped with pinto beans and a tangy white cheese, they called them "sopes," and there was a huge bowl of guacamole, extra-spicy, and another bowl of tortilla chips on the coffee table. More trays of hot food would just suddenly appear in front of the small group. Angie and Rocío kept shuttling to and from the kitchen without missing a beat of the conversation and laughter. After a while, a friend of theirs walked in, Fernando, and he was carrying a guitar which he started strumming and tuning before he sang a Mexican ballad, very softly at first, until the rest of us joined in. I felt a little stupid because I didn't know the words, but everyone was smiling and having a great time, and after the second verse I knew most of the refrain. Fernando sang for a while, one or two or three would join in, sometimes he'd just play without singing, letting us decide whether to join in or just listen to the guitar. I laughed a lot with Angie because she would keep whispering all sorts of things in my ear. We were both a little drunk. Everyone else was too. They only got friendlier with each other, arm in arm at the sound of their favorite rancheras, singing and swaying and declaring to the world that they were Mexican and proud of it. There were serious discussions about death and the purpose of life. We also laughed wildly, at the simplest things. One of them suddenly stood up, took out some papers from his coat pocket—he was the only one wearing a jacket, but no tie—and demanded silence and was greeted first with hoots of excitement and then with a quiet so unnerving I thought I could hear myself perspire in the alcoholic

Angie Luna

heat. He recited some of his own written words in a voice at once passionate and then vulnerable. Poems about love and affliction and not knowing exactly who you were. Poems about courage and even the wretched life of the poor. I saw Angie shed a tear, and others too, including the men, whenever something struck them deeply in the heart. Instead of feeling embarrassed, they were comforted and held by their friends, and I thought I was a part of them. After what seemed centuries of time gone by, Angie squeezed my hand and said we had to go. I stood up, kissed the women goodbye, and shook hands with the men. They asked me to come back, and I said that I would.

As we drove across the international bridge, I could feel Angie's head resting on my shoulder, her hand on my lap, her slow and warm breathing. I thought she might be falling asleep, but when I glanced down she smiled at me and nuzzled my neck. I exited at Airway Boulevard and pulled into the Holiday Inn. Angie said she would wait in the car. When I came back with the room keys, she was combing her hair in the rearview mirror and touching up her lipstick. We drove around and parked facing 1-10, right at one of the entrances to the main part of the building. Our room, on the second floor at the end of a long hallway, was huge, with two queen-size beds, a small denlike area with a couch, a writing desk, a bathroom almost as big as my dorm room, and the perfect quiet we had been looking for. She said it was tremendous, and I agreed. She asked me if I minded relaxing and talking for a while, and I said that I didn't mind at all. I put the chain on the door, found a small radio and turned it to a jazz station from Las Cruces, and sat down with her on the couch. She had already slipped off her shoes so I did too.

We talked about everything. When I would come back to El Paso, and for how long. How many years I still needed to finish my studies. Whether I liked her sisters, and how many brothers and sisters I myself had. If she could save enough money to buy a new car, since her old one was giving her so much trouble. How she would do in her new position, and with what allies and avoiding which enemies. Whether I wanted to come back to El Paso forever. I told her that I wasn't sure. She reached over and took my hand, pulled me closer to her side. We kissed and caressed each other until nothing seemed to matter anymore, not our distance from each other, and not the futility of our love, which wandered far away into the deepest part of my mind. Her perfume enveloped me, took me in, and carried me up. I asked her if she still wanted to be with me. And she asked me if I could turn off the lights.

I held Angie Luna in that room for hours, and I remember the different times we made love like epochs in a civilization, each movement and every touch, apex upon abyss. In the luxury of our bed, we tried every position and every angle. I explored the curves of her body and delighted in seeing the freedom of her ecstasy. Her desperate whispers and pleas. I told her I loved her, and she said she loved me too. We lay in bed with our limbs entangled, in a pacific silence that reminded me of existing on a beach just for the sake of such an existence. I couldn't imagine the world ever becoming better, and for some strange reason the thought slipped into my head that I had suddenly grown to be an old man because I could only hope to repeat, but never improve on, a night like this. I finally took her home sometime when the interstate was empty, and the bridges seemed to lead nowhere, for they were desolate too.

I saw her a few more times before I left for Massachusetts, but nothing shattered me like that particular night, the night of my first Mexican party and my first teary-eyed ranchera, the night when I knew nothing would stop us, and then nothing did. And I just slammed into that black wall. I came back to El Paso for Christmas, having written to her but having received only one brief letter in return. She had returned to Chihuahua, her sister Rocío confirmed this in the empty coldness of a desert winter. Angie had returned to take care of her ailing father when nobody else would. I had never bothered to ask Angie about her mother, and I felt like an idiot. Rocío said that indeed their mother had died many years ago, of breast cancer and its neglect. She told me not to feel guilty about it, most of their friends didn't know either. She told me that Angie had made the decision to go back to Chihuahua, freely and without any remorse. Rocío asked me if I wanted to stay for a drink. I told her I couldn't but only because I thought I was going to choke. She said she would tell Angie I had stopped by. I thanked her for being so kind.

We took Chuy to the ditch behind my
house, Joe, me, and Fernández, and tied
him up. We tied him up tight with a rope I
found in the shed. It must've burned his
wrists 'cause as soon as Joe yanked on the
square knot, Chuy yelped and started
blubbering in the way he does when he's
hungry, but I know he wasn't hungry. It
hadn't been more than ten minutes since I
had given him the Heath bar in front of his
porch, right under his mama's eyes. Hell, I
could smell the frijoles she was cooking in
the kitchen just as I dangled the shiny
wrapper under those stupid eyes. He
followed me like a puppy, and then we tied
him up secret-like.

A Rock Trying
to Be a Stone

Chuy wiggled his shoulders and stood up, his hands dangling in front of him like flippers, but Joe pushed him down hard into a tumbleweed still green from the rain. Nobody could see us in this thicket of mesquite, cattails, and garbage, the best of which was the rusted frame of El Muerto's Buick station wagon lying near the bottom of the ditch. When that stupid pothead had driven into the ditch drunk, he had left us a great place to wait for the bullfrogs to jump out of the mud when the rains came in the summer. And he also punched a tunnel through all the overgrowth and junk in the ditch, a tunnel that ended up at the station wagon with the tinted moonroof, a tunnel we hid from the other pendejos in the neighborhood by covering it with dried-out tumbleweeds. This was our place, only the three of us knew about it, and we swore we wouldn't tell anyone else. Anyway, Joe would have kicked the shit out of anybody who told. He loved that tunnel more than anything else, more than being in his own house. Now we had a prisoner in our tunnel too.

"Now what?" Fernández said, staring at the slobber dripping down Chuy's lips. "I hope he isn't sick."

"Shut up. Get me that other wire over there," Joe demanded and pulled Chuy up to his feet and pushed him down the ditch tunnel toward the station wagon and the slimy green water full of tadpoles and such. "We're gonna tie the re-tard to the Buick, we're gonna tie his legs." Joe slapped Chuy on top of his head, but it wasn't a hard slap.

"What for?" Fernández asked. "What are we gonna do with him?"

"So he can't run away. What good's a prisoner if he runs away?" I said, grabbing the tumbleweed stems behind me and closing up the entrance. The morning had been way too hot already. There weren't any mosquitoes buzzing yet, but the ditch was full of big black shiny flies, the kind that land on dogshit and eat it. Two of 'em buzzed my head, and I jumped back. Hell, I didn't want any shit flies on me.

"Araaaayia! Araaaayia! Araaayiump!"

"Shut up, damn it. Shut the fuck up," Joe said.

"Araaaayia! Araaayiump!"

"Turi, shut him up! Somebody'll hear him," Joe said. He was getting angry. He had that bored look in his eyes, the one before he lunged at whoever was in his face. Steady eyes above a slight smile, his shoulders and arms straight like a tight coil.

"Araaaayia! Araa . . . " The last one died just after it left his lips. His eyes became distracted by the cinnamon jawbreaker I waved in front of him. I pushed it into the fat open mouth, and slobber got all over my fingers. I wiped myself on Fernández's T-shirt, and he slapped it away. Too late. The white saliva slobber was on him, a big foamy wet spot on his chest. I dragged my fingers through the desert dust to get the rest of it off me. I had six more jawbreakers in my jean pockets.

Chuy was sitting in the back seat of the Buick, red foam dripping down his mouth. He seemed happy looking around the bottom of the ditch through the shattered windows, gawking up at the sun through the moonroof. He bounced his tied-up hands on his lap and looked at Joe fiddling with the copper wire around his legs. The wire wasn't long enough to fasten around both legs and the front seat frame.

"Just tie up one leg to the bar," I said, "'cause if he can't run with one leg he can't run with two." Joe looked up and glared at me, but he tied a one-legged tie. We had ourselves a prisoner, if only a happy moron at that.

"Now what?" Fernández asked again, sitting up on the slope of the ditch with his hands on his lap.

"Shut up with your 'now what.' Can't you say anything else?" Joe said, exasperated, just about to pop Fernández one. "I have an idea."

"What?" I said, cutting a cattail off its stalk. It was about the longest I'd seen this summer, longer and thicker than the ones I already had drying on our garage roof for the Fourth of July. As long as a giant Cuban cigar and about as good for lighting firecrackers.

"Let's read the pecker his rights," Joe said, smiling widely.

"His what?" Fernández asked, stupefied. He didn't get it. When he didn't get something, he put on this scrunched-up face as if we were responsible for his mind not grasping what a normal one would. Fernández didn't have much on Chuy, nothing much at all.

"His rights, idiot. Like *Dragnet*," I said.

"Fuck *Dragnet*," Joe said, standing up next to me and reaching for something in his wallet. He was bigger than both of us, older too. No other boys in the neighborhood were friendly with him. My mother had warned me not to hang around Joe. He was a cholo, she said, his family was cursed with the malignant spirit. But I knew he was lonely sometimes, and I knew I was his friend. "I'll read him his Miranda shit."

"What's that?" Fernández asked, standing up and peering at a piece of paper in Joe's hand.

"You have a right to remain silent. . . ."

"It says 'Miranda Rights' on top," I said.

"Anything you say can and will be used against you in a fucking court of law. . . ."

"Who the hell is Miranda? Is it the chick who wrote that?" Fernández asked with his scrunched-up face again. "Who is it?"

"You have a right to an attorney, you have a right to be a re-tard, you have a right to be my slave forever."

"Araaaayia! Araaaayia!"

"Give him another one, Turi. Shut him up. *You* don't have a right to breathe unless I say so," Joe said loudly, stunning Chuy into silence with a raised index finger in his face. I popped another jawbreaker into the fat mouth, a lime-flavored one, and Chuy's face turned up toward the moonroof in beatific happiness again.

"I'm gonna start a fire. I need a smoke," Joe said, stepping away from the station wagon, bored with the game. He strode to an open space among the weeds in the ditch and put his lighter to a dried-up tumbleweed. He threw a piece of cardboard on it and a plank and some scraggly branches. Soon there was a blaze in the open space of our tunnel, about waist-high. Fernández threw rocks at the puddles of slime in the ditch, aiming for two empty beer bottles floating next to a dead frog. I watched Joe roll out a tiny sheet of paper on his knee, sprinkle a sliver of marijuana from a plastic zip-lock bag onto the sheet, and roll it back up tightly into a crooked, lumpy roll. He licked the edge of it before pressing it together.

"Ese Turi, do you want some?" Joe asked, taking his first long inhale of the lighted weed.

"You know I don't. I don't like it," I said. I felt a little stupid myself.

"Well I thought you changed your mind," he said.

"No I didn't," I said.

"I'll smoke it, give me some," Fernández said, looking at me with a smirk. Now I felt ashamed. Fernández was usually a coward.

"Since when are you smoking pot?" Joe challenged, almost like a big brother.

"Since about a week. Roberto Luján gave me some behind the stadium, when I went to play basket at Ysleta High," Fernández said triumphantly. All of a sudden the little thirteen-year-old I knew from down the street, the runt I used to pound into submission with my fists, seemed older, worldly, threatening. I popped a cherry jawbreaker into my mouth.

"Here then," Joe said, holding up the crude cigarette. He didn't seem to care one way or another. Joe was content to sit under the sun, quietly smoking his cigarette with or without company.

Fernández put the cigarette to his lips and expertly inhaled the acrid smoke slowly into his lungs. He didn't move his face on purpose, like a rock trying to be a stone. Fernández handed the cigarette back to Joe, who didn't even look up from scrutinizing the fire. Joe took a toke and suspended the weed between his fingers. Fernández tried to suppress a cough, but he still coughed up a huff of air. I gave him a big smile.

"I know. Let's torture el pinchi Chuy. Let's torture the re-tard," Fernández said, striding down the ditch toward the station wagon. Chuy seemed asleep, his head against the seat, his eyes closed.

"Leave him alone," Joe snapped, his eyes still on the fire. "If he wakes up and starts hollering again, I'm gonna tie *you* up."

I heard my mother calling me from our backyard. The ditch was behind it, running alongside San Lorenzo Street. I could see her peer over the rock wall and search for me up and down the banks of the ditch. My mother went back into the house, and I heard the screen door slam shut.

"I better go. La jefa is calling me," I said, turning to Joe. I could see Fernández stalking the perimeter of the station wagon, jumping over the puddles of water. His eyes were fixed to the ground.

"Ese Turi, can you give me some of your mama's enchiladas again? Just like last week?" he asked quietly, glancing up toward the station wagon to see where Fernández was.

"Well, we might be having flautas tonight," I said.

"Hey, I love flautas. Anything, you know. Just through the back of the fence, just like last week, okay?" he said.

"No problem," I said. I saw that Fernández had gotten a stick, about three feet long, and was taunting Chuy with it, poking him in the stomach.

"Mi jefe beat the crap out of me last night," Joe said, his head down again, his eyes on the fire. "Estaba borracho." I had noticed the welts on his face, his black eye, which was blood red and terribly swollen. I had thought that Joe had been in a fight again, that the other guy must've been dead 'cause Joe could be tough, muscular, mean. I knew Joe always carried a knife in his boot pocket.

"What did you do?" I asked stupidly.

"I let him hit me. He's my father," he said. "I just tried not to get hurt too much. I'm staying here tonight."

I heard the screen door slam shut again. "I'm going. Around seven, okay?" I said and started up the ditch toward the tumbleweed entrance of our tunnel. I remembered, as I walked out onto the ditch bank, that I didn't even know if Joe had a watch. I didn't know if he had *ever* had one.

Now I didn't see firsthand what happened between the time I left the two of them with Chuy and when I heard the commotion in the ditch behind our backyard, with the ambulance siren wailing in the late afternoon and the police cars roaming the neighborhood until dark. Joe told me about it later. This is what he said, as near as I can remember it.

After I left, Joe got up and went to buy a six-pack at Emma's. That's about a twenty-minute walk round-trip from the corner of San Lorenzo and San Simon. That is, if old man Julian isn't asleep in the back room and answers the door right away. Joe didn't say anything about the old geezer, so I assume he was sitting on the porch waiting for anyone to show up. Joe showed up, and he bought what he always buys, a six-pack of Coors. By the time he got back to the tunnel in the ditch, he had already drunk a can of beer and stopped to piss it off behind the González house. I think he had once gone out with Leticia González, and maybe the place seemed familiar to him. Anyway, that's where he pissed.

So he returned to the tunnel in what couldn't have been more than an hour. And guess what the idiot Fernández had done? He had set fire to the tumbleweeds and the grass around the station wagon, he had thrown wood and shit onto it to make it as if he were roasting poor Chuy alive, like a luau pig. He was just fucking

A Rock Trying to Be a Stone

pretending, he said, pretending to put the fire all around the other idiot and burn him up. By the time Joe was walking down the tunnel of brush toward the station wagon, Fernández was trying to stomp the fire out. His sneakers were melting, his pants caught fire, and Joe pushed him away and into the slimy water. Then Joe tried to beat the fire with an old coat somebody had left behind. Chuy was screaming wildly. He screamed and shrieked although the fire still wasn't on him. But it was all around him. The fire was burning up the front seat. The moonroof cracked in the heat and crashed down on Chuy's face. Joe took an empty paint can and was pitching water into the blaze in the back seat, as much as he could with each canful. Fernández stumbled up the ditch bank and ran home. Chuy was jumping up and down and holding his tied-up hands to his face, against the flames in front of him. Jumping up and down and yelling a long scream that Joe said sounded like a freight train's whistle. Joe reached in and pulled Chuy's tied-up foot for a second, pulled it so he could free the other idiot and maybe snap the goddamn wire, but he couldn't. The fire scorched Joe's hand and forearm, burned it like a steak so that his skin wrinkled up and hissed and stung with such a deep pain that he wanted to cut it off to free himself of the agony.

Chuy must've felt the tug at his leg. For as soon as Joe fell back and dunked his fiery arm in the algae water, Chuy jumped off the back seat and discovered his legs and took a step out of the station wagon as if someone had tied his shoe laces together secret-like. Plop. Chuy fell right on top of the blaze outside the car door, his leg still tied up to what was left of the front seat, and the poor bastard wiggled crazily on top of the fire, and hissed and screamed until his burned-up flesh stunk so much that you couldn't smell the slimy water in the ditch anymore. Then he stopped moving and fired up like a Duraflame.

Joe walked home holding up his arm just as the fire raced up the ditch banks in a cloud of black smoke high above Ysleta. The neighbors had seen the smoke and called the fire department, and they had seen Joe but didn't pay him no mind then. That ditch went up in flames at least once a year for as long as I can remember, so whoever happened to junk his cigarette in the tumbleweeds just started what was going to happen sooner or later anyway. It's just that the ditch never burned with some idiot in it before. So after the firemen rode in from Alameda Street with all of their commotion, they started hosing down the grass and the pile of tires and the like. The little cabrones in the neighborhood probably ran after the fire truck like they always do, and climbed on the truck when the firemen weren't looking. And the gringo firemen patted the kids on the head and went about their business stomping the bushes and spraying their waterhoses with that deafening drone from the fire truck. Then, at the bottom of the ditch, I'm sure one of them got real curious. Next to El Muerto's station wagon was something round and blackened and wearing sneakers. They didn't know it was Chuy yet. They just knew it wasn't a charred-up Michelin man.

Joe said he went home. His father wasn't there; the house was empty. With his free arm, Joe broke open a couple of eggs in a dish and patted the egg whites onto the burnt skin on his arm. This made the pain recede. He said he wrapped it up in gauze and sat down to drink a beer before he packed up some clothes in a Safeway bag, his father's Raven MP-25, and whatever cash he could find. Joe never showed me the Raven, but I didn't think he was lying. He didn't care enough to lie. He just did what he did, and that's how he said it. He hid for a while in the ditch behind Carl Longuemare Road. *That* ditch is actually an irrigation canal for the cotton fields on Americas Avenue and for the fields beyond the maquiladoras, unlike the ditch behind my house, which is mostly ornamental,

A Rock Trying to Be a Stone

good for draining off the two or three summer downpours we get in the El Paso desert. But ours is still a good ditch to play in, even after Chuy got himself killed in it.

I knew the police were looking for Joe. They knocked on all the houses on San Lorenzo Street, including mine. Luckily my mother wasn't there. Doña María had called her, and together they had walked down the street to see Doña Lupe, who was hysterical, my mother said later. She loved her little re-tard. So the police came, and I walked out to the fence with Lobo growling and jumping against the chainlink, and I told them my mother wasn't home. They asked if I had seen a José Domínguez of the neighborhood, and I said I hadn't. They went next door with that shithole Don Eugénio, who never returns any of my baseballs, and so on down the street. I never told them anything, and that includes my mother. I should've told them that there was still another stupid idiot in the neighborhood and that his name was Horácio Fernández. But I didn't.

After I ate dinner, I went out back with a plateful of flautas, frijoles, and rice. My mother didn't see me, and my dad was watch-ing TV. I also took some scraps for Lobo, mainly a thick round bone from the brisket for the flautas. This way the dog wouldn't keep begging for what I carried up high on the plate. That was for Joe, if he was still alive and not with a bullet in his chest. I waited out there for a long time. I waited in the dark until I couldn't smell the frijoles anymore, until everything was dead cold. Nothing. I figured the police had already arrested Joe for the fire, but I didn't want to believe it. So I waited some more until I got tired. Then I started feeding a flauta to Lobo in the dark, and the stupid mutt gnawed on one end of it as if it were a giant jawbreaker. The wetness of the muzzle reminded me of Chuy's slobber. I heard "Ese Turi" from behind the rock wall. It was Joe, just another shadow in the dark-ness. I handed him the plate, and he told me what happened, and I told him that the cops were looking for him, and he said he knew that already. "Munch Munch Munch" I heard from somewhere just beyond me, over the fence. I didn't tell him anything about the half-eaten flauta, and he didn't seem to notice 'cause he left the plate clean. I figured I didn't want to add to his troubles. Anyway, he said he was starving, and the dog already had a bone.

That's the last time I ever saw Joe. I don't know what happened to him after that, whether he got to Mexico like he said he wanted to. I'm gonna be a reverse wetback, he said, a mojado without a country. He said that he had some cousins in Delicias who had a farm, that the Chihuahua girls he knew were extra nice. I don't know if he ever got himself a Chihuahua girl. I never saw him again. But I did see el pinchi Fernández again. About a week later. The runt had been playing basket behind Ysleta High again. He was sitting smoking pot behind the stadium with another idiot I didn't recognize. I walked up to him, and he was inhaling the stub of a cigarette. The fire glowed brightly in the afternoon shadow of the stadium. His stupid face was lit up. I punched him right in the mouth with my fist exploding with a hardness I don't remember ever having again. Fernández rolled in the dust and still didn't recognize me. He couldn't even stand up, lost in the stupor of the drug. After that, I never talked to him again either. But I still have a neat round burn scar between the middle knuckles of my left hand, right where I crushed the cigarette on his face.

Horned. White sputum ejaculating from
the abyss of blackness on the contorted face.
Arms upraised toward her like blood-red
streams gushing from the eight-foot hulk of
ghastly malevolence. "¡Maldito Demonio!
Get away from my house!" Doña Dolores
Rivero hissed in a creaky scream, her own
eyes aglare with the image of the evil spirit
outside. "Dios en el cielo, please help this
poor old woman!" She yanked the wooden
crucifix off the nail on the wall next to her
fold-out bed. The defeated manchild, with
His bloody crown of thorns, quivered
against her full breasts and the sheer emerald gauze of her nightgown. "Save me, mi
Dios. Please slay this son of Lucifer!" she
cried, tightly clenching her eyes shut to the

Espíritu Santo

edge of a schizoid blackout. Doña Dolores peered again through her window down to the garden one floor below. She twisted her head to see beyond the thick evergreen bushes abutting her apartment wall. She thought she found a wisp of crimson smoke drifting up into the nothingness of the desert stars. But really, only the wan amber from the streetlight sifted into the shadows, the darkness barely alight. She kissed Jesus on the holy forehead and hung Him up anew to keep a vigil for Lucifer's princes while she slept. She pulled the flowered plastic curtains closed, knelt by her bed, and breathlessly chanted three Hail Marys, glancing at the clutter of framed photographs of her children and grandchildren on the ramshackle dresser. Alone in bed, the gray-haired viejita pulled the coverlet over her head, losing herself in the cave of a halcyon re-prieve.

In the morning, Doña Dolores fired up a burner on her stove and clanked down a teapot half-full of water over the blue flame. Three lonely sparks dissipated in the complex of pipes and wires beneath the fire. After the steam shrieked through the hole barely larger than the eye of a needle, she shot up from a shockable stare. She spooned into her cup two heaps of a chocolate coffee powder that seemed to have a universe of stars sprinkled therein. Doña Dolores drank a gulp that dropped through her throat like a column of apocalyptic fire. She bent over and found a certain deep notch on a splintered two-by-four in front of her kitchen fireplace mantel. Snapped off one end of the wood with a stamp of her foot that rattled the etched mirror behind the mantel cherry. The piece in hand, she fitted it slantwise into the aluminum frame of the kitchen window and jammed it home. The glass cracked a jagged hypot-enuse in one corner of the window. That window was now forever shut. From a Petro Truckstop ashtray on the mantel shelf, she plucked out a cross of palms from a pile of such palm crosses, all blessed and empowered with holy water by Father Emilio Magaña of the Sacred Heart Church on Saint Vrain Street, across from Benny's Tacos y Burritos.

Doña Dolores picked up the other half of the two-by-four and the rusted handsaw she had borrowed from Don Epifanio Mendoza in Apartment Three. She bulled forward through the dead air in the hallway and the bedroom, one implement pendulous in each hand as if she were some aged terminatrix savoring her choice of weapons against an unlucky opponent. The bedroom window was already jammed shut. So was the window in the bathroom. Palm crosses sanctified the light from the impurities and perversities not just of El Segundo Barrio—those she could mostly take care of herself—but also from this nether world impregnate with the malignant spirit. She and palm crosses and two-by-fours against the world. Doña Dolores sat down on her reading chair and peered around her apartment one more time. Maybe she was finally done. "¡Ay, Dios de mi vida!" She shot up from her chair and marched to the living-room window. One lapse, one mistake, and she would be prostrate before Lucifer's machinations! What was she *thinking?* The piece of wood in her hand was three fingers too long for this frame.

"Vámonos, Don Epi. Are you ready?"

No answer from behind the screen door. Doña Dolores couldn't quite make out if that was a man or a shadow draped over the lime loveseat inside Apartment Three. The El Paso sun, a screech of whiteness that pierced every crevice and slant with an explosion and fallout of photons, bounced off the screen door and shimmered into her eyes. She was cold. The wicked November wind seemed to swirl around her like a sentient desert twister and purposefully shoot up under her coat and between her legs. She slammed her fist on the wrought iron diamonds.

Espíritu Santo

"Don Epi!" The shadow stirred, its turtlelike face lit by a streak of sun.

"Doña Lola. I am ready," Don Epifanio said, pushing open the screen door and walking out. Compared to the battle-ready air about Doña Dolores, the old man seemed frail and trapped in slow motion. Indeed, he was eighty-nine years old, once a teenager and young soldier who had ridden with the Villistas at León, Guanajuato, in 1915. Don Epifanio had lost most of his left arm on a day just like today, leaving him with just a flipperlike stump. But at least for one miraculous moment he had seen el General Villa, who had joked to the private about the sexual compromises that had been forced upon Obregón with his own mangled limb. Don Epifanio still remembered the phenomenal rush of pride that had practically raised him off the ground when Villa had touched his wounded shoulder goodbye. From that moment on, Epifanio Mendoza had known in his heart that he had sacrificed not nearly enough for the revolution.

"Well, aren't you going to close the door, señor? Or should I print some invitations for a cholo open house at your place?"

"What? Oh, yes. I forgot, Lolita. My mind is elsewhere today." He locked the door. They shuffled down Olive Street and turned southward on Saint Vrain to cross Paisano in front of the Gedunk Bar. Its neon orange lights palpitated against an absolute black wall. Doña Dolores steadied Don Epifanio over the six inches of curb at the corner. The gutters were littered with shards of burnt sienna glass, flattened condoms like disemboweled earthworms, a Chevy muffler, and the crushed and powdery carcass of a pigeon.

"Are you hungry, Don Epi? María Elena and the girls are cooking pavo and pumpkin pies and mashed potatoes and, of course, stuffing. As much as you want."

"Oh, yes. Tengo mucha hambre," he said, his beady brown eyes riveted on the ground in front of him. Don Epifanio was famous for being a bottomless pit. No one knew how he managed to stuff tortilla after tamale after tostada into that thin, hunched frame. For hours and hours! Sure, each lady was proud of her cooking, but not one of them had the vanity to think that that was the real reason behind this man's miraculous feasting. The speculation was that revolucionarios were all voracious. Somehow, their molecules had speeded up into a permanent frenzy. It was indeed true that the old man could sweat something beyond even powerful.

"You know, your girlfriend Lupita will be there too."

"Oh, *really*," he said, straightening out his plaid clip-on tie.

"Yes. She told me this year El Centro will have music while we eat our cena. Isn't that something?"

"That's very good, I think. Do you think Lupita would dance with me if I asked her?"

"I'm sure she would. But it's classical music, Don Epi, not redovas or polkas."

"Oh, I see."

"Yes, it's a young man from Baltimore. He plays the violin or the cello, I'm not sure. He only plays for viejitos like us. Has a thing called Music Alert, an organization of some sort."

"Too bad. Maybe he knows a good dancing tune on his fiddle. You know, before my fingers got too stiff with arthritis I used to play el acordeón. Music for stomping out the night on a Chihuahua ranch. That and a fiddle was all you needed to be happy."

"You should ask him at the party," Doña Dolores said, smiling. They trudged along Fourth Street. A wholesale warehouse was across the silent street. An ink-black smear of slush opened out into the asphalt from underneath the gigantic gate of corrugated metal as if some secretory monster slug had lumbered to and fro. Three more blocks to reach El Centro, the activity center for senior citizens. From around a corner about half a block away, two young men walked toward them. One wore a T-shirt and what looked like the rainbow of a sarape draped over his shoulders. The other had on a red flannel shirt and a bandanna around the crown of his head. The cholos whispered something to each other and laughed, prancing a menacing gait, gangly, rhythmic, a terrible sway to tempt the gods or anyone else on the streets who might want to taste acrid immortality. "Ay, Dios. Don Epifanio, you stay close to me."

"Let's see what you've got, rukíto," the bandanna blurted out, rifling through Don Epifanio's trouser pockets while the old man raised his hand in fearful bewilderment. His stump was shaking inside the long empty sleeve of his windbreaker.

"Leave us alone! We've got nothing! Please, por Dios, just leave us alone!" Doña Dolores pleaded to the sarape alert in front of them as if to prevent the rabbits from bolting into the alfalfa thickets.

"Give it to me."

"What?"

"La bolsa."

"¡Nunca! You should be ashamed of yourselves!"

"Give it to me or you're *dead,* bitch!" the sarape bellowed in her face, yanking at the purse clutched beneath her arms. He punched her viciously. Doña Dolores collapsed backward and hit the nape of her neck against the chainlink fence in front of the abandoned lot where Kiko's Launderette used to be. The purse was inert on her left knee. The sarape picked it up and dumped the lipstick and tissues and the compact her nieto had given her for her sixtieth cumpleaños. The rosary with the silver crucifix from Rome, eyeliner, a bottle of Tylenol, five quarters, pennies and dimes, two of the old Mexican pesos engraved with the handsome face of José María Morelos, who once had also worn a bandanna on his head, but for a purpose. Her Le Sportsac pocketbook. The sarape zipped open the pocketbook and grabbed the thirty-three dollars folded neatly into a large paperclip.

"¡Malvados! ¡Salvajes! You should be ashamed of attacking old people!" she yelled at their backs as they strode away. The bandanna whipped his muscled torso around and jabbed an ugly middle finger toward the sky. Doña Dolores stared up into the sun. Don Epifanio was shaking convulsively, incontinent, the stains of tears nearly dry on his face. Doña Dolores clawed at the chainlink and raised herself up. The right side of her face felt numb. When she patted it with her fingers, it was puffy like a cotton ball, tender like the meat she pounded with the plane of tiny pyramids of her hammerlike tenderizer. She tasted the bitterness of her blood at the back of her mouth. "Don Epi, are you all right? Señor, please calm down. We're alive. That's what matters."

"I didn't defend you. I'm a useless old fool. Just look at me!"

"Don't worry. We'll clean you up in the bathroom before we go into the auditorium for the cena," she said, picking up her belongings from the sidewalk. Her Matte Épice lipstick was crushed on the ground like a glob of butter on bread.

"I didn't do anything. I'm useless, an invalid coward."

"Don't say such things, Don Epi! It's not your fault. Who knows? Maybe if I had been alone the evil spirit might have pushed them to commit even more unspeakable atrocities. You saved me from that, Don Epi. *That's* what you did."

"You think so? Really?"

"I know it, señor. I know what these cholos are capable of. They're heartless. They have no use for God in their empty souls."

"Well, can I admit something to you, a secret?"

"Of course."

"I was scared."

"We both were. The most courageous people are scared. If you're not, then you don't know the danger you're up against."

"You're right, Doña Lola. The Villistas always said that Álvaro

Obregón cried just before every batalla. He cried getting ready for a fight. We cried after he nearly massacred all of us at León. I'd rather cry like him."

"Don Epi, you know what? I think I know where those malditos live. On Paisano and Stanton. That's where I saw the one with the sarape fixing his car last month. When you go into the bathroom at El Centro, I'll call the police. We'll see if those sinvergüenzas rob anyone else."

"Señora, you look like Jersey Joe after Marciano got through with him. *You* were the brave one. That I know."

The orange dusk fell on Doña Dolores's apartment like the glow of embers on a lonely campfire. Outside, the halfway house across the street was quiet for once. The wretched drug addicts and young hooligans had already retired behind the whitened windows of the first floor and the bedrooms above, their silhouettes immotive. Some were on the roof, gazing at the street below like gargoyles crouched in anticipation of the first light. She had already clicked her deadbolt closed, pushed her sofa on wheels flush against the door. The front drapes were pinned shut with paperclips and long needles. She called Don Epifanio to check that he was safely nestled in his own apartment, reminding him to lock both bolts on his cagelike screen door and to be certain that the four burners on his stove were exactly vertical. Last week Doña Dolores had visited him on a Sunday morning to read *El Diario de Juárez* and the *El Paso Times* together, with a cup of coffee and the banana bread she had baked the night before. She had smelled gas as soon as she had stepped inside his apartment, a faint but definite odor of rotten eggs in the musty air. Sure enough, Don Epi had left one burner on. Now he seemed fine. Doña Dolores laid the receiver down with a soft plastic click. The room was now more gray than orange. She turned on the living room and bedroom lights.

She took out the readings Father Magaña had given her at El Centro, at the cena. The priest had brought them there at her request, having planned to give her some preliminary explanations of these difficult biblical passages. But then he had been taken aback by her fresh facial injuries, the lump of magenta, the languid bloodshot eye. "My Lord, what is the world coming to?" he gasped out loud. Father Magaña had forgotten to list the possible scholarly interpretations of evil in the Bible, whether it was figurative or real, how Saint Augustine had answered the problem of evil in the *City of God*, if evil and the good were somehow inseparable antipodes of God's system for man. The horrified young curate had also forgotten to ask why it was that such matters had concerned Doña Dolores in the first place. Suddenly these things had seemed unimportant and even stupid. Doña Dolores had assured him that she was okay, just a bit sore. She had thanked the young priest and squeezed his hand tenderly. She would find out what was what by herself.

Sitting contently on the green plastic cushions of her reading chair next to the fireplace, Doña Dolores read about the fall of man into evil, in Genesis. Why did Adam and Eve choose evil? Were they already flawed in some way before that choice? That couldn't be. Here it said clearly: "And they were both naked, the man and the woman, and were not ashamed." And here: "And God saw every thing that he had made, and, behold, it was very good." No, Adam and Eve, as created originally, were perfectly good. They would have lived forever, were it not for Satan the snake. Moreover, it was also clear that God Himself created the Tree of Knowledge of Good and Evil, created it and planted it in the Garden of Eden, with Adam and Eve. That much was also clear. So it seemed that God's world already *included* the possibility of evil, that this world was not perfect to start with. From the beginning, this world already possessed a prohibition, namely that one should not eat the fruit of the Tree of Knowledge. Indeed, man did not introduce evil into God's world. Doña Dolores thought about this for a while, why good human beings were put in a world full of possible dangers.

It would be strange, she thought, if God had done this to play a trick on humans, to trap and humiliate them out of some perverse joy. God wasn't mischievous like her grandson Arturo. It was also clear that human beings *could* be good, but often were not, for whatever reason. So just as the world was full of possible dangers, human beings were full of possible evils. What exhorted the world and humans toward good, and against evil? It seemed that they could drift easily from one place to another, like boats lost at sea. Adam and Eve did discover the snake, so maybe they *could* be good, but not perfectly so. If they had been perfect, they would never have chosen to eat Satan's apple in the first place. Maybe they were like children, Doña Dolores thought. If you allowed little ones to act badly at the beginning, soon they would know of no other way to act. You couldn't try to change persons who had acted badly for years and years. This evilness became a part of their character. But it didn't have to end up that way. They just needed a good beginning. But maybe the good beginning would be forever lost if no one could defend *why* one should have a good beginning in the first place. No one was perfect to start with. That was certain. But we lost even the *sense* of perfection the more all of us acted badly. In such a cruel world, acting in a good way would become a joke. Why should one be good to begin with? *That* was the unanswerable question. There was no "answer" but faith. Doña Dolores touched the tenderness of her cheek with the tips of her fingers, stood up, and folded a wash-cloth around four cubes of ice. The sting of the coldness receded. A serenity with the sensation of a stream diffused over the pointed ache.

Soon she fell asleep in her chair, and Genesis slipped off her lap and swooped down in an arc across the floor. Doña Dolores dreamed she was riding a black stallion across a campo dotted with pecan trees, careening through the landscape in a breathless rush at nightfall. The scent of irrigated alfalfa in the fields electrified the wind. The horizon of the Sierra Madre glorified the plains below with a path to the heavens. An eagle, as if confirming this, glided down playfully from a mountaintop, in circles and twists and precipitous plunges. The machinelike horse seemed a part of her. Its chest and haunches exploded with muscle. Its massive blue-black head huffed and swayed as if to exhort the rider into an experience of heaven, like a would-be Pegasus. Suddenly, she heard a clicking noise behind her. A sharp staccato "Click Click Click Click." She turned her head. Behind her, riding on the equine rump, a child sat with its arms reaching to grab her waist. A sinister smile on its face. The fingers contorted like talons. Its teeth snapping together like a puppet's. "Do you want my apple?" the child ghoul repeated to her mantralike.

Doña Dolores opened her eyes. Her living room was raven-black. She fumbled for the knob of her reading lamp, flicked it on and off, and nothing happened. She tried the light switch on the wall next to the TV set. That wasn't working either. She walked back to her reading chair, bumping hard against the metal tube frame with her left shin. Wincing. She rubbed her leg before moving again in this murk. Her legs were sweaty. Beyond the window, on Saint Vrain Street, the streetlights were out. All the red brick tenements and warehouses were blue-black under the moon's glow. The State National Bank, about a mile away, stood like a giant rectangular black hole guarding the pyramids of the Franklin Mountains. Doña Dolores found the box of Diamond matchsticks in her purse and lit the three votive candles in front of the picture of the Virgin Mary on her living room fireplace mantel. She found the box of Purísima candles from Juárez underneath her bed, and some cups and saucers in the kitchen. She scattered the candlelight around her apartment, first to the kitchen table and then to the bureau in her bedroom. The little flames seemed frightened in the thick of this abyss.

At once, her front door rattled wildly, as if some desperate intruder had locked its fingers in the wrought iron to rip it off its hinges. Doña Dolores fell back into her reading chair and crossed herself to plead protection in the name of the Father, the Son, and the Espíritu Santo. A gust of air crashed down through the chimney flue and, apparently animate, swirled in the dead space just below the ceiling, inflamed. A ghastly countenance metamorphosed out of the vermilion matter, screeching at her like a cloud of a thousand sparrows trapped in a fire. The yellow eyes bulged with the thrill of a killing and rolled in their sockets. She breathed in gasps, her torso and legs frozen in near catatonia. The demon's mouth widened into a chasm so dark and engulfing that she forgot the face behind it. Out of its blackness spewed forth first a trail and then a vomit-cloud of flames sulfurous. This wall of blasphemy exploded in front of her face and spawned an ontological hell around her. A cavern of baroque evil spirits, aggrieved serpents, demigods, and shapeless furies. "God save me! ¡Dios, no me abandones! I beg of you, please! Save me!" she uttered gutturally, choking on her pleas, clutching at her breast and fingering the little Christ on the Cross suspended around her neck on a limp chain.

Lucifer's giant face took on a body in mid-air, one tortured with the thrust of metal stakes driven through the outstretched claws and limp feet. An amalgam of chicken, human, and lizard. The Antichrist on its own invisible cross, laughing hideously at her as if to belie all existence of the holy. Swirls of fire like errant kites. Boils and fumes emanating from deep within the earth, like a disease and its malodors from a wretched epidermis. An earthquake underneath her body. Her hope lost. A final persistent ringing. This sonority a respite before her imminent plunge into this extravagance of evil. A ringing again. Angelic ringing. A bell to save her? A straightforward drumbeat of ringing. One final taunt from Lucifer? Doña Dolores opened her eyes again. Lucifer and his princes vanished. A final wisp of smoke wafted gently through the air like a string pulled lazily around by a beetle. Her apartment seemed intact, even quiet. The only movement was the flicker of the flames from her votive candles. That ringing again. She stood up, bumped into a chair, still stupefied, and picked up the phone.

"Doña Dolores. Can you hear me?"

"What?"

"I said, 'Can you hear me, señora?' Are you all right in there?"

"Yes. Yes, I'm fine, Don Epi."

"I just woke up and my lights were out. No electricity. Same with you?"

"Yes, no lights. The whole downtown seems dark. Maybe some sort of accident."

"That's probably right, señora. You're not worried, are you?"

"About what?"

"The lights. That they'll be rioting here like in Los Angeles. Didn't New York City have a riot some years ago when the lights went out?"

"Yes, I think so. But that won't happen here. El Paso is still a good town. More or less. Don't worry, Don Epi. Most of the people here are still gente decente."

"You're right, I'm not going to worry. You know what woke me up, Lolita? A noise. From your place, I thought. A noise like a lion's roar, and laughing. I thought I heard very loud laughing. Maybe I was dreaming. I stood up from my couch and there was nothing coming through your wall. Nothing at all."

"Oh, I see."

Espíritu Santo

"Yes. When I heard the laughing, in my dreams I thought you were in trouble. Isn't that strange? That's why I called so late. It's almost midnight, you know."

"Yes, I know. But I'm glad you called, Don Epi. You call whenever you want, you hear? Don't worry about waking me up. I always like to hear the voice of a friend."

"Thank you, señora. You are very kind. Well, I hope I see you tomorrow."

"Of course. Why don't you come over for an early dinner or late lunch. I'm making flautas and arroz con garbanzos."

"Okay. I'll bring an apple pie from Entenmann's. The one with crunch. I bought it two days ago when I cashed my check."

"That's perfect. I'll see you then. Buenas noches, señor."

"Que duerma con los angelitos. Goodnight, Doña Dolores."

The old man clunked the receiver down and scratched his head. His crooked arm reached out into the soupy darkness, and the stump mimicked its counterpart by dangling further out from his hunched shoulders, athwart. He walked tentatively forward, finding first the rickety coffee table near the sofa and then the smooth open archway to the kitchen and at last the refrigerator door. He tugged at it weakly. When it finally gave way, it slipped out of his hand and crashed into the wall. He held the door wide open; a sheet of cold darkness spilled out. Patting the gnarled hand of his good arm on each shelf, he found the flat box of Entenmann's apple pie, his absolutely favorite culinary delight, and opened the lid. ¡Ay, Chihuahua! he thought, I've already eaten more than half of it.

Don Epifanio held the box aloft for a second, pondering in the milky carbon black whether he should do what he wanted to do. Whether it was right. Of course it was. Certainly he could ask Her about the pie even if he still had money from his government check this month. It's just that he didn't want to walk to the Safeway by himself tomorrow, with his food money in his pocket. It was

Obregón's fear again. That's the only reason he would ask Her now. So he carefully slid the half-eaten apple pie out of the box and wrapped it in aluminum foil and pushed it back into the refrigerator shelf at the bottom. Then the old man carried the empty cardboard box to the kitchen table. Just above the sugar packets, on the rough surface of the plaster wall, an oblong shadow with jagged edges, like a massive tortoise shell, seemed to dance gently as if on water—a vision of Nuestra Señora de Guadalupe. Kneeling beside the table, he pushed the box just under the Virgin's downcast eyes, two slits of light in the darkness. Don Epifanio crossed himself and prayed.

After a while, it came to him. During his third prayer. The idea. Of course that was it! Why hadn't he thought of this before? Oh yes! That was the reason why he had Her. Never had She failed him. His eyes suddenly opened wide and fixed on the bananas. Four black, terribly over-ripe bananas. The ones he had often smeared on toast with peanut butter. The bananas! Today at El Centro he had received a small box of food, with three cans of soup, rice, butter, peas, corn, two cans of tuna, and the oddest thing, a bag of chocolate chips, semi-sweet. What in the world am I going to do with *those?* he had thought. Hah! Of course, it had been a while since he had turned his oven on. But he remembered the recipe well. Sugar, butter, baking soda, baking powder, eggs, flour, chocolate chips, and ripe bananas! He had all of these now. It would take some time to get everything ready. But what else was he going to do tonight in this darkness? Of course, the Virgin would also have to remind him to turn off the stove after he was done. But that would not be a problem.

By morning, the banana chocolate bread had cooled atop the stove. It was just about the best banana chocolate bread he had ever seen. Richly dark brown. The top rising just enough to hint at the delicious morsels inside. Even Doña Dolores exclaimed, when they were sitting down to eat the next day, that she had never tasted a

Espíritu Santo

more wonderful bread. When had he learned to bake, anyway? Oh, he said, it was just something my wife—God rest her soul—taught me years ago. Don Epifanio didn't tell her he had already been handy with the skillet during the revolution. But that was okay. It wasn't the important thing. It was much better just to enjoy this beautiful afternoon together.

There is a man sitting near me. At least I
think it's a man, but I'm not sure. He is
wearing an old, stiff plaid shirt, like what
my grandfather used to wear, a shirt that
desperately needs to be washed, and loose
jeans. I think he wants to kill me. I can see
his beady eyes; they glisten. He doesn't smile
at me, and he pretends as if he's not the least
interested in me. This man, without any
hair, looks straight ahead, a knife in his
hands. His skin sags around his eyes, which
have no color at all. He doesn't seem to care
about anything. Even his hands seem
relaxed, his shoulders slumped. It's as if he's
on the subway, purposely ignoring me and
appearing bored so as not to attract my
attention, or anybody else's. But we are both

*Remembering
Possibilities*

in the dark here. There is no audience except me. This quiet, ugly man is sitting on my sofa. I can see the stars through the living room window above the Hudson River. On 87th Street, a row of lights, from a stairwell, glows weakly, a pale, pulsating light that almost causes me to vomit whenever I see it. But I'm not moving now. The blade—I can see it clearly in this moonlight—shines. I may die tonight. I know that. So I start thinking about Sofia.

I always liked Sofia. In fact, I'm pretty sure I was in love with her at one time. I met her in school in Boston. I'm not going to tell you where we went to school, because then you'll think I'm some sort of arrogant jerk. Suffice it to say that some people who spend their time worrying about such things think it's a good school. I think it was crappy, and it fucking almost ruined my life. But I thought, when I left Las Cruces, that the damn place was near *Chicago,* or someplace like that. I was just an ignorant rural bastard who didn't even know where Chicago was either. But I said what the hell, took off, and got out of there as soon as I could. I probably would've outright quit after a year if I hadn't seen Sofia in Ec-10, in a dark green turtleneck. She always loved turtlenecks for some reason.

I thought she was British when I first saw her clear blue eyes. Those eyes and her pearly complexion. Just the smoothest face I had ever seen, one I'd usually stay away from, a face from the other side of town. But for some reason I didn't. I walked her home after our first section, and she didn't brush me off. In fact, she was immediately shy and also curious at the same time. I remember that as we walked down Mount Auburn together, her porcelain cheeks seemed even more radiant than before. I also noticed that she was strangely composed (maybe frightened?) and kind. She was the sort of girl I thought was much better than me, Mr. Manipulator. She was the one I wanted.

Sofia wasn't British. She was Jewish, from Chicago. We were both majoring in history, and so we'd run into each other a few times, in the same classes. I sometimes invited her for lunch to my House, and she always told me about the parties in her suite. I found out she had a boyfriend already, some dweeb from New York who looked like a hairy mouse. But I knew she liked me, and so I thought, eventually, I might get my chance. I still saw other women, wild and weird and even beautiful. But none was who I wanted. Sofia was the one I could trust. She was the one who made me better than I was. She was the sweetest of friends. The rest of the goddamn phonies at that school should've had their heads held underwater in the Charles. It really was that bad.

My last two years there I had a single suite. It was really just a dark, spooky room with a sooty fireplace, probably the maid's room at one time, and a cold bathroom. But I was happy to be alone. My mattress was on the floor, and the wall in front of my desk was a giant photographic montage of my family. I had taped the best pictures in front of me, to keep from getting too lonely. In the middle of the night, they had rescued me a few times. My mother and father had died in Delicias, Chihuahua, when I was ten years old, and so I had grown up with only my abuelitos. Theirs were the biggest pictures on my wall. I also had pictures of my older brother and his wife and their kids, although I wasn't terribly close to Rogelio. He had stayed in Las Cruces and had always hated my guts, as far as I could tell. Anyway, this was where I worked my ass off, and dreamed about Sofia, and fucking wanted to explode every now and then.

Oh, *fuck!* My face!

"Get the *fuck* up, cracker!" the bald man with the awfully clear eyes screams at me. He's smashed my left cheek with the knife handle and his bony fist. My face is burning with pain. But it's my neck I'm worried about. I smacked the table when I fell over, right on my temple, and twisted the hell out of my neck. I'm probably bleeding, but what the fuck, I'm conscious.

"I can't," I say hoarsely. Why is my voice suddenly gone? He hasn't done anything to my *voice* yet. My wrists, they're numb. I can't feel my fingers. My shoulder is really killing me. My neck and my shoulder. This guy's really a lot stronger than I thought. He's really not old at all, now that I get a closer look. Just wasted, and mean. He's on a cliff, I can tell that now. He's on a cliff just aching to jump off, and I just need to look into his awful eyes with the slightest bit of pride, and he'll jump. He'll jump right on top of me, and plunge that knife into my gut. I really shouldn't have let him tie me up so easily. It's my own fucking fault, really. I should've fought or made a break for it, even if I had gotten cut by his goddamn knife. I would've at least had a chance to escape. Just a chance. I really should've checked out his eyes more carefully when I had the opportunity. Then I would've known. But I couldn't see his fucking eyes when he woke me up. I couldn't see jackshit! Now I'm just fucked. "Please just take whatever you want."

"Shut the *fuck* up!" he screams again, kicking my stomach. He lifts me and the chair as if I'm nothing, and I'm actually a big guy. Maybe this maniac's on drugs. I've heard you get super-human strength when you're high. "Where's your fucking money?"

"The dresser. My wallet. Just take the credit cards. About two hundred dollars are in the first drawer," I say quietly, trying not to get mad, which has never been easy for me, Mr. Hothead. Really, if I had the chance, I'd twist that knife into his gut and smile while he shrieked. But I can't think about that now. I can't push him off that cliff. What would be the point? I really don't want to be buried in New York City. I may have fucked up my life, but I just don't want to end up in Queens somewhere, underneath an overpass, weeds growing through my chest. I hear him smashing things in my bedroom, but at least he's gone for now.

At the beginning of senior year, the first week in fact, I ran into Sofia in the dining hall. I kissed her on the cheek. I was really glad to see her again. Her light brown hair was short now, and straight, and she still had those huge blue eyes, that awfully kind face. I just couldn't keep myself stupid and mean when I was around her. My few friends in school said I usually looked intimidating, or simply angry. But with her, I just felt like I had a chance. My grandfather had just died that summer, so I had stayed home to be with my grandmother, to realize that she wasn't that far behind. But suddenly, with that kiss, none of that seemed to matter for a few seconds. I was happy, and she gave me a big hug too. I even felt like I belonged.

Immediately after that, we started running together regularly. My usual route was down the Cambridge side of the Charles to Fresh Pond, around the pond, and back. It was quiet, incredibly lush and green, and I felt like I escaped my own wretched suffocation for a while. We did that route the first time, but we shouldn't have. When we finished, Sofia was huffing like a quarter horse, beet red, but still smiling and sweet. She really was a trooper. I apologized for going so far and told her we'd shorten our route the next time around. *Our* route. That's exactly how I said it too. She said she enjoyed it, and we went to dinner together. As a surprise, I brought her a sundae dripping with chocolate. She had always been a fanatic for chocolate. I also told her I had another culinary surprise for her later that week. I decided to give her the bars of Mexican chocolate my abuelita had given me for making hot chocolate during the winter. I thought Sofia deserved them more than I did, and nothing else could've made me happier than seeing that smile.

Not long after that first run, I had the best day of my life, with

Sofia. It was early November, two months into the semester, and we were running together again. The leaves had turned and splashed red and yellow and orange everywhere, like a giant festival. I had been thinking that my time was running out, that I was a coward, that it was such a nightmare trying to find out if someone you really cared about, a real friend, also liked you in that special way. Hey, when you wanted just a good time, you asked and found out, just like that. It didn't really matter if they said no. Somebody, eventually, would always say yes. Somebody who wanted it for one night, somebody who thought you were "cute," somebody who was pissed at her boyfriend. But this was entirely different. If I screwed this one up, I'd probably go out and shoot myself. I mean, she could say she just wanted to be friends. I could accept that. I'd cry in my rathole for a while, but I'd accept it. But it couldn't be because I said something stupid, or said it at the wrong moment, or said it in the wrong way. I had been even quieter than I usually was. My head was pounding.

After our run, Sofia and I were walking back alongside the Charles. We found a statue of Longfellow hidden in a cluster of trees on Storrow Drive, his face dripping with stains of green, oxidized copper. It was an alcove just off the roadside, with stone benches in a semicircle around the poet, a bed of crunchy leaves on the ground, a quiet, private place. The gray stone made this place seem colder than it was. My bones were cold. It had been threatening to rain all day, so we had to get back to our dorms soon. There was a certain lack of time here. Sofia sat down in the leaves without a word, and I sat next to her. She asked me about my grandmother, who had started to forget things and constantly saw "un viejo" next to her. My brother had already moved her into his house. I told Sofia that my grandmother was okay, but that she was very old. I told her that she would probably die soon, having lived a good life despite many tragedies. I also told Sofia something I had never said to anyone before, that I regretted coming to the Northeast because I had missed out on my grandparents' final years, that the most vivid picture I had of my grandmother was her look of utter worry whenever she would ask me when I was coming back home again.

We didn't say anything else for a while. In fact, I don't remember having said a *word* after that. Sofia started wiggling her shoulders. She had often told me they became tense for no reason at all. In class I had sometimes seen her arch her back and hold one shoulder up and the other down, back and forth, like she was trying to guide a bead of water straight down her spine. I offered to give her a backrub. After a few seconds, she leaned back, right into my arms, and took one of my hands and kissed it. Just like that. My heart exploded inside my chest. I was breathing, but barely. I couldn't see her face, and I'm glad she couldn't see mine yet. I felt like I had jumped straight into heaven. She gently turned toward me and kissed me, kissed my red hot face, and I remember that my hands were touching her waist as if it might crumble on contact. That was the best day of my life.

Shit! I can't *breathe!* What the fuck is wrong with this guy? Please, don't, don't hit me again! Oh, my stomach! God, what's happening to me? Please help me! Shit! Oh, God! I can't breathe! My lungs!

"What the fuck you looking at, mother-fucker? What the *fuck* you looking at? I asked you a goddamn question, you *prick!*" he screams in his low, booming voice. Is he screaming at me? My mind is almost blank. My entire body's in pain. I'm on the floor. Am I on the floor? I can't really see much anymore, just shadows and a flickering light in the distance. Am I looking at the goddamn stairwell across the street again? There's a hot, pulsating hole in my stomach. It feels as if there's a hole there. But I don't know. I'm gasping for breath.

"Please, just take everything. Please, my God. Just leave me alone. I don't know what else you want," I say, coughing, more hoarse than I've ever been before. I hardly recognize my own voice. I'm actually still in the chair. I can tell that I'm sitting up now. He is in front of me. This He. I hate you. I will always hate you. Nothing matters anymore. Nothing has ever mattered. This life.

"What the *fuck!* You looking at me, prick? Are you the fuck *looking* at me again? Think I done enough? Think so, huh? Fucking bastard! You fucking shit!" God, not that! Anything but *that!* God, please help me. I'll bite it off. I'll goddamn bite it off! You bring it near me and I won't let go until I *tear* it off! I don't care if you kill me! I don't care, I don't care, I, I, I . . . shit. Fuck. This guy's just sick. Look at this. He's fucking peeing on me! Like a dog! Let him do whatever he wants except *that*. That's right. Finish up, you loser. Finish up and leave me alone.

"My closets. A leather jacket. Suits. Jewelry in the blue suit. Cufflinks from my father," I finally stammer, my face dripping wet. My eyes sting, but for some reason I can't smell anything. Suddenly he is not in front of me anymore.

Sofia. My beautiful Sofia. I remember the first time I slept with her. There was the thickest snow on the ground. It was the weekend before Thanksgiving. She had invited me to her house in Chicago for one week. But I didn't have the money to go. I also was nervous about my thesis, and I wanted to keep working on it. One week. I thought about how it would be to meet her parents and stay in their house, but I wasn't going to go anyway, so I never got too worked up about that. She understood. She invited me over for dinner Saturday night. The next morning she'd fly out of Logan.

We were sitting on her couch facing the fire. She and her roommates had actually cleaned up the fireplace, bought a grill to put in front of it, and hauled up a sackful of dry logs next to it. A thick white afghan covered the middle of the living room cement floor. There was a small refrigerator on one side of the couch, and a cabinet of dishes and glasses and a small table for four on the other side. A real New England home almost. The snow outside, and the eaves that sloped toward the couch, focused the warmth in that room toward us. I felt like I could stay here forever. We kissed slowly, and she asked me if I wanted to stay tonight. She said it in such an innocent way. How can I describe her eyes just then? They shimmered, and took me in. Sure, I had thought about this dozens of times since our first kiss at Longfellow Park. I wanted to be with her more than anything else in the world. But that moment, its suddenness and power, made me shudder.

We undressed in the dark cold. I was nervous. Sofia had a single bed, just like everybody else at that goddamn place, and so we couldn't help but hold on to each other. It's about the only thing I've ever appreciated about that school. I remember that her breasts were cool to the touch, and soft and perfect. We didn't make love that night, but decided to "bundle." It was the most wonderful feeling to hear her breathe while she slept, to hold her in my arms. I could see the snow falling outside her third-floor window. I listened as the radiator gurgled and sputtered next to the bed. I remember that I felt complete that night, that for once I did not want to flee my own fear. That was happiness.

After Thanksgiving, Hanukkah, and Christmas, we saw each other often. It was a wretched gauntlet of work before graduation, and we got through it together. I think we fell in love with each other. A few weeks before spring break, after my thesis was finished, she invited me to Chicago again. This time I said yes. I really wanted to celebrate with her after the academic brutality of the final year, and maybe we could start thinking about what to do together after June. I paid my ticket with a new credit card I got in the mail. I decided I could find fifteen dollars every month to keep them off my back. I could add a few hours to my job cleaning bathrooms. I could also spend a little less on pizza at Pinocchio's. I didn't feel as sulky anymore. I felt like I was finally doing things for myself. I was about to graduate with honors, goddamnit! That was a good feeling.

Their house, in a gorgeous, verdant suburb of Chicago, was shockingly huge and modern. I mean, my grandmother's house was nice and clean, but it was in the desert, for starters. One-story, with a brick flower garden my grandfather had put in himself, and linoleum floors swept so often they were worn smooth. But Sofia's house! An intercom system in each room, three stories, if you counted the study in the attic, a kitchen the size of a regular living room, and a *pool!* Her father was a corporate lawyer, and her mother was from an important family in Connecticut. When I walked into that house, I got a little tense immediately. It wasn't the kind of place you could have a sandwich in the living room and admire the two-acre park they had for a backyard. But they seemed friendly enough, and they were definitely thrilled to see their daughter.

Mr. Mossberg was a nice guy. Over dinner my first night there, he asked me what I wanted to do with my life. I told him I didn't know, but that I might apply to law school after a year or so. I kind of threw him a bone, I admit it, but I had to defend myself. These were serious parents with a serious game to play. He said he had grown up in Brooklyn, that his father had owned a deli. He had busted his butt to get where he was. That was the only way to do it, he said. I think Mr. Mossberg saw a little bit of himself in me, and his face really lit up when I told him I had just finished my thesis and received a *magna* for it. "You're on your way, Carlos. Your parents must be really proud of you," Mr. Mossberg said, smiling. I told him the story about my parents and reassured them that I was fine. I broke the ice again by mentioning that I hadn't ever had a pastrami sandwich in Las Cruces and that this was one of my greatest discoveries in college (at Elsie's, actually), better even than reading Plato's *Republic*. They laughed. It was really true. *That* was no bone. He told me that before we left he'd take me to the best deli in Chicago. He did. I still dream about the sandwich I had there.

While Mr. Mossberg was a big guy, tall and round like an ex-linebacker, his wife was sleek and almost frail. She was very shocked when I told her about my parents and seemed to search my eyes for something, as if her sympathy and her mind were in two different places. Mrs. Mossberg said they were very excited about coming to Sofia's graduation in June. It would be great to see the old school again. She was Class of '55. I told her that I thought the school was full of phonies, except for their daughter of course, which won me a wink from Sofia. Mrs. Mossberg kind of smiled politely, probably thinking I was full of shit, and asked me if I wanted more roast beef. I could tell that she thought I was a curiosity at best, an intruder at worse, and was a bit concerned when Sofia ran her fingers down my back as we walked away from the table. Mr. Mossberg didn't seem to notice one way or the other. In fact, he invited me to watch a video they had just rented on their wide-screen TV. I mean, this sucker was the size of two refrigerators! We had a great time.

That week Sofia and I swam in the pool, bopped around her neighborhood visiting old friends, and saw a couple of movies. I was just beginning to feel relaxed around that house when one morning, while Sofia was still in the shower, something happened that changed everything. After my morning run and shower, I sat downstairs at the kitchen table to read the newspaper, just as I had done all week. Mrs. Mossberg was also there drinking coffee. We usually chatted a little, about politics or Chicago or my family or Sofia. This time Mrs. Mossberg asked me how we had met and how long we had been going out. Her grayish blue eyes stared at me when I talked, stared at me when she said something. Her mind was onto something, and I had the feeling I was about to find out what it was. "Are you serious about each other?" she asked quietly, probably making sure Sofia did not overhear. I said that I cared for her daughter, and respected her, which was absolutely true, and that only time would tell what would happen to us. Anything was possible. "Carlos," she said, "you are a nice young man and it's obvious that Sofia likes you. But I have to tell you this and I hope you understand. You are not a Jew." We heard Sofia running down the stairs, and we stared at each other without saying another word. I felt like, all so suddenly, a chasm had opened in front of me and obliterated my mind.

I don't want to say that's why Sofia and I stopped seeing each other after graduation. I never told her what her mother said to me, and I honestly believe Mrs. Mossberg didn't say it in a mean way. She didn't say Jews are better than everyone else, and she didn't say I was full of shit because I wasn't a Jew. She said that her family's culture and religion were really important to them, and to Sofia too, which I already knew. She also meant that it'd be hard to include me completely in their lives because I wasn't a Jew. I think most races and cultures and religions say something similar, if they are serious about what they believe and who they are. To believe in one's "family" often means, by default, to exclude others. There's really no way around this. The question I never answered, however, was could Mrs. Mossberg ever accept me, like I think Sofia already had, if I wasn't a Jew and was still in love with her daughter. Now, I can lay it out nicely, like a puzzle, and think about all these logical possibilities. But I was pretty screwed up when Sofia and I returned to Boston the next day.

"I'm gonna kill you, you mother-fucker! Wake the fuck up!" he screams at me, his face contorted and sweaty, a few inches from mine. Finally, I hear him. Sofia's gone again, and I miss her so much.

"Please. God. Leave me alone. You have everything. Everything. Just leave me alone," I mumble, starting to see him more clearly. I can see his face now, and he's jumping off the cliff. My weakness, my vulnerability pushes him off. My body is shrieking with pain. Am I sitting up? Yes, I think I am. There's a fire in my throat, as if I've been screaming for hours. I think I've shit in my pants. Sofia, I love you so much.

"Hey, you shit! Wake up to *die!*" he screams again. I can see the knife shaking just under my nose, almost dancing. I love you, Mamá. I love you, Papá. Thank you for loving me. I love you too, Sofia. I love all of you. I can see the sack by the door. My friend is about to leave now. I can see everything finally. I am ready. *What?*

"Get away from him, you animal!" What? Harold? Harold? Oh, fuck! Hit him again! Again, Harold! Hit him again! Don't let him get up! God! No! No! Not you, Harold! No, my God! The door swings open. The madman rushes out. Harold, please don't move. Harold, I love you too! Mrs. Litvak peeks through the door and shrieks. Get the police! Get the police! Am I screaming? Can she hear me? Does she understand? Get an ambulance for Harold! I can't move. I'm in a horrible nightmare. Every second seems like an hour. I can see foam coming out of old Harold's mouth. He's bleeding heavily from his stomach, right where the blade pierced him. Good ol' Harold. I'll never forget you. I love you so much. You *had* that bastard. You had him down. You smashed that bat right into his shoulder like DiMaggio. Just like a fucking Yankee, Harold. Why didn't you smash his goddamn neck? Why didn't you crush his skull? God, Harold, you had him. He wasn't going to give you a chance either, if you let him. You didn't look into his eyes, Harold. You didn't see what I saw when he was kicking the shit out of me. Harold, you didn't look, you old bastard! I made that mistake, but *you* paid for it! Harold, I love you. Fucking Harold, please don't die.

I remember the first time I met Harold in the hallway. He gave me a Toblerone chocolate bar just like that, just because he had a couple of 'em in his grocery bag. Harold Aronson. I think he sort of saw me as his grandson, and he said I was just a "kid." I told him I was working my first job in New York, that I just wanted to make some money before I decided what I really wanted to do. He was an ex-longshoreman, a big old guy with a heavy accent, I guess Eastern European. He was a widower, lived on a pension, and occasionally went to visit friends in nursing homes. I think he was lonely, but I didn't mind talking to him because sometimes I was lonely too. I always wondered why he preferred to live alone. He could've lived with his friends. But I guess he just wanted to be independent, and maybe he was taking care of some old sores too, just like me. We had seen a few ballgames on the tube together, just like that.

It had taken me a while before I mentioned Sofia. You see, that was sort of the reason I was in New York in the first place. She had gotten a job in New York, and I also found a job in New York, but we weren't seeing each other anymore. After graduation, we had talked a few times on the phone, but had not gotten together in Manhattan yet. Too busy, too mad (at me, basically), maybe too scared. I wasn't really following her, but I didn't have anywhere else to go either. My grandmother had just died, and when I mentioned it to Harold two weeks ago, that's when I told him about Sofia.

I didn't tell him everything. I just told him that Sofia's mother didn't like me, and that I could be a mean bastard when I wasn't happy. The truth of it was that I had pushed Sofia away after we came back from Chicago. I hated myself, and I hated everything around me. I hated that diploma that this idiot handed to me with his fucking fake smile. I hated what they said about me at the House ceremony, that I was going back to "Latin America" to start a career in "politics." What the *fuck?* I hated political bullshit, and I was born in Texas goddamnit! The whole place was really fucked up. I just didn't want to be around Sofia. I didn't want to see her parents. I was glad when she told me I was "selfish" and "self-destructive." I think she knew me pretty well. When she said it was over, I felt like

I had just twisted a knife into my own gut. I cried for three days straight, alone. Anyway, I never told Harold all these gory details.

But I remember exactly what he told me. He said to call Sofia and apologize for being an "idiot." He said it just like that. Idiot. Harold got pretty worked up about it too, just like when his Yankees were losing and he'd blurt out something like "Hey! You dumb son-of-a-bitches!" Except that it always came out garbled like "Hayi sonnu-a-butches!" because his mouth watered when he got agitated. So not only did he call me an idiot, but old Harold kind of spat on me too, in an agitated, inadvertent way. He said I wouldn't be marrying the mother, and that if I loved this "Sofuya" I should call her up and tell her so, just like that. The family shit would take care of itself. I finally did believe him.

I don't really remember much else about Sofia, except her eyes. I guess I could believe them too. I mean, when I was acting like a jerk and I wanted her to kill me, because only she could, I remember her blue eyes. They were really telling me not to go away, not to be so fucked up all the time. But I wasn't listening. I couldn't listen. It's kind of a serious mental problem, this extreme self-flagellation I have. It kind of gets revved up and keeps me from doing what I should do. It's all a matter of not being so messed up inside. I guess everyone climbs out of their shithole one way or another. The real lucky ones get out before it's too late.

The chubby boy slammed the wrought-iron screen door and ran behind the trunk of the weeping willow in one corner of the yard. It was very quiet here. Whenever it rained hard, particularly after those thunderstorms that swept up the dust and drenched the desert in El Paso during April and May, Tuyi could find small frogs slithering through the mud and jumping in his mother's flower beds. At night he could hear the groans of the bullfrogs in the canal behind his house. It had not rained for days now. The ground was clumped into thick white patches that crumbled into sand if he dug them out and crushed them. But he was not looking for anything now. He just wanted to be alone. A large German

The Snake

shepherd, with a luminous black coat and a shield of gray fur on its muscular chest, shuffled slowly toward him across the patio pavement and sat down, puffing and apparently smiling at the boy. He grabbed the dog's head and kissed it just above the nose.

"Ay, Princey hermoso. They hate me. I think I was adopted. I'm not going into that house ever again! I hate being here, I hate it." Tuyi put his face into the dog's thick neck. It smelled stale and dusty. The German shepherd twisted its head and licked the back of the boy's neck. Tuyi was crying. The teardrops that fell to the ground, not on the dog's fur nor on Tuyi's Boston Celtics T-shirt, splashed into the dust and rolled up into little balls as if recoiling from their new and unforgiving environment.

"They give everything to my stupid sister and my stupid brothers and I get nothing. They're so stupid! I always work hard, I'm the one who got straight As again, and when I want a bicycle for the summer, they say I have to work for it, midiendo. I don't want to, I already have twenty-two dollars saved up, Oscar got a bicycle last year, a ten-speed, and he didn't even have anything saved up. He didn't have to go midiendo. Diana is going to Canada with the stupid drum corps this summer, they're probably spending hundreds of dollars for that, and they won't give me a bicycle! I don't want to sit there in the car waiting all day while Papá talks to these stupid people who want a new bathroom. I don't want to waste my summer in the hot sun midiendo, measuring these stupid empty lots, measuring this and that, climbing over rose bushes to put the tape right against the corner. I hate it. Why don't they make Oscar or Ariel go! Just because Oscar is in high school doesn't mean he can't go midiendo. Or Ariel could go too, he's not so small, he's not a baby anymore. And why don't they put Diana to work! Just because she's a girl. I wish I was a girl so I could get everything I wanted to for free. They hate me in this house."

"Tuyi! Tuyi!" his mother yelled from behind the screen door.
"¿En dónde estás, muchacho? Get over here at once! You're not
going outside until you throw out the trash in the kitchen and in
every room in this house. Then I want you to wash the trashcans
with the hose and sweep around the trash bins outside. I don't want
cucarachas crawling into this house from the canal. When I was
your age, young man," she said as he silently lifted the plastic trash
bag out of the tall kitchen can and yanked it tightly closed with the
yellow tie, "I was working twelve hours a day on a ranch in Chihuahua. We didn't have any *summer* vacation." As he lugged it to the
backyard, to the corner where the rock wall had two chest-high
wooden doors leading to the street and a brick enclosure over which
he would attempt to dump the trash bag into metal bins, a horrible,
putrid smell of fish—he hated fish, they had had fish last night—
wafted up to Tuyi's nose and seemed to hover around his head like a
cloud.

"¡Oye, gordito! Do you want to play? We need a fielder," said a
muscular boy, about fifteen years old, holding a bat while six or
seven other boys ran around the dead end on San Simon Street,
which had just finally been paved by the city. When the Martínez
family had moved into one of the corner lots on San Simon and San
Lorenzo, Tuyi remembered, there had been nothing but dirt roads
and scores of empty lots where they would play baseball after school.
His older brother, Oscar, was a very good player. He could smack
the softball all the way to Carranza Street and easily jog around the
bases before somebody finally found it stuck underneath a parked
car and threw it back. When it rained, however, the dirt streets got
muddy and filthy. Tuyi's mother hated that. The mud wrecked her
floors and carpets. No matter how much she yelled at the boys to
leave their sneakers outside they would forget and track it all in. But

now there was black pavement, and they could play all the time, especially in the morning during the summer. You couldn't slide home, though. You would tear up your knee.

"Déjalo. He's no good, he's too fat," a short boy with unkempt red hair said, Johnny Gutiérrez from across the street.

"Yeah. He's afraid of flies. He drops them all the time in school and el coach yells at him in P.E.," Chuy sneered.

"Shut up, pendejos. We need a fielder," the older boy interrupted again, looking at Tuyi. "Do you want to play, Tuyi?"

"No, I don't want to. But Oscar will be back from washing the car, and I think he wants to play," Tuyi said, pointing to their driveway as he began to walk away, down San Lorenzo Street. He knew Oscar would play if they only asked him.

"Ándale pues. Chuy, you and Mundis and Pelón will be on my team, and Maiyello, you have the rest of them. Okay? When Oscar comes we'll make new teams and play over there," he said, pointing to a row of empty lots down the street. "There's more room and we can slide. I'll be the fielder, you pitch, Pelón. And don't throw it so slow!"

Tuyi looked back at them as he walked down the new sidewalk, with its edges still sharp and rough where the two-by-fours had kept the cement squared. Here someone had scrawled "J + L 4/ever" and surrounded it with a slightly askew heart when the cement had been wet. Tuyi (no one called him Rodolfo, not even his parents) was happy to have won a reprieve from midiendo and from cutting the grass. He was not about to waste it playing baseball with those cabrones. He just wanted to be alone. His father had called home and had told his mother to meet him after work today. They were going to Juárez, first to a movie with Cantinflas and then maybe for some tortas on 16 de Septiembre Street, near the plaza where they had met some twenty years before. Tuyi had heard this story so many times he knew it by heart. His father, José Martínez, an

agronomy and engineering student at the Hermanos Escobar
School, had walked with some of his university buddies to the plaza.
There, young people in the 1950s, at least those in Chihuahua,
would stroll around the center. The boys, in stiff shirts with small
collars and baggy, cuffed slacks, looking at the girls. The girls, in
dresses tight at the waist and ruffled out in vertical waves toward the
hem, glancing at the boys. If a boy stopped to talk to a girl, her
friends would keep walking. Sometimes whole groups would just
stop to talk to each other. In any case, this was where Papá had first
seen Mamá, in a white cotton dress and black patent leather shoes.
Mamá had been a department store model, Tuyi remembered his
father had said, and she was the most beautiful woman Papá had
ever seen. It took him, Papá told Tuyi, five years of going steady just
to hold her hand. They were novios for a total of eight years before
they even got married! Today they were going to the movies just as
they had done so many times before. His father had told his mother
that he and Tuyi could instead go midiendo tomorrow, for a project
in Eastwood, on the east side of El Paso, just north of the freeway
from where they lived. Mr. Martínez was a construction engineer at
Cooper and Blunt in downtown El Paso. On the side he would take
up design projects for home additions, bathrooms, porches, new
bedrooms, and the like. The elder Martínez had already added a new
carport to his house and was planning to add another bathroom. He
would do the construction work himself, on the weekends, and his
sons would help. But today he wanted to go to the movies with his
wife. They were such a sappy couple.

"Buenos días, Rodolfito. Where are you going, my child?" a
woman asked, clipping off the heads of dried roses and wearing
thick black gloves. The house behind her was freshly painted white,
with a burnt orange trim. A large Doberman pinscher slept on the
threshold of the front door, breathing heavily, its paws stretched out
toward nothing in particular.

The Snake

"Buenos días, Señora Jiménez. I'm just going for a walk," Tuyi answered politely, not knowing whether to keep walking or to stop, so he stopped. His mother had told him not to be rude to the neighbors and to say hello whenever he saw them on his walks.

"Is your mother at home? I want to invite her to my niece's quinceañera this Saturday at the Blue Goose. There's going to be mariachis and lots of food. I think Glenda is going too. You and Glenda will be in 8-1 next year, in Mr. Smith's class, isn't that right?"

"Yes, señora, I'll be in 8-1. My mother is at home now, I can tell her about the party."

"You know, you're welcome to come too. It will be lots of fun. Glenda told me how the whole class was so proud of you when you won those medals in math for South Loop School. I'm glad you showed those snotty Eastwood types that a Mexicano can beat them with his mind."

"I'll tell my mother about the party. Hasta luego, señora," Tuyi muttered as he walked away quickly, embarrassed, his face flushed and nervously smiling. As he rounded the corner onto Southside Street, his stomach churned and gurgled. He thought he was going to throw up, yet he only felt a surge of gases build somewhere inside his body. He farted only when he was sure no one else was nearby. He had never figured out how he had won three first places in the citywide Number Sense competition. He had never even wanted to be in the stupid competition, but Mr. Smith and some other teachers had asked him to join the math club at school, pressured him in fact. Tuyi finally stopped avoiding them with his stoic politeness and relented when he found out Laura Downing was in Number Sense already. He had a crush on her; she was so beautiful. Anyway, they would get to leave school early on Fridays when a meet was in town. Tuyi hated the competition, however. His stomach always got upset. Time would be running out and he hadn't finished every single problem, or he hadn't checked to see if his answers were absolutely right. His bladder would be exploding, and he had to tighten his legs together to keep from bursting. Or Laura would be there, and he would be embarrassed. He couldn't talk to her; he was too fat and ugly. Or he wanted to fart again, five minutes to go in the math test. After he won his first gold medal, all hell broke loose at South Loop. The school had never won before. The principal, Mr. Jácquez, announced it over the intercom after the pledge of allegiance and the club and pep rally announcements. Rodolfo Martínez won? The kids in Tuyi's class, in 7-1, stared at Tuyi, the fat boy everybody ignored, the one who was always last running laps in P.E. Then, led by Mrs. Sherman, they began to applaud. He wanted to vomit. After he won the third gold medal in the last competition of the year at Parkland High School, he didn't want to go to school the next day. He begged his parents to let him stay at home. He pleaded with them, but they said no. The day before the principal had called to tell them about what Tuyi had done. He should be proud of himself, his mother and father said, it was good that he had worked so hard and won for Ysleta. The neighborhood was proud of him. His parents didn't tell him this, but Mr. Jácquez had told them that there would be a special presentation for Tuyi at the last pep rally of the year. He *had* to go to school that day. When Mr. Jácquez called him up to the stage in the school's auditorium, in front of the entire school, Tuyi wanted to die. A rush of adrenaline seemed to blind him into a stupor. He didn't want to move. He wasn't going to move. But two boys sitting behind him nearly lifted him up. Others yelled at him to go up to the stage. As he walked down the aisle toward the stage, he didn't notice the wild clapping or the cheering by hundreds of kids. He didn't see Laura Downing staring dreamily at him in the third row as she clutched her spiral notebook. Everything seemed supernaturally still. He couldn't breathe. Tuyi didn't remember what the principal had said on the stage. Tuyi just stared blankly at the space in front of him and wished and prayed that he could sit down again. He felt a trickle of water down his left leg which he forced to stop as his face exploded with hotness. Thank God he was wearing his new jeans! They were dark blue; nobody could notice anything. Afterward, instead of going back to his seat, he left the stage through the side exit and cleaned himself in the boy's bathroom in front of the counselor's office. The next day, on the last day of school, when the final bell rang at 3:30, as he walked home on San Lorenzo Street with everything from his locker clutched in his arms, he was the happiest person alive in Ysleta. He was free.

Tuyi walked toward the old, twisted tree just before Americas Avenue, where diesel trucks full of propane gas rumbled toward the Zaragoza International Bridge. He did not notice the Franklin Mountains to the west. The huge and jagged wall in the horizon would explode with brilliant orange streaks at dusk, but now, at mid-morning, was just gray rock against the pale blue of the big sky. His shoulders were slumped forward. He stared at the powdery dirt atop the bank of the canal, stopping every once in a while to pick up a rock and hurl it into the rows of cotton around him. He threw a rock against the 30 mph sign on the road. A horribly unpeaceful clang shattered the quiet and startled him. A huge dog—he was terrified of every dog but his own—lunged at him from behind the chainlink fence of the last house on the block. The black mutt bared its teeth at him and scratched its paws into the dust like a bull wanting so much to charge and annihilate its target. At the end of the cotton field and in front of Americas Avenue, Tuyi waited until a red Corvette zoomed by going north, and then ran across the black pavement and down the hill onto a perpendicular dirt road that hugged the canal on the other side of Americas. There would be no one here now. But maybe during the early evening some cars would pull up alongside the trees that lined this old road. Trees that grew so huge toward the heavens only because they could suck up the moisture of the irrigation canal. The cars would stop under the giant shade, and groups of men, and occasionally a few women, would sit and laugh, drink some beers, throw and smash the bottles onto rocks, just wasting time until dark, when the mosquitoes would swarm and it was just better to be inside. Walking by these trees, Tuyi had often seen used condoms lying like flattened centipedes that had dried under the sun. He knew what they were. Some stupid kids had brought condoms to school for show and whipped them around their heads at lunchtime, or hurled them at each other like giant rubber-band bombs. Tuyi had also found a ring once, made of shiny silver and with the initials "SAT" inside. He didn't know anyone with these initials. And even if he had, he probably wouldn't have returned the ring anyway: he had found it, it was his. Tuyi imagined names that might fit such initials: Sarah Archuleta Treviño, Sócrates Arturo Téllez, Sigifredo Antonio Torres, Sulema Anita Terrazas, or maybe Sam Alex Thompson, Steve Andrew Tillman, Sue Aretha Troy. After he brought the ring back home and hid it behind the books on the shelves his father had built for him, he decided that "SAT" didn't stand for a name at all but for "Such Amazing Toinkers," where toinkers originally referred to Laura Downing's breasts, then later to any amazing breasts, and then finally to anything that was breathtaking and memorable. The sun sinking behind the Franklin Mountains and leaving behind a spray of lights and shadows was a "toinker sun." The cold reddish middle of a watermelon "toinked" in his mouth whenever he first bit into its wonderful juices.

About a half mile up the dirt road, Tuyi stopped. He was at his favorite spot. He shuffled around the trunk of the oak tree and found a broken branch, which he then trimmed by snapping off its smaller branches. In the canal, he pushed his stick into mud—the water was only a couple of inches deep—and flung out globs of

The Snake

mud. He was looking for tadpoles. The last time he had found one, he had brought it up to a rock near the tree. Its tail was slimy and slick. He found a styrofoam cup, which he filled up with water. Under the tree, he watched it slither around the cup, with tiny black dots on its tail and a dark army green on its bulletlike body. After a few minutes, he flicked open his Swiss army knife and slit the tadpole open from head to tail. The creature's body quivered for a second or two and then just lay flat like green jelly smeared on a sandwich. Tuyi noticed a little tube running from the top of the tadpole's head to the bottom, and a series of smaller veins branching off into the clear green gelatinous inside. He found what he took to be one of the eyes and sliced it off with the blade. It was just a black mass of more gushy stuff, which was easily mashed with the slightest pressure. He cut the entire body of the tadpole in thin slices from head to tail and tried to see what he could see, what might explain how this thing ate, whether it had any recognizable organs, if its color inside was different from the color of its skin.

But today he didn't find anything in the mud except an old Pepsi bottlecap and more black mud. He walked toward the edge of the cotton field abutting the canal. Here he found something fascinating indeed. An army of large black ants scurried in and out of a massive anthole, those going inside carrying something on their backs, leaves or twigs or white bits that looked like pieces of bread, and those marching out of the hole following, in the opposite direction, the paths of the incoming. The ants would constantly bump into each other, go around, and then follow the trail back toward whatever it was that kept them busy. How could ants follow such a trail and be so organized? Did they see their way there? But then they wouldn't be bumping into each other all the time. Or did they smell their way up the trail and back home? Maybe they smelled each other to say hello, such as one might whose world was the nothingness of darkness. Tuyi wondered if these black ants were somehow communicating with each other as they scurried up and down blades of grass and sand and rocks, never wavering very far from their trails. Was this talking audible to them? Was there an ant language? There had to be some sort of communication going on among these ants. They were too organized in their little marching rows for this to be random. Maybe they recognized each other by smell. He thought this might be the answer because he remembered what a stink a small red ant had left on his finger after he had crushed it between his fingertips. This might be its way of saying, "Don't crush any more red ants or you'll be smeared with this sickly sweet smell," although this admonition could be of no help to one already pulverized. This warning might have been to help the red ants of the future. Maybe, ultimately, red ants didn't care if any one of them died as long as red ants in general survived and thrived without being crushed by giant fingers. Anyway, this would make red ants quite different from humans, who were individualistic and often didn't really care about anyone else except themselves. For the most part, humans were a stupid, egotistical mob. Tuyi decided to find out if black ants could somehow talk to each other.

Finding one ant astray from the rest, Tuyi pinned it down with his stick. This ant, wriggling underneath the wooden tip, was a good two feet from one of the trails near the anthole. Its legs flailed wildly against the stick, tried to grab on to it and push it off, while its head bobbed up and down against the ground. After a few seconds of this maniacal desperation—maybe this ant was screaming for help, Tuyi thought—six or seven black ants broke off from a nearby trail and rushed around the pinned ant, coming right to its head and body and onto the stick. They climbed up the stick, and just before they reached Tuyi's fingers, he let it drop to the ground. It worked. They had freed their friend from the giant stick. Tuyi looked up, satisfied that he had an answer to whether ants communicated with each other. Just about halfway up from his crouch he froze: about three

The Snake

feet away, a rattlesnake slithered over the chunks of earth churned up by the rows of cotton and onto the caked desert floor. He still couldn't hear the rattle, although the snake's tail shook violently a few inches from the ground. Tuyi was a little hard of hearing, probably just too much wax in his head. The snake stopped. It had been crawling toward him, and now it just stopped. Its long, thick body twisted tightly behind it while its raised tail still shook in the hot air. He didn't move; he was terrified. Should he run, or would it spring toward him and bite him? He stared at its head, which swayed slowly from left to right. It was going to bite him. He had to get out of there. But if he moved, it would certainly bite him, and he couldn't move fast enough to get out of its way when it lunged. He was about to jump back and run when he heard a loud crack to his right. The snake's head exploded. Orange fluid was splattered over the ground. The headless body wiggled in convulsions over the sand.

"God-damn! Git outta' there boy! Whatcha doin' playin' w'th a rattler? Ain't ye got no *sense?* Git over here!" yelled a burly, red-headed Anglo man with a pistol in his hand. There was a great, dissipating cloud of dust behind him; his truck's door was flung open. It was an INS truck, pale green with a red siren and search lights on top of the cabin.

"Is that damn thing dead? It coulda' killed you, son. ¿Hablas español? Damn it," he muttered as he looked at his gun and pushed it back into the holster strapped to his waist, "I'm gonna haf'ta make a report on firin' this weapon."

"I wasn't playing with it. I was looking at ants. I didn't see the snake."

"Well, whatcha doin' lookin' at ants? Seems you should be playin' somewhere else anyways. Do you live 'round here, boy? What's yer name?"

"Rodolfo Martínez. I live over there," Tuyi said, pointing at the cluster of houses beyond the cotton fields. "You work for the Immigration, right? Can you shoot mojados with your gun, or do you just hit them with something? How do you stop them if they're running away?"

"I don't. I corner the bastards and they usually giv' up pretty easy. I'm takin' you home, boy. Git in the truck."

"Mister, can I take the snake with me? I've never seen a snake up close before and I'd like to look at it."

"Whatha hell you want w'th a dead snake? It's gonna stink up your momma's house and I know she won't be happy 'bout that. Shit, if you wanna take it, take it. But don't git the thang all over my truck. Are you some kinda' scientist, or what?"

"I just want to see what's inside. Maybe I could take the skin off and save it. Don't they make boots out of snake skin?"

"They sure as hell do! Nice ones too. They also make 'em outta elephant and shark, but ye don't see *mae* cutting up those an'mals in my backyard. Here, put the damn thang in here." The border patrolman handed him a plastic Safeway bag. Tuyi shoved the headless carcass of the snake into the bag with his stick. The snake was much heavier than he thought, and stiff like a thick tube of solid rubber. He looked around for the head and finally found it, what was left of it, underneath the first row of cotton in the vast cotton field behind him. As the INS truck stopped in front of the Martínez home on San Lorenzo Street, and Tuyi and the border patrolman walked up the driveway, the baseball game on San Simon stopped. A couple of kids ran up to look inside the truck and see what they could see.

"They finally got him. I told ya' he was weird! He's probably a mojado, from Canada. They arrested him, el pinchi gordito."

"Shut up, you idiot. Let's finish the game. We're leading 12 to 8.

The Snake

Maybe la migra just gave him a ride. Why the hell would they bring 'em back home if he was arrested?"

"Maybe they don't arrest kids. He's in trouble, wait till his father gets home. He's gonna be pissed off. They're gonna smack him up, I know it."

"Come on! Let's finish the game or I'm going home. *Look* it, there's blood on the seat, or something."

"I told ya, he's in trouble. Maybe he threw a rock at the guy and he came to tell his parents. Maybe he hit 'em on the head with a rock. I tell ya, that Tuyi is always doin' something weird by himself. I saw him in the canal last week, digging up dirt and throwing rocks. He's loco."

"Let's go, I'm going back. Who cares about the stupid migra anyway?"

"Ay, este niño, I can't believe what he does sometimes. And what did the migra guy tell you, was he friendly?" asked Mr. Martínez, glancing back at the metal clanging in the back of the pickup as he and his wife pulled up into the driveway. The moon was bright tonight. Stars twinkled in the clear desert sky like millions of jewels in a giant cavern of space.

"Oh, Mr. Jenkins was muy gente. I wish I could've given him lunch or something, but he said he had to go. He told me Tuyi wanted to keep the snake. Can you believe that? I can't even stand the thought of those things. I told Tuyi to keep it in the backyard, in the shed. The bag was dripping all over the kitchen and it smelled horrible. I hope the dog doesn't get it and eat it."

"It looks like everyone's asleep. All the lights are out. Let me get this thing out of the truck while you open the door. Do you have your keys? Here, take mine.

"I'm gonna put it in the living room, está bien? That way we can surprise him tomorrow. Pobrecito. He must've been scared. Can you imagine being attacked by a snake? This was a good idea. I know he'll be happy. He did so well in school too."

"Well, if it keeps him out of trouble, I'll be happy. I hope he doesn't get run over by a car, though," said Mrs. Martínez while pouring milk into a pan on the stove. Only the small light over the stove was on, and that was nearly covered up as she stood waiting for the milk to bubble. "¿Quieres leche? I'm going to drink a cup and watch the news. I'm tired, but I'm not really sleepy yet."

The house was quiet except for the German shepherd in the backyard who scratched at the shed door, smelling something powerful and new just beyond it. Princey looked around, sniffed the floor around the door, licked it, and after trotting over to the metal gate to the backyard lay down with a thump against the gate, panting quietly into the dry night air. Inside the house, every room was dark except for the one in the back corner from which glimmered the bluish light of a television set, splashing against the white walls in sharp, spasmodic bursts. In the living room, a new ten-speed bicycle, blue with white stripes and black tape over the handlebars, reclined against its metal stop. Some tags were still dangling from its gears. The tires needed to be pressurized correctly because it had just been the demonstration model at the Wal-Mart on McCrae Boulevard. It was the last ten-speed they had.

Ignacio Aragón didn't really like himself,
and that's why he always wanted to sleep.
He was sitting at his creaky wooden chair in
the kitchen, looking at the children swinging their lunchboxes on their way to South
Loop School. El viejo Aragón wanted to
close his eyes and go back to the dream
world of his bed. It was November in Ysleta,
and really there was almost no reason to go
outside. The leaves were brittle on the
mulberry trees beyond his window. The
wind swirled through San Lorenzo Street
like a party of witches and warlocks. The
doors were locked. The street gate was
closed. A little girl with a Selena lunchbox
banged the gate inadvertently and ran up

Time Magician

the street and disappeared behind Doña María's fence. Ignacio Aragón was completely alone.

His wife had died many years ago, and his children had disappeared into adulthood. Don Aragón had never hated himself. That was much too extreme. But after he retired from being head janitor at South Loop—el tetón, they had always snickered not even behind his back, these little savages—he had finally had the time to think about himself. He did not like what he found. He did, indeed, have the small breasts of a woman, even though he wasn't fat. His face was really pockmarked, and his eyes were doglike and fearful. Moreover, his legs, in this old age, had become spindly, like chicken legs. Yes, he was a misshapen old man.

But that wasn't the worst part. As he sat in his house, day after day, he remembered that he had yelled at his wife way too often. Rosita had had her ways too, nitpicking him to death or simply ignoring him sometimes. But she had never deserved his tirades, even when Jiménez had scolded him. Maybe she had deserved a rebuke or two, but not these hysterical fits of anger, which had often consumed him after a long, hot day of mopping floors. It was a lack of character, Don Aragón had finally decided. He had been terribly at fault, and now he couldn't do anything about it. Last year, in a dark and relentless fit, he had switched on the gas burners without the pilot light. That was as close as he ever got to really hating himself. But then, just as suddenly, before he fainted under the cloud of fumes, he realized there was no point to that either. He just didn't like himself anymore, and that was that.

"At least I'm not going to be a pendejo about it."

Don Aragón had slept late into the morning again. He had just washed his face, and his wispy white hair above his big ears was still damp. His eyes fluttered close as the wooden chair slowly cracked and snapped under his weight. An angel came to him. A dark shadow surrounded by brilliant light. It was Rosita, or some form of her. Don Aragón, wherever he was, could barely keep his eyes on her as she slowly approached him. But it was she. There was a coldness in his heart, an awful fear.

"Why are you here?" he asked, still blinded and weak and afraid. "I am sorry I yelled at you. I am sorry I was cruel sometimes."

There was no answer. The angel-woman hovered near him, her face obscure as if in a watery grave, yet her brown eyes did stare at him. She seemed to encircle him.

"There is this horrible feeling in my heart, Rosita. For stupid little things, because I was tired, because I hated Jiménez with all my life, especially after that thing with el niño Rodrigo. I don't know. Maybe because I was a janitor with breasts who never made any money and kept you in rags! For these things, I don't know, I mistreated you. I never deserved you. I know now that I never deserved you!

"Remember that time when you offered me a bowl of frijoles con queso and I had just walked in from work and I was holding my dirty workshirt in one hand and my lunchbox in the other? I yanked the bowl from your hands and dumped it in the trash can. I will never forget the look on your face. I never apologized, I even went to sleep without kissing you goodnight, and we never talked about it. How could we? I was a madman and you just wanted to stay away until I became normal again! I was a monster! Your face was looking at a monster and I suddenly realized, after all these years, that in a way I was looking at myself. It was horrible! It is even more horrible to me now.

"I never told you this, but I hated your kindness at that moment. I hated that you offered me the frijoles just as my head was still escaping the burdens of my work. I hated that my hands were full, that you didn't care that my hands were full, that you didn't just *see* what was simmering inside my head! It was a simple act of exasperation, Rosita, can you understand that? When I saw your face, when it turned from your little crooked smile to that wide-eyed, fearful look of surprise, dear God, that was the dagger I wanted into my heart! Nothing could've caused me more pain. You think it didn't affect me, that I went to bed simply in a 'bad mood'? Oh, Rosita! I *created* that face! It should not have existed for one moment in this world! If I could just take the thousand times, if, if I could somehow take them back and have your smile instead, my kissing you and pushing my troubles behind me even during my worst moments— oh, dear God, please help me!"

The angel-woman's face seemed to smile ever so slightly. She shimmered and faded away and opened her mouth as if to say something, and then simply glowed brightly, like a perfect photograph, still here and nowhere. Her thick black hair flowed behind her as if she were falling forward, and her moon-shaped face seemed extraordinarily young, forever young. In her eyes, two fiery jewels, there were no questions or doubts.

"Rosita, Rosita! But I didn't know! I didn't know these thousand instances would suddenly become a lifetime. You come home from work and your back is in pain and you're worried about what other thing your boss will attack you for, and you're not *thinking*. You respond like the worst kind of animal. It's a jump of the mind into, into, I don't know! Oblivion! Hatred! A twisted desire to plunge into your awful fate in this world! It's a knife into my own gut! Oh, Rosita! Why was I like this? I had you! I did have something. I had *you*," Don Aragón sobbed fitfully. His tears blinded him completely, as if he had suddenly lunged into a black cave. When he finally wiped his eyes clean, the angel-woman was gone. His heart seemed to skip a beat, he gasped, and the silent world around him fell back into place with a shudder.

It was the middle of the night. His clock, as he turned toward it, read 3:32, although who knew if that was right. That damn thing seemed to have a mind of its own. All the clocks in this house, it seemed, possessed wildly different times. It didn't matter anyway. Don Ignacio Aragón got up when he felt like it, when he knew that if he didn't get up soon he would never get up again. Maybe he had heard a noise. Maybe that's why his eyes had suddenly popped open. The air was cold and dark around him. The phone rang. It was a shrill, spine-tingling sound. Was he asleep or awake? It rang again. A weird sensation floated through his stomach, like a bowel movement. It was as if his muscles wanted to answer the phone, but *he* didn't. An eerie conscious paralysis.

"Hello," Don Aragón whispered hoarsely. Could he see his breath in this deadly chill? Had he also neglected to pay the heating bill?

"Yes, hello. Mister Aragón? Is this the house of Ignacio Aragón?" a soft, quiet little voice said tentatively, almost inaudibly. A young man's voice.

"Yes. This is Ignacio Aragón. Who's this? What time is it anyway? Why are you calling me now, at this hour?" Don Aragón retorted harshly. He cleared his throat and rubbed his eyes. The weakness on the other side of the line, this timidity, immediately jabbed at him and woke him up. It was an old, almost forgotten reflex.

"I'm very sorry, Mister Aragón. But I need to talk to you. I leave El Paso in three days and I need to talk to you before then," the little voice blurted out sharply, almost squeaking at the last word. Was it simply nervous, or was it shrill, like a madman's voice? It was hard to tell. "It's Rodrigo Peña. From South Loop School. I don't know if you remember me, Mister Aragón."

"Oh, I remember you. Just ring the doorbell by the mailbox at noon," Don Aragón said, his eyes burning with pain, his head suddenly pounding. The receiver clicked on top of the phone with what seemed a soft, sickening click in this silence. A tear rolled down his cheek, and he clenched his fists, and his whole body shook, as if electrified, and if a butcher knife had been handy, he

Time Magician

would've stabbed the air, and maybe stabbed himself, for this hateful present, and what could've been, and what could now never be changed. He half-fainted on the bed and fell in and out of sleep and did not dream of anything at all. But instantly, he remembered every detail.

Rodrigo Peña. It had happened almost thirteen years ago. It should've probably, blessedly, been left in the past, like an old wound that's now a white scar. It should've remained buried with his wife in Mount Carmel Cemetery, among those things which are immutable and tragic and cursed because they have no place to go anymore, because they have played out their existence, however ill or well. It really should've just stayed hidden in the recesses of an old man's life. A bitter episode possessed of a familiar, but not fresh, pain anymore. But now, here it was again.

One day in late spring, on the last day of school at South Loop, Don Aragón had just finished stacking the dozens of chairs in the middle hallway. The lower grades had left early, as usual, and these rooms would be repainted during the summer. Jiménez had also told him that these fire-orange plastic chairs would be replaced. Three first graders had been pinched terribly by the cracks in the hard plastic just this week. The district had finally declared the chairs a hazard. Don Aragón could hear the music from the southern hallway, the far side of the E-shaped building where the seventh and eighth graders partied and laughed and made out and said goodbye to each other. E for South Loop Eagles.

He had been perspiring heavily after moving so much furniture, and one side of his lower back flashed with pain. He grabbed the large wooden push broom and started sweeping out each room, one by one. The thin white T-shirt he wore, an old cotton V-neck, clung to his skin but snapped clear and sucked in fresh air with each push and pull of the broom handle. At least he wasn't bending over anymore. There was something to this quiet rhythm that he almost enjoyed, and he had always considered it the best part of his job. It was relatively easy, and he could think while doing it, or he could simply let his mind float into the freedom of the late afternoon. Often he wondered what Rosita might cook for dinner, or he imagined how he might kiss her on the back of her neck, just to surprise her. But when it really mattered, when he saw her, he forgot these thoughts and seemed stuck in the moment. But maybe this time he wouldn't forget.

Don Aragón carried his broom and buckets and sponges, for the blackboards, to the southern hallway. A few of the parties were still winding down. But he could start on the empty science and music rooms now. A couple of kids told him to have a good summer as they cleared their lockers or simply hung around waiting to see what their friends would do. But most of them just ignored him, as they often did, or studiously looked away as he walked by. When they had been the babies of the middle hallway, these niños had smiled at him, asked him all sorts of questions, and even grabbed an occasional sponge and cheerfully wiped down the blackboard for him. But by the time they were ready to leave South Loop School, he vanished in most of their eyes, or worse, he became an object of their derision. That's just the way it had always been, and always would be. From innocence to savagery, in what seemed only a handful of seasons.

Mrs. Bennett's room was never very dirty. But she did have the habit of leaving the windows open, which overlooked the cottonfields, so when the wind picked up it became awfully dusty. Suddenly three boys were at the open door, in the hallway. Lalo Quintana, and his brother Raúl Quintana, who had been caught smoking pot in the ditch outside the school fence twice, and Rodrigo Peña. Lalo was younger, Rodrigo's age, popular, and even occasionally sweet. But he did follow his older brother around. Rodrigo was Lalo's friend, but not really a best friend simply because he seemed too quiet for the Quintanas. Maybe they were neighbors, or maybe their families knew each other. Don Aragón had seen them, and others, huddled around the basketball courts and laughing after school. Against the chainlink fence around the blacktop, he had picked up—along with brown paper bags, candy wrappers, and odd pages of math homework already graded—magazine pages of naked women.

"Ese, Nacho, what are you doing this summer?" Lalo said, grinning and glancing quickly at his older brother Raúl. Lalo's eyes were a light brownish green and seemed vaguely phosphorescent, like cat eyes. His light brown hair was as thick as a helmet, and dusty.

"Órale pues," Raúl complained, pushing Rodrigo, who glared back at the older boy as if he were really angry at him. Rodrigo took a step forward, just inside the door, and didn't move. Raúl frowned, a tall lanky shadow that always seemed restless, almost on fire. He shifted his weight, from one sneaker to another, as if he were about to leave them behind once and for all.

"Nada. Trabajar como siempre. Ya saben. To live one must work. That's how it is," Don Aragón said, almost smiling, still pushing the dust and crumpled papers toward them with his broom. "¿Y ustedes?"

"Don't know, pero que bueno que ya se acabó la escuelín," Lalo chirped, at the other side of the doorway. "I'm glad the summer's here." He glanced quickly at his older brother again, who still seemed impatient. "Ese, Nacho, el pinchi Rodrigo wanted to show you something. Go ahead, Rodrigo, no te hagas pendejo." Lalo softly kicked Rodrigo in the butt. Rodrigo almost raised a fist at his grinning friend, yet he walked forward slowly and took out a paper from one of his notebooks. Rodrigo's crew cut and chubby cheeks somehow gave him the appearance of a little boy. He handed the paper to Don Aragón.

As the old janitor focused his eyes on the paper, something startling happened. It took a while to connect the pain his brain realized with the act, and finally with its cause. The episode must have taken a total of three seconds, but its shock and severity ingrained it in his mind like a torture. A sharp, sudden agony, as if a pencil was stabbed into one side of his chest. That wretched, gratuitous, almost gleeful twisting of his flesh. The tiny hand, that evil hand, its greedy fingers clamped tightly around his nipple. The thumb viselike and angry and secure. His breast pinched rose red, and all he could do, in that precious moment, was feebly twist his shoulder to try to deflect that outstretched claw. The running away and the laughter. Those uproarious guffaws in the hallway, their echoes out in the playground. Like more invisible hands repeatedly shooting at his injured chest.

"¡Cabrones! Come back here! Go to hell! I hope you go straight to *hell!* Do you hear me?"

Don Aragón never told his wife, or anybody else, about the humiliation and shame he had felt that day. For hours afterward, it felt as if a red-hot cinder pulsed inside his chest. In the janitor's closet, he lifted up his T-shirt and gently rubbed at the red welt, to possess it somehow, but his brown skin felt only raw. He tried to forget it, to tell himself that these were just idiotic kids who did this, and much worse, to each other every day. But whenever he moved, when he bent over to pick up another trashcan, when there was the slightest jiggle to his chest, the shame tumbled back into his throat, as if someone had just slapped him. He was just a poor old man, but they did not have to do that to him.

It was a cold sunny day, and the wind had suddenly picked up considerable force. The thick dried leaves from the three moros in the frontyard spun into the air and crashed loudly against the windows. The old man's house seemed desolate in this desert landscape. The flat roof sagged to one side, like a pancake just over the edge of a plate. The two-by-sixes jutting out unevenly from the roof were black and rotten. The white plaster walls themselves were cracked, and one had partially buckled, the adobe bricks bulging like a tumor underneath the plaster. It could've easily been mistaken for an old haunted house, full of yesteryear's ghosts and tragedies, bespeaking of what could have been and what almost was, were it not for a few crucial moments. And yet, there he was still in this house. Ignacio Aragón. At least he still possessed his dreams.

It was a few minutes before noon, and Don Aragón waited for Rodrigo Peña. So many things had flooded the old man's mind in anticipation of this "confrontation." What else could he call it? First he thought that he would scream at the boy for the cruel adolescent trick that had embittered him. He even imagined that he would hit the boy with a saucepan, that he would exact revenge in a very painful and surprising manner. But then Don Aragón began to fear this meeting. What if this young man, stronger and more agile than him, decided to take a pair of pliers and torment him in more unspeakable ways? Oh, it could be awful! How could an old, half-crazed fool defend himself against such raw power? Why in the world had he agreed to meet him? He should have simply left the past in the past and moved on now, to making the few ticks left on his clock really matter. What on earth had he done?

"Hello, Nacho," a smiling young man said to Ignacio Aragón as soon as the old man opened his eyes. Rodrigo was wearing jeans and a pullover sweater, and carried a heavy metal toolbox in one hand, a thick leather jacket in the other. The face of Rodrigo the boy was still there, but now fuller and more angular, even gaunt. The hair, like all boys' hair, still seemed dusty and unkempt, even wild.

"My God! How did you get into my house?" Don Aragón stammered, his eyes still fighting against the sun's splashy glare outside. His eyes watered inadvertently, stupidly. The old man felt a great coldness surround him.

"You let me in, don't you remember? You remember everything here all alone, but you forget when it matters. You forget *now*. What's the point of remembering every detail in your mind if you're going to forget when we're face-to-face?"

"You hurt me, you son-of-a-bitch. I hated you and your stupid friends for so long. I remember *that*. I don't want your apologies."

"I am not here to apologize, Nachito. I'm sorry you thought that. I can see how you would think that, how you might even wait for such an apology for years. But I'm not here for that."

"Well, then, what the hell do you want? If I was not such an old man, I'd take a swing at you. Bah! Do whatever the hell you want. I don't care."

"You know why I'm here. You *asked* me to come here. Or don't you remember that either?"

"You're a goddamn liar, that's what you are! You were an awful boy and now you've become an unrepentant liar. *You* called me," the old man said, shaking, his mind inside a cloud of brightness that completely blinded him. "That's what I know!"

"You *wanted* me to call. You wanted me to come here and apologize. You probably wanted me to turn back the clock and not listen to the Quintanas that day and just show you, oh-so-proudly, the A on my homework! Like a time magician! You are such a dreamer, Nacho. You really should've just tried to control what you *could* control. You know, boys will be boys."

"Get the hell out of my house. You're simply taking advantage of me again. I'd kick you out if I could. With one good goddamn kick in the culo. I don't need anything from you."

"Oh, you poor little victim. I feel sorry for you. I feel so very sorry for you. Isn't that what you want, what you've always wanted?

You do need something from me. And here it is. Pobrecito Nachito. What a terrible life you had! Circumstances beyond your control! Shall we cry together? I'll help you cry if you want. Better yet. Why don't you just hit me?"

"You fucking cabrón. I'll kick your ass in a minute. I'll kick your ass, I tell you!" the old man shouted, slowly pushing himself up from his creaky chair. His knees felt weak, and the blood seemed to rush away from his face. He almost fainted. Don Aragón refocused his eyes on the resplendent figure in front of him. His heart suddenly started thumping loudly inside his chest, like a jackhammer. It was Rosita again, smiling at him.

"No, no, no. Siéntate, mi rey. I'll bring you another cup of soup. It will make you feel much better. Descansa, Ignacio. I know you are so very tired," Rosita said, her right palm held up to stop him, ready to turn around and fulfill her promise.

"Rosita, my dear. I don't know what's going on anymore. I don't know anything at all. Please don't go. Just for one moment. Please don't leave me," Don Aragón said, overcome with emotion, tears streaking down his cheeks. His entire body trembled violently. It felt as if he were floating in midair, in an ether that held both of them for only a few seconds. There was no time to lose. "I loved you all my life. I love you now more than ever. Why didn't I say that one thousand times more before you died? Why was I such an idiot all my life?"

"I'm here now. I love you too."

"Rosita, mi preciosa. I never meant to be so cruel to you. I meant to love you. I wanted to fight my anger. I wanted it not to consume me. But it did. I love you, do you hear me? Do you understand that?"

"Yes, I know that. Don't worry. I always knew that. I love you too. Let's not fight anymore. Let's never fight. I don't even remember most of our fights. I didn't think about them as much as you did,

Ignacio. I had too many things to do. Too many things around the house. Our children. My work. I simply left you alone when you were angry. You were a good man, don't worry."

"I know I wasn't. Please don't say things only to make me feel better. I know what you're doing. I want the truth now! Enough of these lies! Enough!"

"What should I do? Simply join you in your quest for pain? Let's both look at the worst things in life and call that the 'truth.' Is that what you want? We had a difficult life. We both know that," she said quietly. Her voice was almost a whisper now. Her face, her brown eyes, shimmered and then almost disappeared altogether. Don Ignacio gasped. "But I took what we had and found the good things I could find there. Friendships. Our babies. Just a pleasant moment here and there. Maybe that was just foolish."

"Rosita, I am terribly scared of dying."

"So was I."

"I am scared that I wasted my life with stupidities. That truth, my God, just *crushes* me. Why was I like that? Why? I, I just want to set everything right, to carve it in granite. Now I just want to go back and change everything. But it's impossible now! My head lurched from one hateful impossibility to another! Oh God, what have I done?"

"Nothing, Ignacio. I know you might think this too cruel again, but you have done nothing. That *is* the truth. But that should have been okay. It should have been enough. We did have our little moments here and there. And that should have been enough. It's not something that is easily understood."

"I guess I understand now."

"I know you do, my dear. I know you do."

The old grandmother glared into the hot street. Her lazy eye wandered about while the fierce eye centered her steady gaze. Damn that man, she thought. Es un coyote bien hecho. He always tries to get through the day by doing nothing, yet he still pretends to be tired from all the work that he did. Damn him. Just wait until I see him—he'll wish that he was somewhere else then. We'll see what excuse he mumbles out today.

"Here is the chicken and the milk," he said, giving her the paper bag with groceries, four bills, and coins. She looked at the money, and then she stared at him. She could not count, and the American bills seemed the same to her, although she

The Abuelita

usually recognized Lincoln's beard. This afternoon he was being honest, because he already had enough money for his cigarettes.

"Where's the rest of it? I know you took more money today. Cabrón. Bastard."

"Here is the receipt, señora. That is what I bought, and that's how much it cost. Esta señora no le tiene confianza a nadie. You don't believe me, but there it is. I took nothing." He looked away: his arched back shielded him from the gleaming gray eyes.

"Why did it take you so long? You brought nothing, yet it still takes you half the day to run an errand. Come here!" she shrieked while her head trembled. He was in the next room, where he had quickly shuffled away in search of a quiet reprieve.

"Go bring me a dozen eggs and some vegetables. I forgot the vegetables. Here. Take it and go!" She flung the money at his dark, outstretched hands. Not quick enough, he watched the coins fall to his feet. Almost daring to challenge her for this reckless impatience, he jerked up and shook his tiny bald head in disgust. But he only condemned her silently.

"¡Ándale! ¡Levantalos! Pick them up and get going!" her voice exploded into the hot afternoon air. Slowly he placed his right knee on the floor and then his left, while his beady green eyes scanned the floor for quarters, pennies, and dimes. Finally he shuffled toward the door and yanked his sagging brown pants over his belly before stepping outside. Otra vez, he thought. Again I must go to Paisano Market; but I'd rather be out there than in here.

"And don't take all day!" he heard from behind the fuzzy gray of the screen door just when he dropped his weight on the throbbing corn in his left foot. Yes, it's much better out here under the hot summer sun.

In El Paso, the heat of the day lingered within the black asphalt of the streets after the sunset. This radiant heat reminded people of the day's difficulties and of the need to endure them for only a while longer. The nights were cool and dry, however, and often a desert breeze joined the distant clanging of a freight train to welcome a deep, forgetful sleep. This soothing repose was the night's contribution to the vitality of the coming day.

The old couple lived in downtown El Paso, slightly north of El Segundo Barrio, the area of the city that passed for the poor district. Yet it was not really poor like Harlem or South Boston; it was only comfortable and familiar. The proper and proprietary sons and daughters of the city could not understand the concept of a neighborhood, and they certainly could not understand this neighborhood. They lived in suburbs that had sprung forth from the desert with the guiding hand of the developer. The matching barbecue pits, rock walls, and cactus landscapes betrayed a cold and barren land where people merely existed next to each other. A nastily self-righteous individualism pervaded the fashionably new neighborhoods, and rightfully freeway restaurants and drive-up gas stations engulfed them. But the area of El Segundo Barrio lay, as did all of downtown El Paso and central Juárez, at the ancient pass that cut through the pyramidal Franklin and Chihuahua Mountains. The heart of El Paso had always been at this mountain pass.

The history that created the progressive Sunbelt city from the Old West town of mining and railroads was eagerly overstepped by the modernists, and only El Segundo Barrio lived reluctantly with this whole history. Red brick warehouses, cracked streets, and abandoned apparel factories were girdled by clothing-by-the-pound stores, foreign exchange houses, and tenements. Old people abounded: grandmothers, grandfathers, viejitos, and solitary oldsters. Some owned modest homes that were built forty or fifty years ago, while others stayed in government housing or inexpensive apartments. Here in El Segundo Barrio, the street life burst with a peculiarly patient mortality forged out of a life that was present as history. This life expected and understood the present as if this moment was at once disarmingly familiar and, yet, still alive with a newly aroused power. At any second, it seemed, the mortality of the barrio could hurl itself heavenward, into laughter, or toward death. Each way could just as easily rip away the looming seriousness. And only then could history seize the present.

Intermixed with this place were the glossy outposts of the Sunbelt city, and Lolita's favorite was La Gallina, the fast-food chicken restaurant on Paisano Street. She would send José to the restaurant on the third day of each month when the government checks arrived in the mail. She liked their crispy wings.

"¿Qué está pasando, qué quiere ahora el maldito viejo?" she asked, pointing to a television picture of Ronald Reagan on the evening news.

"They are saying," José's eyes beamed with a distant pride, "that el Presidente wants a war with a country called Iran." He had learned English while laboring in the copper and gold mines of Colorado during the 1920s.

"Parece que está loco. Why doesn't that crazy man go fight himself? What does he have against these poor people? This man talks too much and does nothing. He reminds me of you, José. I remember el General Villa riding into Chihuahua City with his revolutionary troops when I was a little girl. Villa would hang men like this Ree-gaan on the spot. El General hated politicians and bankers.

"Pobrecitos. These poor people look as if they have nothing to eat. How can they fight the Americans?" she said, looking at a news report on the famine in Ethiopia. "They seem in worse shape than the Mexicans. Look at the eyes of this child: he is crying without tears. The mother must think this world is only for terrible suffering. You know who's at fault? The governments, they're to blame for not helping the people. They steal everything from you, and then they step on you to keep you in line. It's just like Mexico."

José went into the kitchen to wash the dishes. She watched the television silently for a few minutes and then turned it off. In the bathroom, she began to clean her aged face. The left side of her mouth drooped, and it just quivered whenever she spoke. Recounted repeatedly by her older sister, the story of the drooping mouth began when Lolita was a young woman working on her father's cattle ranch. Apparently, a bolt of lightening had struck the ground nearby and shocked Lolita into this facial disfigurement. Since strong hands and a sturdy back were the most important tools to have in those days, nobody thought twice about a doctor's cure. Anyway, the nearest healer was in Chihuahua City, which was 112 miles from El Charco. Now she not only had that mouth and the lazy eye, but also her back was arched into a hump. The stoop forced her to look up into the mirror whenever she wanted to see her reflection in the bathroom. Slowly she stroked her bluish gray hair with a comb, and her steady gaze dominated that mirror.

The sounds of the summer crickets alternated with José's heavy breathing. They lay on a folding bed that provided them with just enough room to turn in their sleep. Lolita was still awake, however. On her back she was quiet, and she attempted to distinguish the various sounds of the night, her eyes twitching nervously from left to right. Her frail and crooked body was resting, and the leg that was injured last week when she misjudged the curb on Olive Street had only a weakly pulsating pain emanating from the bruise.

Her mind jumped from a worried thought about her grandson, Arturo, to a faith in a God who resolved all the problems of the world. Arturo se va volver loco. ¿Para qué estudia tanto ese muchacho? That combative and moody child, now a young man, studied too much, and he would go insane, she thought, if he did not stop working. He should begin to enjoy the sweetest fruits of life. Usually Arturo called whenever he was deep within a frenzied state, and he would ask his grandmother for advice. Sometimes he called just to hear a steady voice imbedded in the world of pot-boiled chickens and mashed sweet potatoes. He was studying at Yale, where he was homesick and alone, and the phone bills to Texas only added poverty to his miseries. ¿Por qué no te vienes a la casa? ¡Ya no te mortifiques! She told him to come home and forget his self-imposed torment. Why was he suffering when he was handsome and had a college education? Arturo, the one blessed with such bounty, did not listen to his beloved abuelita. She worried about him tonight because he had not called her in two weeks. Tomorrow, she thought, I will say a prayer for him at the Church of the Sacred Heart, and I will ask Lupita to say one for him too. Esa señora es una santa. Lupita's prayers are always answered. That woman is God's angel of mercy.

When the sun erupted over the stark desert landscape and filled the morning shadows with an orange glow, a courageous enthusiasm often overtook the solemn solitude of the night and pushed the staggering heat of the day into the distant future. With a creaking stiffness in her back, Lolita removed the safety pins that closed the living room curtains. Then she dislodged the wooden boards that jammed shut the windows. The cool morning air soon swept into the room.

"¡Levántate! ¡Vas a llegar tarde con la señora Smith! Hurry up and drink your coffee! And get dressed for God's sake!" she yelled to José. Today he would work for Mrs. Smith, who had a ten-acre farm on the east side of town. Each week José waited eagerly for this day. For years he had worked regularly for four days during the winter, and six days during the spring and summer. Everybody was impressed with this kindly, hardworking old man who defied time with a toothy grin and a viselike grip. Yet eventually, time slowed him. Soon the people looking for someone to cut their grass, or trim tree branches, or pull weeds called young kids or professional gardeners for the job instead. After José smashed into a slow-moving locomotive on the Saint Vrain tracks, his 1956 Chevy station wagon was destroyed. Distraught and fatalistically angry, he called his grandson, who took him to Legal Aid Services. José finally received nine hundred dollars from the C & O Railroad Company after two months, yet this was only a bitter recompense: his working life had ended, even in his hopeful eyes.

The people who had already contemplated his replacement quickly dismissed him when he could no longer move his yard equipment after the accident. He was an old, slow man. They patted him on the back and gave him a farewell bonus, but they saw only their escape from a difficult decision, and not his plaintive eyes. Finally José even lost his job with the ornery, but loyal Colonel, a sixty-five-year-old stocky ex-marine. After much dillydallying, which ended when loneliness overcame the need for independence, the Colonel decided to move north to Missouri with his grandchildren. He had always looked at José with the begrudging respect that military men gave other survivors. This respect was like a rough sympathy toward another. The Colonel saw the uncommon vigor in José's work, and like a battle leader who admired the sacrifices of his men, he responded to this nobility with unflinching loyalty until the end. To give was to be needed. Now Mrs. Smith did the same. Tuesday was another work day. Another day for uncommon vigor, another day for uncommon respect.

"All right. I'll be done in just one minute, señora. Stop hurrying me! I'll catch the bus with plenty of time to spare," he said, bending over his shoes and pulling up his socks.

"¡Viejo roñoso! When you come back today, I'm going to wash those filthy pants. You look like a street bum. Don't you feel any

shame for looking like that? At least pull your pants up, so everybody doesn't stare at you as if you have some disease." She handed
him his sack lunch, which contained two jelly-and-cheese sandwiches and one ripe black banana.

"I'll be back late. After work, I have to get a loaf of bread at
Safeway. Do you want anything else?"

"Get some cigarettes and a box of doughnuts. They're on special
today."

The screen door slammed shut, and she was alone. She sat down
in the living room, holding her mug of black coffee, and looked out
into the street. From there she could watch the entrance of her two-
story apartment building and still enjoy the breeze. She stared at the
sparrows that drank water from the two plastic bowls under the
shrubs. She worried about Arturo. Why did he enjoy being separated from his family, why did he go away to attend that school? I
know he is suffering, she thought, because he is alone over there; he
is without his familia. The jobs and the schools in El Paso are not as
good as the ones over there. But the family is here, and he needs to
be with his family. I do not understand why he is over there. Mi
Dios lo va a cuidar. El verá que Arturo no se vuelva loco. She asked
God to care for her grandson and to keep him near the Holy Spirit.

Without warning, a sharp pain ripped through her lower
abdomen. She uttered a soft cry as she clutched herself, and stooped
over in the chair as if she were plunging into an abyss. Her eyes
watered while the abdominal pain intensified to a peak. Hoping that
the pain would quickly leave her body, she tried to remain still in the
chair. "God, please help me," she whispered. "Help me now with
this pain, please help me." Her grimace further distorted her blood-
less face, and the perspiration covering her neck and shoulders so
cooled her spotted brown skin that she lost her bodily sensation. She
was dizzy. She reached for the nearby sofa with her left hand. "God,
I don't want to die, please help me. Ayúdame Dios, por favor,

ayúdame." She collapsed onto the sofa and lay there breathing heavily. The stillness in her apartment was interrupted only by the whirring of passing cars, the squeaky chirping of the birds, and the spasmodic gasps of her guttural breathing. Soon the pain receded, and she fell asleep exhausted.

"Señora, wake up, Lolita," said a high-pitched voice from behind the screen door. It was Margarita, a good friend who lived next door.

"No, Margarita. I can't go today. I don't feel very well."

"The girls will be disappointed. We are starting to make our plans for the Christmas celebration, and since you are the second oldest member at El Centro you will be a princess in the parade this year."

"I know. But today is not a good day for me. I need to rest," Lolita said. Finally she lifted herself from the sofa and sat in the chair, her legs quivering after the sudden motion. "Can you please ask Lupita or María to finish my side of the quilt? I'm falling behind and I don't want everybody to wait for me."

"Of course. Do you want me to bring you food from the cafeteria? I'll just ask Rodrigo to give me a plate for you. I'm sure he'll give me double portions too, you know how much he likes you."

"You are an angel of God, Margarita. Thank you for helping this poor old woman." Margarita left, and through the window Lolita saw her friend disappear into the brightness of Saint Vrain Street. She enjoyed seeing everybody at El Centro, and for many years she had never missed a day. There the oldsters were taught how to make stuffed animals for their grandchildren, colorful quilts, and dolls. Each month they also went on field trips, to the zoo or to neighborhood parks. The best part of each day at El Centro was lunch, when Lolita and her friends sat in the corner of the cafeteria next to the coffee machine. She led the largest and most popular table during lunch, a boisterous gathering of real friends. When she had first gone to El Centro, however, she had sat alone, and later with Elsa, a

The Abuelita

pretty widow who had just retired and moved into the government housing on San Antonio Street. Unlike others at El Centro, Lolita easily ignored or dismissed the notions that became the tenets of the day in the reinforcing swirl of the demagogic cliques. Her jokes and ready smile were interrupted by quick and pointed comments that seemed to cleanse the musty air. This critical gaiety surprised the shy and controlled people who sought only quiet company, and alienated those cynically lonely victims who came to El Centro only to suffer before an audience. Soon, most of the señoras and señores, the gray-haired and the dark-skinned, began to seek Lolita's table at lunch. Some came timidly hoping to be near the merriment and irreverence, while others sprang forth into the tumble with their dormant personalities enticed by her laughing eyes. Last year she had ceased her daily visits to El Centro because she was often tired. This month she had already missed one week. Today she did not go.

She sat still as the pain lingered in her abdomen like a faint pulse. The late morning yielded to midday, and the enlivening freshness gave way to an intensive heat that subdued the day. She concentrated on the pain, which focused her on the fragility of her body. Her eyes, glazed and tearful, first stared at the floor and then glanced outside at the birds splashing in the water. When she shifted her body in the chair, the remnants of the pain suddenly sharpened into prickly points against this deep and dull vagueness inside her body. Even the tilt of her head became a concentrated, gentle motion haunted by a lurking distress. "Dios, no quiero morir. Pero cuando me muera, espero estar en Tus manos y en Tu gloria," she repeated in a breathless chant. Knowing that the time to face death was not now, she prayed to God. She prayed because that time was not now, and thus she could still hope. The attacks her failing body endured, however, could only remind her of this irrepressible time that would soon come. This horrible time that was no time at all.

The desperation and the fear finally surrendered to a time where she could wait for death again. A time and a place where death was not here now, although it lurked nearby. She prayed after these attacks because praying was the best way to unveil and to confront the waiting. Usually, pain constricted the body and the mind like a foe attacking the ramparts. The self retrenched. In the young, however, the healthy presence of the body overran the self's embankments and spilled out into the world in a euphoric wave of pride. For Lolita, her waiting anticipated death as an important event in a vigorous life. But this anticipation was not a morbid ideal in a life dragging itself through an abyss to live, strangely and gloriously, within a kingdom of defeat. Lolita's waiting came from her life's roaring engagement with the world. A worthy life faced death like one confronting an unkind intruder who demanded a severe review of the past: the melancholy and fear in the response to the dreaded inquiry were joined with the joy and fulfillment of having acted already on these questions in life. Most never wanted to die, but a few were ready.

Lolita prayed to be able to face the time when the pain reached an apex of intensity. Amid the overflowing and uncontrollable pain, she would sense a stillness that eventually ceded to a soothing return from sheer pain. During several attacks, she eagerly anticipated this stillness: it was the beginning of the end of the ordeal. Today, for the first time, she contemplated the possibility of not returning from this peak. She thought about the time beyond the stillness. She did not know what to think; she did not know how to comprehend the time when the waiting was not proceeded by a return. She prayed and asked God to help her. She asked not for life but to be in the time after death. I am in your hands, she thought, please let me enter your kingdom of justice so that I can live in your glory forever. Slowly she lifted herself from the chair and walked to the kitchen.

She heated chicken broth on the stove for lunch. As she sipped the broth from a cup, she was tranquil. I know that I will die, and when the Lord calls me to heaven, I shall go into His hands. I hope that José remembers my cigarettes.

The cool air of the evening brought back the vivid life of the morning. Soaking his callous feet in salty hot water, José was in the kitchen. His limp and dusty trousers gently unrolled into the steamy water while his bald head reclined against the wall. His rigidly concave back almost pushed him onto the floor. He was sitting on a kitchen chair and resting. His eyes were closed.

Pobrecito, she thought, the poor man is tired. She looked at him for a moment and quietly shuffled to the bathroom, where she was scrubbing his foamy work pants on an aluminum washboard. I hope he already ate dinner and washed the dishes because the news will be on soon.

"José, José!" she yelled from her supplicating position in front of the tub. "Levantate y prende las noticias. No te quedes dormido en la silla como un perro. Get up and turn on the television. You can sleep after the news!" José grumbled something about the need to pace yourself, yet rose to his feet to finish the dishes. His soggy trousers left a trail of water droplets across the kitchen floor. The telephone rang, and Lolita answered it in the bedroom.

"Hallo," she said.

"¡Abuelita loca!" screamed a man's voice. "How are you and El Tigre? Have you been good, señora? I miss both of you."

"Arturo," she responded with a sigh. "Why haven't you called? I was worried about you. How do we know you are okay when you don't answer the phone? We called you about two days ago and nobody answered."

"¡Ay, señora!" he said enthusiastically. "I've been working almost as much as the Tiger works under the hot sun. Instead of pulling weeds, I've been sitting in the library reading and writing. I was probably in the library when you called. Usually I stay there until it closes at midnight. I am the nocturnal gremlin who explores the darkness, you know. But don't worry about me, abuela, I'm fine. I'm just tired of studying so much." Actually, the solitary Arturo was fighting off desperation. The mixture of an intense academic burden with his longing for the simplicity of life at home caused him to almost suffocate some nights, when matter seemed to torment even his quietest movements. Add to that his insistence on studying philosophy and his use of this critique as a relentless self-destruction of beliefs, and the world of Arturo thus fluctuated violently. He used his uneasy self, like a bustling laboratory, to foment and experience new ideas. But periodically, the experiments went awry, beyond his own nature, and his world rocked dangerously on the edge of an abyss, almost ready to fall.

"Where is the Tiger?" asked Arturo, the pace of his bouncing right leg even quicker than before.

"Aquí estoy," José said firmly, "your abuelita is in the bedroom and I have the kitchen phone."

"How are my parents and the rest of the family?" Arturo asked after a short silence.

"Everybody is fine. Your mother and father were here two days ago. They were going to the movies in Juárez. They're always out, having fun and enjoying themselves. I hope they don't neglect your brother," she said.

"Don't worry about Rudy, he can take care of himself. I am also well, but I'm tired and I miss being at home. Sometimes I feel so lonely that I can't read another page. They give us too much work at this school. Sometimes I want to give up on everything," Arturo said, resting his head on the cool wood of his writing desk. He needed to hear their voices to feel calm. By appreciating the worth in their lives, Arturo indirectly searched for and found self-respect.

The Abuelita

To care was to see the fragility of this ephemeral world, where man sacrificed himself in order to possess the good life. When he called his abuelitos, Arturo felt needed, and they felt needed too.

"Well, if you don't like it there, get out," Lolita said, "just get out. Didn't you finish school already, didn't you tell me that? What are you doing there anyway?"

"Yes, señora, but this is for another degree. I want to improve myself and I want to learn more things so I will be an educated person." Arturo explained simply so that his grandparents understood why he was still in school at the age of twenty-five. "Remember what you told me: El que adelante no ve atrás se queda." He who does not look forward is left behind.

"That's right, but why are you killing yourself with all that work? Why do you want to read all the time? You're going to drive yourself crazy."

"I'm studying because I think I have important ideas. My schooling is important to me and I must do it," Arturo responded in a loud, nearly shrill tone. When he studied furiously, he was isolated from the world, and he called them to claw at his loneliness. "I'm studying some German philosophers. One of them is called Heidegger. That is, HEI-DEG-GER," he repeated clearly, so that they could understand the name.

"Who is this Hi-ger?" Lolita asked. "Aren't these Germans hated by many countries, are they not a bad people? Why are you studying them?"

"No, abuelita. Not all Germans are gente mala. They're often very intelligent. This HEI-DEG-GER writes about death and about how it should be important to people during life. What do you think of that?"

"Ese viejo está loco. That man is a lunatic. How can death be important during your life when you have so many reasons to live? If you continue to read those philosophers, you're going to be as crazy as they are. That idiot Hi-ger probably never had a happy day in his life.

"Look, my son," she continued, "drop those books, and go outside for a walk, or go out with some of your friends. Stop studying too much and don't be a crazy hermit. Remember what I told you: El que adelante no ve atrás se queda. Do you know what that means? It means that you should stop waiting for death and let the Germans worry about that. Find contentment and happiness in your life before you realize that your time to live is almost over. Use each day to make yourself and others happy, and then you will never have regrets in your life. I'm an old woman now, but I will only stop when the good Lord brings me down with his own two hands."

"Gracias, abuelita. I'll be okay, don't worry about me. I just felt lonely and depressed, but I feel better now," he answered.

"Arturo, you are only beginning to live. You're young. Enjoy the rest of your life. And don't waste it by studying all the time. The only things that you'll get from plunging into your books are depression, blindness, and insanity. Have faith in God and he will show you what is life. I will pray for you on Sunday, and I'll ask God to help you when you are lonely and afraid. I'll also ask Lupita to pray for you. She is an angel of mercy," said Lolita.

"Go out and have a beer, or go to a party," José interrupted, his tight skin yielding to a grin.

"Don't pay attention to that drunken old fool! How can you tell him to do that? That may be the answer for a useless old man like you. Go ahead, go out and get yourself drunk. I'll leave you out there in the streets with the stray dogs! And if I don't punish you first, the Lord will surely toss you into the dark pit with the horned one. Don't pay attention to him, Arturo," she said.

"Ay, señora, you always take everything I say the wrong way," José responded resignedly.

"Please don't fight. I didn't call to listen to a fight. I have to go

The Abuelita

now. I have a lot of work and I also don't want to stay up late," Arturo said.

"Okay. But remember what I told you. Don't drive yourself crazy. Relax and enjoy yourself," she said. "And call us again whenever you can. I'll tell your parents that you are well. Do you want me to send you more hot chocolate packets and homemade cookies? I'll wrap them up and I'll tell your brother to put them in the mail. And Arturo, please don't suffer all the time. That is no way to live."

"Thank you, señora. Don't worry about me, I'll survive. I miss the family. Please say hello to everyone. Goodbye, Tiger. Don't let la abuelita get the best of you. You know how she is. Hasta luego, we'll talk again soon."

Lolita walked into the kitchen while José was placing the leftovers in the refrigerator. She looked at him and almost said something, but returned to the bedroom and undressed. She was happy after having talked with Arturo, yet as she pulled her airy white nightgown over her knees, her eyes looked plaintively at the ground. How can he be preoccupied with death at his age? That Hi-ger is probably a poor bastard with nothing to love; maybe he doesn't have a God, she thought. Poor lonely bastard. I'm not surprised he writes all the time; he probably thinks writing is all there is in life. And my pobrecito Arturo, alone and separated from his family, he must be digging himself into an early grave of insanity by working too hard. That damn German is the only companion he has over there.

She folded the bedspread and uncovered the soft white sheets. José was washing his face and shaving. Both were soon in bed, and the apartment was dark and quiet. Yet Lolita was still awake.

Death.

She remembered the abdominal pain. She could pose the question about death but did not know how to answer it. Without knowing how to find an adequate answer, she asked about her life and the end that would be death. The dark stillness of the room seemed to crush her into an existence where she faced herself alone, although she also seemed everywhere. She remembered Arturo and the anxiety that he felt when he studied too much and when he was alone. Why does he do that? He only needs to live his life and to enjoy it. I am old—what choice do I have? I must think about death because I know I will not live forever. I feel old, she thought, my body reminds me each day that I will be here for only a while longer. I think about death because I can see clearly that it will soon be a part of my life. When you are young, you can live forever, and you can make a life that is as ferocious as an angry lion's life. When you are old, however, you must retreat from this ferocity and become an old child: you live each day with your eyes open to the world, knowing that this wonderful creation will soon be taken from your hands. Why does Arturo plunge himself into these pits of torment? He needn't worry about death. Of course, he will also die, but not soon. And with the Lord's help, he will live a long life. Then why think about death now? Why?

She closed her eyes, attempting to impose rest by command. There must be something else that Arturo is trying to do, she thought. I can't believe he is tormenting himself for nothing. Well, whatever it is, it seems a waste of time. That crazy Hi-ger just put some notions into poor Arturo's head.

She shifted her weight to find an elusive comfort, yet a persistent tenderness spread through her body like a gentle wave. The pain in her abdomen slowly swelled from a gaseous sensation to an intense pain that drained her mind. She braced herself for the attack, rigidly fixing herself and hoping this posture would discourage the agony assaulting her body. The pain was now a roaring, evil wave, and she began to choke, her larynx contracting with one giant spasm. Her extremities twitched with the convulsions reverberating throughout her body. José stirred, yet remained in a deep sleep. On the bed with her hands clenching her stomach, she winced at the blinding light pounding her exposed face. Her forehead was pale, and the loose skin under her neck tightened as she pushed her head into the pillow.

Damn death.

I'm going to fight you; energy to kill is energy to live. Damn this pain. Stop, God, please stop. If I die, God help me, please help me God. She reached the apex of intensity. Everything in the world was still while she was uncontrollably spinning, and then suddenly she was motionless while the world itself was shaking violently. Nausea. The darkness of the room became a life of specificity and sheer intensity—she could discern the minutest detail in the mass of darkness. She breathed deeply, and the pain finally receded. Her pillow and gown were soaked. Attempting to regain her balance and trying to quell the rising vomit in her stomach, she lay in bed for a moment.

Damn, she thought, as she slowly rose from the bed. Tomorrow I will go to El Centro, and I will get ready for the Christmas parade. She lit a cigarette on the kitchen stove and sat quietly puffing away great clouds of smoke. Tomorrow I will get someone to take me to Licon's Dairy; I want asaderos and cheese for my chile con calabazas. Gently the night yielded to the dawn, and Lolita sensed the cold desert breeze coming in through the open window.

Don Chechepe Martínez was asleep under
the pecan tree, his mouth as wide open and
dry as the caked earth in the cotton fields
under the Ysleta sun. The old man was lying
in a ditch. He had on a red flannel shirt and
brown, mud-smeared trousers. Near the
ditch was a red wheelbarrow with a pile of
plastic flowerpots. Most of the pots were
empty except for the six begonia seedlings
next to the canvas work gloves and the
trowel at the back of the wheelbarrow. A
gust of wind swept through the yard, rustled
the leaves against the fence, and brought
down with it two sparrows that danced and
splashed in the pool of dirty water in the
birdbath. In the frontyard, beyond the trees,
the trunks of which had been neatly

The Gardener

splashed with lime, a screen door creaked slowly open. There was silence again, the peaceful silence of spring. Suddenly the birds flew off as a head of white hair poked out from the corner of the shed. The latch of the chainlink gate flipped open with a metallic clang. An old woman, her shoulders hunched over, shuffled into the yard. She didn't close the gate behind her. At the fence alongside the ditch in the back, she slowed down considerably, which meant she was barely walking forward since Maggie Johnson, at her best, skidded forward in tiny jerks. She stepped gingerly around the dried leaves so as not to make a sound and found Don Chechepe happily asleep, a ray of sun on his dark brown cheek. She smiled.

She opened the back fence gate carefully and stood a couple of steps from the old man, who snored a muffled honk through his nose. She didn't close this gate either. Maggie shuffled a few feet away from Don Chechepe, toward the end of her property, which extended for two acres on Socorro Road. The city had not yet paved this road, and she preferred it that way. Once in a while a farm truck with cotton might rumble by and stir up a lot of white dust. But that would be nothing compared to the traffic and the *pandemonium* she expected once Socorro was paved. Anyway, what could she do, by herself, widowed, with no family left in Texas and none within six hundred miles. She wrote several letters but received only polite responses from those *bureaucrats*. So she had Don Chechepe plant thick evergreen bushes along Socorro Road, well inside her property line. This would be her wall against the onslaught of a city growing wildly, beyond the sensible proportions of peace and quiet.

Standing at the end of the ditch that irrigated her property, Maggie yanked open the metal trapdoor that kept the water in the main ditch from the field. She glanced back: Don Chechepe was still deep in an exquisite slumber. A gush of water rushed in, too much water, and so she tapped the door down with her palm to slow the flow into the ditch. She didn't want to drown the poor man. She just wanted to trick him. She started shuffling as quickly as she could, passing the steady trickle of water that crept toward Don Chechepe. Hurrying, she swung the back gate closed, rushed past the birdbath, her pale legs speeding up to a near walk, and stood panting and perspiring. Behind the front gate, Maggie could see Don Chechepe still asleep in the ditch, the water about two feet away. Let's see if he doesn't come into the house now, she thought. He'll be as wet as a seal!

"¿Qué diablo? ¡Ay Dios! Ya me moje todo," Don Chechepe mumbled, barely awake, the water gurgling behind his back, into his trousers, against his waist. Still bewildered, the old man planted his hands against the ditch bank to push himself up. Water and mud splashed onto his face. Maggie snorted out a laugh but quickly put her hand over her mouth. Don Chechepe finally held up his head and sat up. The water was now running coolly through his underwear. He spotted the open trapdoor at one end of the ditch, searched the field to the dead tree trunk at the edge of Mrs. Johnson's property line, but saw no one. "!Malditos!"

A screen door creaked slowly open again.

"My goodness! What in blazes haeppened to you, Chepis?" said Maggie, standing under the garage door, holding Don Chechepe's twenty dollar bill in her hand. With her Southwestern twang, she mutilated what was already a mutilated name. "Chechepe" had been "José" when Don Chechepe was born in El Ojo del Obispo, near Chihuahua City. After he moved to El Paso and worked on a poultry farm on the outskirts of town, his friends called him "Pepe," which was later changed to "Chihuahua Pepe" to distinguish him from all the other Pepes working on the farm. "Chihuahua Pepe" became "Chechepe" after a while, and then "*Don* Chechepe" when

The Gardener

he began to lose his hair, and now finally "Chepis" with Mrs. Johnson. He didn't mind what they called him. They were all good people.

"Well, señora, I reelly donno. But mebee I do, mebee."

"Dang it, Chepis. What do you maean?"

"Well, los indios, I t'ink."

"Did them Tigua boys open up the irrigation again? *Goodness!* I'm gonna have to spaeak to their mommas. So the ditch wuz fillin' with water and you fell in?"

"Sí, señora. Somet'ing like daat."

"Did you hurt yourself?"

"No. I'em okay. But, no, I'em wet. I donno. Mebee I go home ahorita, 'n' dry a little bit. I'em okay."

"That's a bunch'a you-know-what, Chepis. You're gonna be dry befowar goin' home. Other-wise, you're gonna be seeick. I have some old pants and shirts from Doctor Johnson. I never did throw 'em out. They've been there yaears."

"Okay, señora. Gracias."

Don Chechepe followed Mrs. Johnson through the back door of the house. He had worked for her for eight years now, and yet he had never really been inside. He had stepped just inside the threshold a couple of times, waiting for her to get something for him, usually his twenty dollars. She would invite him in, but he would just stay by the door so as not to be impolite. And impolite he never was, and never could be, which was something most people knew already. They knew he was a good man. In any case, he was usually filthy from his work, and he didn't want to track mud and dirt into her home. So he never went inside, that is, until today.

Eight years with the Widow Johnson. It didn't seem that long to him. Don Chechepe had first been introduced to Mrs. Johnson by Colonel Wilfred Smith, who also lived on Socorro Road but further east, toward the city of Socorro itself. Don Chechepe had worked for Colonel Smith for almost fifteen years now. Fridays and Saturdays Don Chechepe took Bus 80 from his little apartment in El Segundo Barrio in downtown El Paso to Colonel Smith's. The fare was only a dime with his senior citizen's card. Mondays and Wednesdays he worked for Mrs. Johnson. The old man had always liked working outside. It was peaceful and reminded him of growing up on a farm in Chihuahua. Don Chechepe had first been a chicken hauler, then a sweeper at the poultry farm, and finally a gardener. Outside, under the sun again, whenever his bones ached, he would take a nap and, soon enough, get up and do some more work and stick his hands into the black moistness of the earth to plant another seed for the spring.

"Here. You come in here and git out of your clothin'. There's a towel inside the door. I'll brang you somethin' nice and dry."

"Gracias, señora." Don Chechepe turned slowly around in the small space of the bathroom. It was clean, with white and black ceramic tiles on the walls, and an old cast-iron bathtub with white, cross-shaped faucets.

"Chepis. You might as well take a bath. The 80 goes on by in another hour or so. You cain take that one," he heard suddenly from the other side of the door. Don Chechepe, hunched over and crooked, turned his head slowly around the bathroom like an ancient turtle, then unbuckled his belt and pushed off his shoes.

"Chepis. I'm laeavin' your clothin' by the door," he heard again, sitting inside the bathtub, the steamy water lapping up against his leathery brown skin and loosening up the black grime inside the ridges etched into his hands and feet.

He finished his bath and climbed out of the bathtub with such a slow deliberateness that it seemed there was more stopping than moving in his creaky limbs. His biceps were still taut and sinewy, as were the muscles on his legs. His belly was bloated and tight as a drum, which gave him the appearance of a beetle. He opened the door slowly, grabbed the clothes on the floor, and pushed the door shut with his back. With his chapped and calloused fingers, he passed his hand over the smooth gray wool of the cuffed slacks and squeezed the springy argyle socks. He had an entire outfit here: undershorts, an undershirt, a black leather belt, Bostonian black shoes, a pair of slacks, socks, a blue oxford shirt, and a wool sweater vest. The doctor must have been some looker, he thought.

"My, my. Well don't you look haendsome!" exclaimed Mrs. Johnson. She was sitting on the living room couch, a red brocade with silvery white pillow cushions tucked into each corner. "Set yourself down right here, Chepis. How'r you feelin'?"

"Okay, señora. T'ank you for the ropa. I breeing it back on Monday."

"You ain't brangin' back nothin'. I should'a given them to you yaears ago. They ain't doin' no good in the closet."

"Gracias, señora."

"And plaeaze, stop callin' mae seynora. It makes mae feel ready for the grave. Call mae Maggie. All my fraiends call mae Maggie and I consider you my fraiend."

"T'ank you, Maggee. Si somos amigos, then, pleeze call me José."

"All raighty, Hosae. That's much, much better." Maggie got up and shuffled to the kitchen and brought back two cups of black coffee on a pushcart. Next to the cups were a matching sugar bowl and creamer of Lancaster English ironstone china, two spoons, and a tray of sugar cookies. "Let's have a cup of coffee, Hosae."

"Gracias, Maggee."

"You know, Hosae, I'm here all by my loanesome. It's been that way for yaears. You live alone too, is that raight?"

"Yes, señora Maggee. Mi esposa se murio hace seis años."

"Yaes. My husband died about nine yaears ago too, just befowar you caeme here. He wuz a good man." She put the cup to her lips, took a sip, and placed it carefully next to the sugar cookies. He was sitting next to her on the other side of the sofa, his coffee cup on his knee. Outside it was getting dark. The thick, black clouds of a desert storm were about to unleash themselves on the ground. The smell of rain swirled in the violent wind. Fat drops of water pattered against the window.

"Well, you know, Hosae, I would be so plaeased if you stayed for dinner. We could talk about gardening and such."

"T'ank you, Maggee. Con mucho gusto."

"Well, that's simply wonderful! Do you like pot roast and sweet paotatoes? I put some carrots and prunes in too."

"Oh, sí. D'at sounds reeal good. You know, señora Maggee, we could plant a jardín of vegetables theeze year."

"Oh, yaes!"

"Tomate, chile california, jalapeño, calabaza, pepino."

"That sounds so excitin'!"

Don Chechepe was quiet for a moment, staring at the pushcart in front of him and the fireplace beyond, thinking. He pushed his legs out from the sofa and leaned back to find something in his pocket.

"Señora Maggee. Here, I don want theeze. I can't." With his fingers, thick and nicked with small cuts, he put the twenty dollars on the pushcart.

"But Hosae! You work so ha-rd, that money is yours!"

"No, Maggee. I can't take any dinero from my frieends. I weell not."

"Hosae, what are you doin'? Dang it, that money is yours!"

"No. No voy a aceptar dinero de mis amigos. Daat's the way it weell be."

"No it ain't! If you think you're stubborn, well, my fraiend, you don't know what stubborn is!" said Maggie, turning red, walking deliberately toward the kitchen. Don Chechepe couldn't really see what she was doing from the sofa, but he heard a pot cover clang against some other metal and then nothing. Silence. Maggie came back and sat down. She was still red.

"Hosae, are you takin' the money?"

"No, señora."

"Okay, but plaeaze no more seynoras, at least not today. Maybe I should start callin' you 'Mister Hosae,' see how *you* like it."

"No, Maggee."

"Okay, then. I want you to think about what I'm gonna ask you. But befowar I ask it, you need to know this is somethin' a *fraiend* would ask of you. And I do maean fraiend, okay?"

"Ándale pues."

"You like workin' in my garden, raight?"

"Yes."

"And I'm glad you do too. But you won't take money for it. Well, Hosae, I want you to keep workin' in my garden. I like that you're here."

"T'ank you, Maggee. I like beeing here."

"Go-od. You and I live aloane, in separate places. Yet you still want to work here and I want you to work here, but you won't take any money. Raight?

"Sí."

"All raight. Now I want to ask you, as a fraiend, would you like .to move into this house with mae? Into one of the empty bedrooms. I got three of 'em. This way, you could work on my garden, we could be together, as *fraiends,* and you wouldn't have to take your bus all the way downtown. You wouldn't be aloane, we would be fraiends livin' together. What do you say about that?"

Don Chechepe stared at the pushcart for a moment, looked at

the fireplace again, and turned around to look at Maggie with his face down. When he looked into her eyes, he could look at them for only a moment, as if he were looking into the sun. "Okay, señora Maggee. I agree to daat."

"Wonderful! Simply wonderful. I think dinner's rea-dy, *Mister* Hosae. Why don't we talk about the details in the kitchen, all raight?"

"Okay."

As Maggie followed Don Chechepe into the kitchen, both of them shuffling along in a slow-moving convoy, the kettle in the kitchen hissed with steam and spat out droplets of water. The rain outside, with the wind, seemed to want to get inside through the window and put an end to all the fuss on the stove.

The young woman yanked open the
venetian blinds and snapped at the little boy
in the troubled sleep in one corner of the
colorful and cluttered bedroom.

"Juanito! I'm not going to wait for you
today. Get up or you'll have to walk to
school alone."

She stood over the single bed in a tight
blue dress, her hands on her hips, and
pulled off the bedcover printed with
whimsically colored freight trains and
dropped it on the floor. The little boy, still
half-huddled inside his dream, finally
turned over and rubbed his eyes against the
bright light. His cheeks felt raw and wet. He
got up, walked past his oldest sister without

*The Last
Tortilla*

even glancing at her, and stumbled into the bathroom in the hallway.

Alejandra Márquez marched back to her bedroom but couldn't find her Pink Sérénade lipstick on her bureau, where it usually was. She walked into the empty bedroom across from Juanito's, Teresa's old room, and found a good enough substitute in her absent sister's vast array of perfumes and powders and lotions. Who knew if Terry would come home for Christmas anyway? The last Alejandra had heard about her youngest sister's plans was that she might go skiing with a group from business school during the holidays. Skiing? Alejandra thought for a moment. Was la mariposa really going skiing instead of coming home? What's wrong with these people anyway?

Alejandra walked to the end of the upstairs hallway, on the wall of which hung, just outside her own bedroom door, a large rectangular mirror in a gaudy golden frame. She pressed and patted the lipstick over her full lips meticulously so that the lines would be straight and smooth and thicker toward the center of her mouth. She pressed her mouth into a Kleenex, leaving behind a fuzzy and delicate outline of her lips, like an old family photograph. She stared at her face in the mirror, brushed away a strand of her straight, shoulder-length jet black hair which sometimes wandered over her forehead. Studiously she rubbed a few specks of makeup into her light and creamy skin. Alejandra wasn't sleek and athletic like her sister Teresa, and she wasn't, certainly, the thin reed Rosanna was. Yet this one, the eldest of them all, was still shapely. Alejandra wasn't even afraid to show her hourglass figure in tight dresses at the Electric Q in Juárez whenever her best friend, Carmen Priego, goaded her into a night of dancing. However, Alejandra would not wear short dresses anymore, because this wouldn't look right at Dillard's. She'd look trampy.

Alejandra stared at the mirror again, with a full view of herself this time, and suddenly turned to the bathroom door.

"Juanito! Twenty minutes! Be ready or Ofelia will drive you to school. Or you'll have to walk. ¡Apúrate!"

She pushed the tube of lipstick into her purse and rapped on the bathroom door. There was no response from the other side of the door, yet she did hear the drumming of the water pellets stop and the shower curtain dragging open. She stepped quickly over the thick hallway carpet and tiptoed down the stairs so that she wouldn't slip in her high heels.

"Buenos días, Ofelia. ¿Cómo amanecieron?"

"Bien, ya sabes. A bit tired. The rheumatism in my spine woke me up again. It's been hurting me all morning, mi hija."

Mi hija? Alejandra almost winced. Why in the world did she say *that?* Ofelia's high-pitched, grating voice, her incessant whining, were bad enough. But now *mi hija?* Alejandra suppressed a choking sensation in her throat.

"Pobrecita. Hope you feel better when the weather gets warmer. Only a month to go, more or less," Alejandra said finally, sitting down at the kitchen table too, with a cup of coffee. "¿Y mi papá?"

"He left already. I think he's finishing the bank calendars now. For New Year's. The machines need to be warmed up early. ¡Ay, como trabaja este hombre! I think he might just work on Christmas Day!"

"Ay, no. But we're having la cena, we're eating *together!* That's what we talked about last night."

"Yes, of course, mi hija. Don't worry. I'll talk him into it. I'll take care of it," Ofelia said and nodded like a bug-eyed doll with a spring inside its wooden head. That's what was always a bit odd about this wiry woman in her early fifties. The green eyes, behind cat-eyed glasses. The eyes pouncing from object to object in a steadily

The Last Tortilla

nervous commotion. These seemingly shell-shocked eyes, and that head in tow.

"I'm going to call him. Why does he float around everything? He's here. He's not here. He says he'll do something for us, then he forgets. What's the matter with him? I'm going to call him."

"No, no, no," Ofelia said, her eyes skipping around the room even more furiously. She fidgeted in her chair as if it were about to undergo spontaneous combustion.

"I'm going to call him and ask him. Why *not?* Why is he going to work on Christmas Day and miss la cena?" Alejandra asked, feigning indignation. She knew her stepmother was lying. Another one of her little manipulations. But this aspect of Ofelia's character had actually never bothered Alejandra too much. In a way, she understood why her stepmother did these things. Alejandra simply took it as a game that was occasionally even diverting. Ofelia was promising to make something happen that would happen anyway, promising to *deliver* her father to her, like a basket of tortillas. But if Alejandra knew anything, she knew that her father was a stubborn and ritualistic creature. Juan Márquez had never worked on a Christmas Day in his life, no matter how many customers clamored for their idiotic calendars early. Even if the old man just wolfed down his Christmas dinner and watched TV like a zombie, he still wouldn't go back to work until the day after Christmas. Just out of habit, of course.

"No, Alejandra. Please, por Dios santo! You'll disturb him. Don't worry. I'll talk to him."

"Well, let me just give him a quick call, to clear things up. What's his new number at the print shop, do you know?" Alejandra asked slyly, picking up the yellow kitchen phone on the wall. She placed the receiver to her ear and waited. She was really enjoying this. Ofelia looked as if she were on fire herself finally, her face ashen and panicked, her mouth O-shaped and out of breath, all so suddenly. Alejandra put the phone down. "Maybe you're right. Talk to him.

Convince him to come to Christmas dinner with his family. I hope you can."

"Sí, Alejandra, sí. Don't worry. I'll talk to him as soon as he gets home," Ofelia said, the blotchy brown returning to her face again. She stood up slowly from her chair, not quite completely straight, like an old abuelita, and shuffled to the refrigerator door for a refill of her prune juice glass. Before she sat down again, Ofelia rubbed her own back in long, methodical strokes. "Ay, what a beautiful dress you have on today. Are you going out with your friends tonight?"

"Think so."

"To Juárez again?"

"Yes."

"¡Ay, qué horror!" Ofelia exclaimed, her back to Alejandra, shaking her head again and tapping the sugar bowl and salt and pepper shakers so that they would be in a perfectly straight line. "Juárez is such a nightmare. Full of thieves and beggars."

"Why do you say *that?*"

"Because it's true. I wouldn't go to Juárez if you paid me." Ofelia's eyes jumped to the plastic tablecloth of daisies, and she pinched the two corners in front of her, then straightened out the edge dangling just above her bony lap.

"But not everyone en el otro lado is a thief or a beggar."

"You know what I mean. Mexico's a disaster. It's dirty, disgusting. The people on the street, oh my God! I can't stand them when they're over here, in El Paso. You know they're the ones who steal most of the cars and pickups at the mall."

"But didn't you grow up in Juárez too?"

"Ay, Alejandra, mi hija. That's entirely different. I grew up with a certain class of people. Not la gente raspa. Here there are laws, there is order. Over there, nothing but esos Mexicanitos begging for food and smearing their grimy paws on your windshield."

"Ay, querida Ofelia. You're exaggerating. I can't believe what you're saying," Alejandra said, suddenly feeling much younger than her thirty years. She really did not want to be polite. When was the last time she had censored herself before an adult who wasn't her father or mother or abuelito or abuelita? But somehow, peace was more important. Peace was more important than earth-shattering pain. Even this uncomfortable, fragile peace. "It's really not that bad."

"The child is waiting for you."

Alejandra turned her head. Juanito stood at the foot of the stairs, in jeans and a navy sweatshirt. His gray Dallas Cowboys jacket dangled from his arm and dragged on the floor. Suddenly he looked like a baby again, and not an eleven-year-old, like a baby puzzled by this sometime cordial dislike between adults. Alejandra asked him whether he wanted cereal or huevos rancheros or avena, stroking the wet black hair on his pallid forehead as he sat down in his chair, trying to relax the tightness she perceived in his perfect little face. Without looking at Ofelia, Juanito said he wanted Captain Crunch. Alejandra quickly reached for the cereal box and a bowl and a half-gallon of whole milk and put them in front of him. Juanito first pushed the small squares into the milk and then gulped them down in big spoonfuls. He kept his eyes on the bowl or on the dead space just beyond it, not fearful or nervous anymore, just wary. Ofelia, who had not taken her eyes off the boy, pouted and said good morning to the little face in front of her, in a singsong voice she thought was friendly. But from the other side of the table, she looked like a giant leopard about to lunge for his food.

Juanito mumbled a good morning, to the empty air, it seemed, but would not look into Ofelia's eyes. He turned his head toward Alejandra, who smiled at him as she leaned against the Formica counter of the kitchen sink, her coffee cup in hand. Finally, the little boy grabbed the bowl with both hands and pitched the rest of the milk and cereal into his mouth. Milk dribbled down his chin and onto his sweatshirt. Ofelia frowned. Standing up, he wiped his mouth on his sleeve and picked up his jacket and the math book and the two spiral notebooks on the stairs, and walked out into the driveway. Only when the screen door slammed shut did he look up again, as if the air suddenly possessed a sweeter scent outside. Alejandra picked up her long white sweater and her purse from an empty chair, smiled politely at Ofelia, and waved goodbye. The red 1968 Mustang, its chrome shiny and clean, backed out slowly onto Socorro Road and after a few minutes turned on Yaya Lane and again on Carl Longuemare.

"Oye, Juanito. You should be nicer to Ofelia, you know."

"Okay," the little boy said, looking straight ahead to see if he could spot the Doberman pinscher that had lunged at him on Carranza Street last month. "Today's the last day of school. Vacation for two whole weeks."

"Muy bien, mi niño. Want to go to midnight mass on Christmas Eve? Carmen Priego will be there. Remember her from last year? Está un poquito loca, como tú," Alejandra said and tousled his hair.

"Yeah."

"Maybe after mass we can eat menudo at Taco Cabana."

"But I don't like the panzas."

"So? We'll take the meat out. Just eat the pozole."

"We could go to Little Caesar's."

"¡Ay no! Mexicanos eat menudo at midnight. Only gringos eat pizza then. ¿Eres gringo?"

"Nooo. But I still like pizza."

"Well, tell me what you want to eat. Carmen and I are Mexicanas."

"Okay, we'll go to Taco Cabana."

The car pulled into the South Loop School parking lot, and Alejandra stopped the Mustang at the walkway to the front entrance. Next to the glass double doors, a huge eagle, fierce, its talons ready for a fight, leapt out from a sea of tiny, multicolored ceramic squares embedded in the brick wall.

"¿Qué pasa? You're going to be late."

"Can I ask you a question, Ále?"

"Sí. What?"

"Do you ever think of Mom?"

"Of course. All the time. Why do you ask, mi hijo?"

"I had a dream about her last night."

"Really? What was she doing?"

"She was talking to me, she was holding my hand. I could see her. She was wearing her favorite dress, the yellow one."

"I miss her too, my honey. I wish she was here," Alejandra said, a huge lump in her throat, stroking back his hair and caressing his cheek. Suddenly, she wanted to cry, but she didn't. It had been a while since she had been able to push away this bleak and merciless storm of pain into the horizon. She had merely been caught off guard this time.

"Ále, I think she *is* here."

"¿Qué dices?"

"I think she's around us all the time."

"I don't know about that, mi rey. I think she's in our hearts, I think we keep her alive by thinking about her. I miss her a lot too. If you want, we can light an ofrenda for her on Christmas Eve. I know she would like that. Nuestra madre era muy católica."

"Okay. See you later, Ále-gator."

Alejandra watched him trudge up the long walkway toward the double glass doors. His jeans seemed a bit rumpled. His hair crested up into black spikes as a gush of air swept through the empty and ominous canyon of yellow brick walls and flat, dry grass. The vastness of the space seemed to open up and swallow the little boy. He walked straight into it, swinging his books on his arm, happy, or at least oblivious to the deadness all around him.

Dillard's was packed with Christmas shoppers. The escalators and elevators at the center of the first floor clanged incessantly, the bass to the chatter of voices hovering in the air. In one area, the air seemed particularly festive and electric, at the makeup and perfume counters to one side of the elevators. The giant faces of beautiful models glowed above each counter, smiling, teasing, and rejoicing for no particular reason at all. The neon-lit counters sparkled with gold and amber and emerald. Mirrors, small round ones, some on swiveling arms, rectangular ones in chrome frames, refracted the ubiquitous, yet subdued light every which way. A magical world. Alejandra finally caught the eye of a young woman across the aisle from the Clinique makeup counter and gave her a thumbs-up. Carmen pretended to keep listening to the matronly woman who brushed her eyelids ever so delicately and chatted about her husband, her children, her neighbors, this difficult life. Finally, Carmen winked at Alejandra and almost broke out into an indecorous grin. Another woman, in a mock fur coat and clutching a shiny black handbag, suddenly stopped right under Alejandra's eyes and waited impatiently for her attention.

"Señorita. If you would please assist me, I would be most grateful."

"Of course," Alejandra said, smiling. "How can I help you?"

"I bought this Lancôme foundation two days ago and I was not given the free gift. The lipstick, the mascara, the moisturizer, the makeup remover, and the body lotion. Here is the receipt for the purchase."

"I understand that, señora. But the Lancôme free gift began yesterday. Not two days ago. I'm sorry."

"But then the señorita who helped me should have told me that. I would have waited to buy the makeup today when I knew I would be back for my layaway at J. C. Penney."

The Last Tortilla

"I'm sorry, señora. That wasn't her responsibility. In fact, we had ads in the paper two days ago about the free gift."

"So you are *not* going to help me?"

"No, I'm sorry. But I can't."

"Señorita, I spend a lot of money in this store! I am an excellent customer, I have been coming here for *years!*" the woman shot back angrily at Alejandra's face, snatching the receipt from the counter with her manicured hands. "What is your name?"

"Alejandra Márquez, para servirle."

"I would like to see your manager, señorita, and tell him how rude you and your little friends have been to me. You young ladies should learn more about *respect!*"

"The manager is not here today. *She* is out sick, señora. But I'm the assistant manager, and you can file any complaint with me," Alejandra said, still smiling.

"Oh, this is absurd! I will never shop here again!" the woman hissed and stomped down the aisle.

"Vieja estúpida," Alejandra muttered quietly. Carmen caught her eye from across the aisle and winked again. Alejandra fished out the inventory sheets from underneath the cash register and began totaling up the categories when she glanced up and caught a familiar face in front of the glass doors of the Texas Street entrance.

"Rosanna! Where have you *been?* I haven't seen your face since Thanksgiving, mi hija," Alejandra said, hugging her sister tightly and planting a big kiss on her cheek. They shared a definite family resemblance: straight, inky black hair, a pearly complexion, huge brown eyes, high cheekbones, and a face shaped like the moon. But strangers might have easily confused them for an off-kilter mother-daughter team in which the mother looked too young, or the daughter too old. Alejandra was voluptuous, a traditional beauty, who embarked on her thirties with just a hint of crow's feet around her eyes and the slightest softness to her chin. Everyone had always said she was her mother's younger twin. Rosanna, however, was boyish, slim and pretty without any makeup. More nervous, like her father, and practical too, but without his toughness. Rosanna's gray skirt was loose, almost too big for her, and even a bit frumpy. She looked like a newly minted undergraduate at her first job, although she was only two years younger than Alejandra. "You look so *thin*. You're not working this Saturday, are you?"

"It's all right," Rosanna said, sitting on the stool in front of the cosmetics counter and lifting her leather portfolio onto the glass. That way she could at least avoid the mirror underneath the counter. "I just have enough for Roberto's computer. I'm buying it tonight. Can't wait to see his face when he opens it." She caught a glimpse of her own face in another mirror. What a horror show! she thought. Why was she parading around with that helmet of hair from the 1950s? And this face! A red, puffy patch just below the corner of her mouth, as if she had been slugged. What a pimple that would be! Rosanna glanced at her older sister leaning casually against the glass counter and was just the slightest bit jealous of her, as she had always been. Alejandra could *still* have any man she wanted, if she only decided to settle down.

"He better be really nice to you too."

"Don't worry. I know he's been planning something, but I don't know what it is yet. Somebody pulled a knife on him yesterday," Rosanna said, slowly stroking the red spot of her cheek with her index finger.

"¡No me digas! Was he hurt?" Alejandra exclaimed, almost out of breath with astonishment, at the opposite side of the counter again, in front of the cash register.

"No, not at all. The cholo pissed in his pants when Roberto pulled out his gun. You should've heard him last night. *Laughing.* He almost *cried* he laughed so hard. His partner was with him."

"Ay, qué hombre. A cop. Why did he ever want to be a *cop?*"

The Last Tortilla

"It's not as exciting as it is on TV. Maybe in New York, but not here in the middle of nowhere," Rosanna said, fishing out the three documents she had to file at the county courthouse before the end of her lunch break. She also clicked open her compact.

"You know Teresa's probably not coming home for Christmas."

"Yeah, she called me."

"She *called* you? I haven't spoken to her in four *months!*" Alejandra retorted, a bit angry. That was typical. Her two younger sisters always excluded her. Particularly Teresa. She would always try to drag Rosanna to her side, a stupid game which, thankfully, Rosi had more or less stopped playing after she got married, and certainly after what happened to their mother. "Well, I don't really care if she comes. She can do whatever she wants. Isn't that what everybody's doing?"

"It's a new boyfriend, that's why. She thinks she really loves him, and he does sound like a nice guy."

"Really? Who is he?"

"Oh, just a guy from business school," Rosanna said, smoothing the cover-up over her chin and cheeks. *She already thinks I'm just a self-absorbed bitch. Don't tell her! I'm telling you because I trust you. Please just don't tell her. Alejandra will just say I'm a bitch and a slut, you know she will. What does she know about love anyway? Who does she think she is? Mom? It just happened. He invited me out to lunch. He's really handsome and caring. I wasn't thinking about anything. It just happened. Sure, I got an A in his class. But it's not because of that. You know I'm good at finance. God, Alejandra would never let me off the hook with her looks of disapproval. Promise me, Rosi. Don't ever tell her. Yeah, he's married, but they've been separated for three months. His wife doesn't know.* "Yesterday Roberto got the tickets to the Sun Bowl. Right on the fifty-yard line. Sure you don't want to go with us?"

"Yes, I'm sure. But Juanito can't wait. You know, I think he still misses Mamá a lot. Today he told me he was dreaming about her. Thinks she's floating around the house or something. I don't know what to do with him sometimes," Alejandra said, reaching up to Rosanna's white collar and brushing off a few specks of makeup.

"Oh, God. Poor child. I miss her too."

"El niño still will not talk to Ofelia too much. At least it's better than a couple of months ago. After a while he'll be okay."

"I don't understand why Papá married that woman. It's as if he didn't care what we thought. As if he didn't respect our mother's memory. I mean, I know it's been two years almost. But why *Ofelia?* I always thought, when I walked to South Loop, that her old white house was haunted, the House of the Dead. Remember that ugly black dog she had? The barren old widow and her mean black dog. Come on, really, you don't think he was having an affair with her while Mamá was alive, do you?" Rosanna said, combing her hair in the round mirror next to her.

"Not *that* again! It's kind of disgusting to even keep *thinking* that," Alejandra said quickly, having thought about that very same thing once in a while. It simply wasn't a possibility. Maybe Papá and Ofelia had flirted with each other over the years. They certainly knew each other, but her parents had also known everyone else in this neighborhood. It was that kind of neighborhood, where everyone had begun with an empty, dusty lot and slowly built up a house, piece by piece. Now there were almost no children left. It was becoming a neighborhood of old people, and their old memories. "I think el viejo was just super-lonely and wanted someone to cook his dinner and wash his clothes, and Ofelia was right there. Convenient. Another lonely person in the neighborhood. I guess he could've waited longer, but for what? They get along. But she can be tan insoportable, that woman."

"She's a bitch. I *hate* her. She's picky and manipulating. Every time I see her she's always trying to ingratiate herself with me. She just wants attention. Or she's making these horrible little comments. I feel like I'm being pinched to death," Rosanna said, shaking with an abrupt anger. She didn't cry, but her eyes glistened, and she blinked away the sting.

"I'm not going to defend her. I know what you mean, mi hija. But can you imagine being in her position? Coming into a family like that? Anyway, it's his house. He can do whatever he wants with it. Oh, I think Carmen's found an apartment for us," Alejandra said, keeping an eye on three teenage girls who were loitering near the silk panties and camisoles across the floor, in the next department. She started to walk around the glass counter when the girls saw her and walked quickly to the up escalators, toward the mezzanine. Rosanna was about to say something, but Alejandra held her hand up and phoned her friend Julie upstairs.

"*What?* Really?" Rosanna said, surprised. Finally! It was about time! Alejandra wasn't really too old. She could still find someone if she tried, if she wasn't at home trying to be everybody's mother instead. She had her own life to lead. It was really about time. How great to be single again, and *not* have to live at home. Rosanna herself had never been that lucky.

"Maybe next week. Her primo's moving out to Los Angeles and needs to rent his house. Three bedrooms, with a nice backyard. Offered it to us for only three hundred dollars a month."

"Have you told Papá?"

"Not yet. You know how he is. He's busy with his business. He's hardly ever home anyway. I'm sure he'll be happy that I've found what I want. I should've moved out years ago. I don't know what I was thinking," Alejandra said serenely. What would her mother have said? It was true: her mother would have never allowed her to move out. And Alejandra had loved her mother with all her heart. But now, well, nothing was the same anymore.

"I'm happy for you. I have to go, Ále. My boss will kill me if I don't file these today."

"Ándale pues. Oye, don't forget your buñuelos next week," Alejandra said, standing up straight again, smoothing out her dress.

"Yeah. Hope it's better than last year. It was so hard not having Mamá there, but at least we didn't have Ofelia yet."

"Don't worry. It'll be festive. I promise."

"Ah! I almost forgot *why* I came! You know I forget *everything*," Rosanna said, beaming with pride. There was a certain mischievous spark to her eyes.

"¡Ay no!"

"Yes. I think we finally did it. I'll tell you for sure next week. You and Roberto are the only ones who know."

"That's wonderful! That's the best news for Christmas! You just made my year! I'm so happy for both of you," Alejandra gushed, hugging her sister again. Suddenly, just like that, the world seemed right again. "I can't believe you weren't going to tell me until next week! I can't believe you *forgot!*"

"Now you know. I just told Roberto yesterday. He lifted me up with a big bear hug! But *please,* don't tell anybody else yet. I'll tell you what the doctor says next week. Okay?"

"Cuidate, mi hija. Hasta luego," Alejandra said, radiant. She watched Rosanna zigzag through the maze of counters until her sister skipped up three steps and through the glass doors on Texas Street. Alejandra suddenly remembered when her little sister had rushed home from South Loop and burst into her room, crying and muttering about a fight. Rosannita had smacked a boy, and he had laughed at her, and she had smacked him some more, and he still laughed because she was bleeding between her legs. The bleeding wouldn't stop, and Rosannita had tried to stop it with the stiff brown paper towels in the girls' restroom. Don't cry, Alejandra had said, it's all right. She tried to explain it to her in the same beautiful way Mamá had once told her. It's a natural thing, mi hija. In many ways, this makes us *special*. Talk to Mamá, she'll tell you. But Rosannita was horrified! How could she tell Mamá about this? Only Alejandra could really understand how idiotic boys could be. Long ago, in another life, it seems, they, and everything around them, had been together in one place.

Ofelia sat on the living room sofa. Her eyes were fixed on the flashes of light emanating from the television in front of her. She didn't have her tinted cat-eyed glasses. They were on the coffee table. The venetian blinds were drawn shut although it was early Monday afternoon, still an hour before she needed to start dinner. The room was dark and smoky. She liked it that way, to keep her eyes from aching in the consuming brightness outside. She had heard Juanito come in and out all day, but she hadn't actually seen him in the house yet. His books had been by the staircase since Friday night, untouched. The boy was on vacation. Suddenly she heard the door slam again and thought she caught a glimpse of the little boy running outside with other kids from the neighborhood. She took a drag of her cigarette.

"¡Ay, qué horror!" she whispered at the TV, still transfixed by the flickering images on the screen.

The daughter slept with her stepfather. He claims the young tramp seduced him during dinner one night, when the two were alone and he was drunk and didn't know what he was doing. The mother herself, the talk-show host says with a smirk on his face, was forced to have sex with her first husband and two of his brothers during their honeymoon. It was sort of a "family wedding," he quips with another generous smile. I wasn't responsible for being a bad role model to my daughter, the mother pleads to the audience. I had also been abused by her daddy. And two other siblings in this incredible family are now having sex regularly! They've bought a house to live together! And here they are! the host screams into the camera. The brother and sister hold hands as they prance onto the stage. He plants a big kiss on her lips just as they sit down. The audience roars. The host beams, the microphone just below his lips, and then sprints to different audience members to give them a voice in all of this. Was the sex *good?* somebody asks. What's it like to nail your own sister? a young man chimes in, smiling widely. You people are disgusting! a middle-aged woman interjects before the host cuts for a commercial.

Ofelia took another drag of her cigarette. The glow lit up her face in the darkness. She got up to heat water on the stove for a cup of instant coffee and slumped into the sofa again, one eye on the blue fire beneath the kettle.

The sister doesn't see anything wrong with sleeping with her brother. At least he doesn't have AIDS, she says defiantly. Actually, the talk-show host interrupts loudly, reading from an index card in front of his bulbous microphone, the three of them, these two sisters and brother, have even had a ménage à trois several times. The audience gasps and laughs. Several hands shoot up in the air. Have you gone and done it with the *dog?* a hoarse person squawks into the microphone. How do you know who's your real father anyway? someone else asks. Why are all of you on this show? a third demands, having snatched the microphone away from the host. Why are you making a spectacle of yourselves? At least have the decency to do this in private. They paid us good money, the young tramp responds happily. I thought we were gonna try and work out our problems, the mother adds. That's what the producer told me. Wait, wait, wait, the host protests, holding up one hand, the microphone by his side again. We just wanted them to have a chance to share their incredible story. We thought it would be interesting. Music. Cut to another commercial.

The Last Tortilla

Ofelia turned around and found Juanito standing by the doorway, a baseball bat in his hand. She grinned hard at the boy. He managed a shy smile.

"Do you need something, niño?"

He shook his head and galloped up the stairs, pushing the thick part of the bat onto each step. Ofelia, in her smoky murk, tapped her cigarette on the glass ashtray and turned her eyes to the TV again. The kettle's shrill sliced through the air. She stood up and poured herself that cup of black coffee.

Juanito jumped on Alejandra's bed, rolled over, and sprang to his feet on the other side, just inches from the TV set atop her white bureau. He clicked it on. The white numbers of the alarm clock flipped over: it was exactly 4:30 P.M. He changed the channels until he reached *Canal Dos: La Voz de México* and waited for the opening credits of *Los Ricos También Lloran.* His mother's favorite novela. Whenever he had come home from school, she had been watching it. He would sit down in the kitchen and show her his latest quiz or homework assignment. She would turn off the volume of her show and carefully study his homework. His mother had always been so proud of him, mounting each A on the refrigerator for a week. He had been, and still was, an excellent student in math and American history. Juanito again stared at the TV screen.

A young woman scrubs the floor in front of a brass fireplace. Dark-haired, with big brown eyes, and pretty. She wipes her sweaty brow with her arm while melancholic music drenches the opening scene. The pointy heels of some proper señora stop just in front of the young woman's eyes. She peers up at this unseen face, at once submissive and proud, and listens attentively for a few seconds. There is a tired but innocent beauty in these eyes. Suddenly, the pointy heels turn smartly away. The young woman follows them for a moment and then begins to scrub the floor again. At once, the scene is outside. The same young woman pins wet clothes to a line.

The music soars to a crescendo, as if climbing the backdrop of verdant mountains behind her. The serene light of the sun flitters on the bleached sheets like a movie projected onto a spastic screen. A well-dressed young man sneaks up to the young woman from behind, takes her by the waist. Their faces are near each other, almost touching. She pulls back, resisting. But he kisses her lovingly. Finally, the wet shirt in her hand falls softly to the earth. The new episode begins.

I love you with all my heart, she says on the phone to him. Why would I embezzle money from your parents, why would I do anything to hurt your family? I swear that I'm not the one who's guilty, please believe me! The handsome young man, in an avocado-colored polo shirt, is silent and hangs up the phone. A tear rolls down his cheek; he seems desperate, trapped. He grabs the picture next to his bed, and kisses it, and swears to God he'll find out who's tearing them apart. I believe you! I believe you now, I'll always believe you. Cut to an older woman, the young man's mother, and her best friend at a café. I knew she was stealing from us all this time. Who else could it have been? Now she's trying to trap mi hijo with her wicked charms, the mother says angrily over the place setting of fine bone china. And you discovered the missing bank notes in her possession? the best friend asks, astonished. The police found them, in her bedroom. They also found some *photographs,* the mother answers in a whisper, leaning over the table. Cut to another young woman, the daughter of the mother's best friend, working out on a Stairmaster at a health club. She turns to a girlfriend, who is also slim and attractive and is wearing a leotard. I love him so much, I'll do anything to keep him, *anything!* she says to the camera, angry, unrepentant. Our families have been together for years, we were meant for each other. Luckily, her girlfriend quips, you won't have to worry about that pobrecita anymore. The girlfriend laughs. Suddenly her own face turns deadly serious. She is thinking about that same young man. She also loves him. Cut to a baby food commercial.

Juanito leaned back onto the bed after turning the TV off. He clicked his sneakers together. With his foot, he pushed the door closed. The sun streamed into Alejandra's bedroom and held the silence within to a fuller existence. Each perfume bottle in front of the mirror on the bureau contained an amber or lime or rose liquid in finely etched glass. The lines and corners refracted the light. Microbursts of sun gleamed on the glass and in the mirror. The tint in the air intermingled with the scent of Alejandra's perfumes. The little boy flipped onto his stomach. A whiff of air from the flowered bedspread floated over his face, surrounding him in warm comfort. His eyes fluttered to a close, and he fell asleep in this fine and peaceful silence.

The gravel in front of the old Ysleta Mission was wet and muddy. Even in the darkness, Juanito could see José's white tunic dragging in the mud. The sneakers of the soon-to-be father of the Christ child were caked with gobs of mud too. Why didn't he just hike up his skirt? Maybe, Juanito thought, he's too busy making sure he doesn't trip over his wooden staff and hit the donkey. The Virgin Mary, a large black umbrella over her head, sat unsteadily on the old animal, her skinny legs pressed together, her face down. The lady parishioner holding the umbrella slowly followed the lead singer, another woman in black with a loud and whiny voice, and guided the donkey with a rope around its hairy neck. About three dozen peregrinos marched across the parking lot behind the donkey, toward Mount Carmel, this the final leg of the nine posadas before Christmas.

Juanito held his hand high over the candle, yet the heat still brushed against his skin and burned him. He cupped his hand around the dancing flame, at least keeping the wind from blowing it out. The thick clouds sprinkled a gauzy drizzle over them. The muted gray seemed like the smoky sky an hour before a desert dawn. Carmen's candle had already blown out. Instead she held up a Bic butane lighter toward the heavens. She grinned at Juanito, but he didn't see her. He stared at his sister Alejandra, who sang with a bright voice and seemed in a buoyant mood. The group stopped in front of the church and formed a semicircle around the donkey, Mary, and José. Their singing echoed against the adobe walls of the Tigua Indian Reservation, bounced around the cinder blocks of the church, and faded into the vast and dark space beneath the clouds. It was a joyous singing, mysterious and awesome and elusive, in strange words Juanito did not completely understand, singsong words, words of God, Spanish words:

Por Misericordia
Te imploro posada.
Viene padeciendo
Mi esposa adorada.

> Aquí no es alberge.
> Sigan caminando.
> Temo que al abrir
> Me vayan robando.

No obres con crueldad.
Tengan mas amor,
Pues el Ser Supremo
Te compensará.

> Ya pueden seguir
> Y no fastidiar,
> Porque si me enojo
> Les voy a pegar.

The Last Tortilla

Llegamos cansados
Desde Nazareth.
Soy un carpintero.
Mi nombre es José.

No quiero tu nombre.
Quiero descansar.
Porque ya te dije
No puedes entrar.

Alberge te implora,
Dueño de la casa,
A pasar la noche
La Virgen María.

Pues si es la Virgen
Y quiere entrar ahorita,
Parece en la noche
Una huerfanita.[1]

Suddenly, from behind, Juanito heard a clunk and a voice yelling. He stopped listening to the song and peered across the parking lot. An old bull trotted to a nearby tree and rubbed its massive head and horns against the rough, lime-splashed bark. Two boys ran toward it with a lasso in hand. Four men also rushed to help them. Two picked up the wooden beam the bull had knocked over, cradled it in their arms, and fixed it again on the metal hooks jutting out from the thick posts of the makeshift corral. Then they tied rope tightly around the beam to keep it in place and swung open the gate to let the bull go back where it belonged. But the bull wouldn't go. It didn't run away either. It just didn't budge at all. It rocked its head from side to side and scratched against the tree.

Somebody slipped a rope around its neck and gently tried to tug the bull back into the corral. But the stubborn bull shook its head, and the rope fell off. The bull lurched a few steps forward and leaned against the tree, scratching its ribs and rump against the bark so hard that dried chunks of it crumbled to the ground. The tree shook terribly. Dried leaves and bits of branches drifted to the ground. Somebody else yelled, and one of the boys sprinted across the gravel and into the Tigua restaurant. The others surrounded the bull and waited until the boy came back and handed one of them a bundle wrapped in a brown paper bag. A man wearing a baseball cap took out a carrot from the bag and fed it to the bull. Suddenly it stopped scratching and leaned away from the tree. The man took out two more carrots and fed another to the bull as he started to walk slowly toward the corral. The bull took a step forward, chomped on the carrot, followed the man into the corral, and ate the rest of the carrots in the bag. Then the man jumped out of the corral. Juanito turned around. Everyone was already inside Mount Carmel. The donkey stood quietly next to a tree. A rope hung loosely from its neck and swooped up into one of the dead branches above. The little boy walked inside, found his sister and Carmen in a pew toward the front, and slipped into the empty space his sister had saved him.

The bespectacled old priest read from the Bible, in Spanish, while Mary and José stood next to him in front of the altar, staring forlornly at a basket on a bed of hay. Juanito couldn't quite see what was inside the basket, except for a bright light. He saw that the boy and the girl sometimes blinked and looked at the congregation because the hot light was too bright. The Christ child was probably on fire next to that hot light, he thought. The Christ child was a doll melting. Maybe the Christ child was nothing but a socket with a powerful lightbulb. Juanito stared above the altar, above the faces transfixed by such a mixture of solemnity and joy. The great bloody Christ hung on His cross high above them, life-size, His head and shoulders slumped forward. Christ was apparently looking at all of them. Juanito stared at Him and waited for Him to move.

The bones of this Christ almost poked out from the taut pallid skin. His eyes were half-closed, frozen just at the moment before they closed forever. Blood dripped down the side of His chest, right where a Roman guard had stabbed Him with a spear just for good measure, having offered Him a sponge with vinegar to stanch His thirst. One day after Sunday mass, Juanito had asked his mother about this wound. She had told him the story about the hateful guard and the vinegar and Jesus crying, "My God, my God, why have you abandoned me?" God is everywhere, she had said. He is there where you can't see. He is there when you don't believe in Him. He is inside of you and in all of us. Then God, Juanito had thought, must also be even in a figurine of Himself. He must know that I want to see Him. He must know that He should be here, in Ysleta, at least every once in a while. Maybe Jesus Christ walks around only at night, like an insomniac. Maybe God floats around invisibly, and that's why I can't see Him move. But if I look hard enough, I'll catch Him moving. This was what Juanito had thought after attending church with his mother one day. The day before she died.

He squinted at the Christ on the cross again, but He didn't move this time either. Jesus Christ dangled inertly on the cross. Maybe God didn't like people to stare at Him when He was helpless and in pain. Maybe God *hated* that. Maybe, God especially hated people who wouldn't look away from His wounds, who expected Him to move. Juanito understood what this God had done to him. This evil God had taken his mother away from her home because once he had demanded to see Christ on the cross move. It was true. Everyone had said God had taken his mother now. She lived in the kingdom of Heaven with the Almighty. Soon, Juanito himself would be with his mother in this eternal life. Yes, that's how Alejandra had explained his mother's death to him. But nobody knew he and Mom had been in church together, that he had been stupid enough to ask his mother these questions about the statue and the blood and His death. Nobody knew, but God. He was everywhere. He listened to everything, like an undetectable and powerful spy.

Juanito knew exactly why his mother had died. He knew the reasons for God's anger against him. It had not been an accident at all. God had *murdered* his mother. This manipulative and cruel God was just like the Roman guard who had once tortured Him. Instead of killing Juanito directly, the one who had dared to ask these horrible questions, God taunted and tortured him by taking his mother away to an alien world. This God was not just judgmental and vengeful. He also wanted to teach people a lesson and display how fragile life was under His dominion. But Juanito wasn't afraid; he wasn't really angry anymore. One day this God would come for him too. This great Being would take him to the jail of Heaven where his own mother was trapped. That's why he could feel her around the house: she was trying to escape from this evil kingdom, trying to tell him they would one day be together again. And that's all Juanito wanted. He wanted to be with his mother again. So he wasn't afraid of this God anymore. He wasn't afraid of God's gift of death. One day He would move toward him, this great He, and that would be the best day of Juanito's life.

"Vámonos," Alejandra said, tugging at Juanito's shirt.

Suddenly he felt the stiffness in his knees. He stood up from kneeling on the padded board on the floor. Carmen was already walking toward the foyer. A woman in a white shawl tapped her shoulder from behind, and they gasped and hugged and started laughing. Alejandra, still waiting for Juanito at the end of the pew, recognized the woman, Margie Jiménez, a friend of Carmen who had worked at the J. C. Penney across the street from Dillard's. Alejandra started to walk up the aisle toward them, but stopped as soon as she noticed Juanito had also stopped a few feet behind her. "¿Qué pasa ahora?" she asked.

"You said I could light a candle for Mom."

"Juanito."

"You *promised. Lela, please.*"

"Okay. Pero rápido. I still have to start cooking for la cena. And I know Carmen wants to go to Taco Cabana for a drink and menudo. Ándale pues."

Alejandra watched him run toward the front of the altar. The old priest was putting away José's staff, Mary's garment, and the basket with the Christ child into a closet to one side. At the other side of the main altar, Juanito had stopped in front of the statue of Nuestra Señora de Guadalupe, in an alcove painted in ivory, the demure Virgin in malachite green and gold. The Queen of Heaven was surrounded by fresh red roses, tiny ex-votos pinned onto a bulletin board, and a small wrought-iron stand with rows of votive candles flickering and burning, like tiny muted stars. He dropped a handful of coins into a metal box, took a thin lightstick from a tray on top of the box, and lit the middle candle on the row closest to the Virgin, just beneath Her big brown eyes. He dropped to his knees in front of the candle.

"Is he on his knees again?" Carmen sneered after they had said goodbye to Margie. "Alejandra, my dear, you better watch that your little brother doesn't become a religious fanatic."

Alejandra had known she would regret it, and she did. It was seven o'clock on Christmas morning, and she had thick ojeras under her eyes. But at least she would still be one of the first in line. Last night, after bringing Juanito home from Taco Cabana, she had returned to the revelry at the restaurant for another hour. She really shouldn't have listened to Carmen; she should've just stayed home and gone to sleep too, like her little brother. And sure, Alejandra had also promised Leonardo, Margie's cousin, that she'd return for another drink. But *they* weren't getting up to cook tamales the next morning. Their mothers would do that. At least, when she finally came home, in the wee hours of the morning, she had not forgotten to set her alarm clock and had even left herself a note reminding her to get the masa in the morning. But now she was dead tired. She skipped breakfast, only a Whataburger coffee mug in her lap, and raced to La Modesta.

When Alejandra pulled her Mustang into the parking lot, her heart sank. Already there was a long line of people out the door. Mostly the mothers and grandmothers of Ysleta, anxiously cradling huge vats in their hands or limply holding empty pots at their sides. La Modesta was probably the only tortilleria on the entire east side of El Paso that was open on Christmas morning solely for the purpose of selling masa to those too fussy to buy it beforehand. The great tamales, the ones with a singularly airy and delicate consistency, began with the freshest cornmeal dough. The store-bought tamales were just not the same thing. Alejandra took her place in line but had to run back for the large white-speckled black pot in her trunk. A new person was already in front of her by the time she got back in line. Another car pulled into the parking lot. She heard an abuelita in front tell her grandchild to ask the cashier how much was left. The child returned with good news: they still had four hundred pounds of masa. Even if everyone in front of Alejandra bought twenty pounds, there would still be enough for her own tamales.

Nobody was awake when Alejandra got back. She was sure Juanito would be up to open his gifts, but he wasn't. Actually, there were not many gifts to open. A three-foot plastic tree, which Ofelia had bought at K-mart, was surrounded only by Alejandra's and Rosanna's gifts. Teresa had not sent anybody anything. Maybe she had forgotten because she was too busy with her work. Maybe she'd bring their Christmas gifts later, when she came home from her ski trip. Maybe. Maybe not. Ofelia had already parceled out the presents from her and Papá the day before, leaving them for each person on the bed during the day, unwrapped, no note, the price tag pinched off the store plastic.

Alejandra turned off the stove. She took the broth from the chunks of lean pork she had already simmered for hours and dumped it into an empty pot. She carefully sliced off the fat from the pork and shredded the meat. The meat steamed, so her fingers had to be nimble to avoid this searing heat. Her face was perspiring. Ten pounds of pork for ten pounds of masa, her mother had always repeated to her like a mantra. Alejandra put the shredded pork in another black pot and added a splash of the broth and clicked on a burner extra low. She collected the strips of chile nuevo méxico, the seeds and stems of which she had already removed the night before. She sliced the chile into smaller strips, brittle and red, and pushed them into the blender with a diced onion, a clove of garlic, oregano, and water. The whir of the blender was incredibly loud, but nobody seemed to stir upstairs. In the meantime, she started the coffeepot. Her head pounded with a headache. The coffeepot groaned and sputtered to a start. As the chile was pulverized and then liquefied under this roar, the kitchen was suffused with an invisible but choking odor of chile. Alejandra sneezed in spasms, covered her face with a washcloth, and finally turned off the blender. She poured herself a cup of coffee and sat down for a minute. Then she dumped the lavalike chile liquid onto the heap of pork in the pot and mixed it. The meat was done, or at least on its way. Now she only needed to watch that it didn't dry out, add salt, and stir it to achieve her savory carne enchilada.

No, mi hija, we don't want those cornhusks. The ones from Juárez are much better. I know they're trying. Look at these wonderful chiles and tortillas and hominy and tripe. But not those cornhusks. Sure,

Smith's wraps them in plastic bags, neat and clean. The ones from Juárez are dirty. You might even find a worm or two in them! But don't be fooled. Look, I'll show you. Just like my abuelita showed me. We'll buy these gringo cornhusks and we'll also get the ones from Juárez tonight. We'll compare tomorrow. You can help me cook.

Es muy fácil hacer tamales. Let's take a look at the cornhusks from Smith's. See? They're smaller and are falling apart, even after they've been in water for so long. Oh! Don't let Juanito grab that pan or he'll pour it all over himself. Okay, mi hermoso, no llores. Here, play with this. Now. See these? They're fresher, almost tender. Sure, it took a while to clean them properly, but that's how it is. Good work produces good results. Sloppy work? Well, let's take a look at what really matters, how they taste.

Try these, Alejandra. I only cooked six of them. You'll see why. Not bad, but definitely not delicious. Right? Now try these. The husks are from Juárez. Those are the ones everyone will eat tonight. Notice the difference? Right! This one tastes like a wilted white tortilla wrapped around nothing. And this tastes like real corn, like the earth. Even the carne enchilada has colored this tamale nice and pink. See? Your mamá would never tell you a lie. I know. Why don't we just give those tamales to the dog. That animal will eat whatever you put in its bowl.

Alejandra stirred the meat again. The shredded pork was evenly red and bubbled like a thick stew. The cornhusks were soaking, free of the fibrous hair and the specks of dirt from the fields. Once the masa was ready, she would spread a thick layer of it on each husk, add two or three spoonfuls of pork meat right in the center, and slowly wrap the tamale so that neither the meat nor the masa would squeeze out before the whole tamale was cooked. But getting the masa just right was the hardest part.

Alejandra lifted the ten-pound slab of dough from La Modesta and dropped it into a large round pan about three inches high, the shape of a miniature bullring. Into the pan she added broth, salt, lard, and baking powder. Slowly, with her sleeves rolled up to her elbows, she mixed the large white mass together, into a larger and softer mass, which she seemed to push and pull into submission like a recalcitrant ghost. After half an hour of this kneading and mixing, her arms were tired, but her headache had disappeared. She lifted her shoulder to wipe off the perspiration on her brow. A blue car, with shiny chrome headers, rumbled slowly in front of the picture window in the dining room, on Socorro Road. Like a blue ghost.

Alejandra, can I talk to you for a minute? Just leave that, Carmen will take over. In my office, please. Sit down. Alejandra, I just got a call from your father. Your mother's been in an accident. She's at Hotel Dieu right now. I think it's serious. This is the number he left me, but go. Don't worry about anything here. Carmen is going with you. She'll drive. I'll take care of the registers. Don't worry about anything here at all. If I can do anything, anything at all, just ask me. I'm praying for you and your mother.

Someone from upstairs walked across the hallway and closed a door hard. Alejandra could hear the water hissing through the pipes as the shower was turned on. She flicked the bits of dough off her fingers, picked up her coffee by clamping it tightly between her index finger and thumb, and gulped down half a cup of the luke-warm liquid in one swallow. She rinsed her hands with cold water and grabbed the hand mixer she had given her mother on her forty-fifth birthday. She plugged the mixer into the socket next to the masa and began to push the metal beaters into the soft whiteness. The machine churned and sputtered and sometimes clogged up. Alejandra had to vary the depth of the beaters in the masa to keep them churning. She added another spurt of broth to the pan. After an hour, the masa seemed finally ready. She filled a glass with water, pinched a glob from the flat white mass in the pan, and dropped it into the glass. If the glob still floated in water after a minute or so, her mother had said, then it would be *real* tamale masa. And so it did.

Alejandra, my dear, you know how much I loved your mother. She was my best friend. I can't believe it's been a whole year. God has her now, you know that, don't you? The pain is still so fresh for me too, my little Alejandra. Look at how many people remembered! Even after a year! I think it's the most tragic thing that's ever happened in our neighborhood. Everyone loved your mamá. I want to tell you one thing, now that almost everyone's gone. You know it happened almost in front of my house. Your mother even might've been coming over for a visit, I don't know. I've had nightmares about it, Alejandra. Sometimes I just don't want to sleep. But I have to tell you this, for both of us.

I saw it happen. I was watering my bushes when I heard that evil car roaring down the street. I'm glad that idiot's in jail for the rest of his life. You know they still do it all the time, they think Socorro's a race-track or something. Your mother was just on the edge of the road. She must've heard the car. I think she was looking straight at it. I was praying for her to move. It was about five seconds after I knew she had seen the car. "Adelita, my precious one, step to one side. My God, Adelita, please get out of the way!" But she didn't. I don't know why she didn't. I keep imagining this scene in my head again and again. It's terrifying. Only God knows all the answers to these questions. Certainly only God. Maybe your mamá was just frozen with fear.

Alejandra's work was almost done. She spread the masa onto one cornhusk, filled it with pork, and folded it into a pouch, tamale after tamale. She began to fill up one large black vat inside of which was a steamer and water. Dozens of tamales. Rows and rows of tamales neatly stacked next to each other. Rows on top of more rows. An army of fat little tamales with a trace of red on their bellies. After she finished one vat, she turned the burner on low and began to fill up another one. She still had nearly half of the masa left.

"Buenos días, Alejandra. My goodness, so many tamales. I hope they eat most of them this afternoon," Ofelia said, walking stiffly to the kitchen counter in her pink bathrobe and peering into the vat in front of Alejandra.

"Oh, I hope so. How are you feeling today?"

"Not bad, not bad at all. Mi estómago felt a little tight last night. Something I ate, I guess. But I feel better now. I won't eat anything too heavy today."

"No tamales? I hope you can try them, at least one."

"No sé, Alejandra. We'll see. I never really liked them anyway."

"I'm sorry. I didn't know that. I'll make you something else for la cena."

"No, no, no, Alejandra, mi hija. No te molestes. I'll do it myself. Maybe I'll make some chicken broth. A cup of it will do," Ofelia said in the scratchy voice of her self-pity, pouring herself a cup of coffee. "And your father?"

"Outside. Reading the newspaper, I think."

Ofelia shuffled outside, banging the screen door behind her. Alejandra could hear a few faint murmurs followed by long silences and more murmurs. She could hear Ofelia's slippers dragging slowly across the patio pavement. The screen door creaked open, and Ofelia walked into the kitchen again.

"My dear, may I use one of the burners on the stove?" Ofelia asked in a voice high-pitched and seemingly meek, waiting ever so attentively for Alejandra's response as if this decorum were not only a matter of course in the kitchen but of great importance. The two back burners were empty.

"Of course. Let me move the tamales to the back," Alejandra said, grabbing the heavy vat with her fingers caked in white and gently lowering it onto a back burner. Alejandra returned to folding and stuffing her tamales on the kitchen table. She was almost done. "Is that okay?"

"Sí, gracias. Your father wants huevos estrellados for breakfast," Ofelia said to no one in particular, facing the front of the stove. She looked in the cabinet underneath the kitchen counter. As she bent over, she braced her back with one hand and, in slow motion, straightened up with a black skillet in her other hand, dropping it on the stove with a metallic bang.

"Is your back hurting you again, Ofelia?"

"Well, you know how it is. My body's the cross I have to bear in this world," she said, opening the refrigerator door and grabbing two eggs.

"Maybe you should go see a doctor."

"I did. Dr. Johnson on Alameda."

"¿Y qué dijo?" Alejandra asked. Her arms were really tired. The muscles between her shoulders also ached.

"Well, he said there was nothing *physically* wrong with me. That maybe my nerves were getting the best of me. But I don't believe that, Alejandra."

"Why not? He didn't find anything wrong. Maybe it's in your head somehow."

"What are you saying, my dear? ¿Que estoy loca?" Ofelia snapped back, stirring the hot oil onto the egg yolks.

"No, of course not. I'm just saying, really repeating, what the doctor said. If there's nothing wrong with your body, maybe it's something else."

"That doctor's a quack. What does he know. I know what I feel, and my back and my head are in pain, my entire *body*."

"I'm sorry to hear that," Alejandra said, staring at Ofelia's back and gently placing the last tamale into the second vat. Alejandra covered the vat with its lid and carried it to the stove. "Con su permiso." Ofelia stepped back from her eggs, glared at Alejandra for a moment, and drained the greasy eggs on a paper towel after Alejandra had adjusted the burners under both vats. A screen door creaked open and crashed shut. Rosanna walked into the dining room.

"Ay, mi hijita. I thought you would never get here," Alejandra said to her younger sister, kissing her on the cheek as Rosanna hugged her. "I'm already done with the tamales."

"No! I don't believe it. You must've been up at six."

"¿Y Roberto?"

"He's coming. He'll be here by four, don't worry. Some of his friends from work stopped by to give us Christmas presents this morning, and they started to watch a stupid football game on TV. But I told him to be here on time," Rosanna said, finally turning to see Ofelia stirring frijoles on the stove in the kitchen. "Good morning, Ofelia."

"¿Cómo estás, Rosanna? And your husband left you all alone?"

"Not really. He's watching a game."

"I see," Ofelia said, looking up briefly from her work on the stove and forcing her face to grin politely at Rosanna.

"Siéntate, niña. I'll get you some coffee. Decaf, right?" Alejandra said and winked at her sister, who blushed and nodded and plucked a Sweet and Low from the tray in front of her.

"I'm sorry I wasn't here to help you. But I made the buñuelos yesterday. Should I just leave them here?"

"Yes, yes, yes. Let me try one," Alejandra said, peeking into the large paper bag filled with triangular fritters sprinkled with sugar and cinnamon. Alejandra took one out and munched on it. "Oh, those are so deadly. You haven't lost your touch, mi hija. You were always the best at buñuelos."

"If you say so. I really only make them once a year now. Too much of those and I'll get fatter than fat. Would you like one, Ofelia?"

"No thank you, Rosanna. My stomach's not right, you see," Ofelia said, the breakfast plate ready next to the stove. Two eggs fried for three minutes without breaking the yokes, two scoops of beans using the large blue spoon, and exactly three tortillas on the side, just as el viejo liked it. She shuffled outside through the carport door to call her husband to the table.

"What a witch!" Rosanna muttered under her breath. Alejandra looked up in mock astonishment and smiled.

"Oh, just ignore her. Es muy amarga, esa mujer. I don't know why. Rosannita, did you talk to Papá when you came in?" Alejandra asked, stroking her sister's black hair with the palm of her hand.

"Yeah, I did. I told him we were having a baby."

"What did he say?"

"Seemed happy. Asked me if I had a good doctor, how Roberto felt."

"What's wrong, mi hija? What's wrong? Por favor, stop crying."

"I wish Mamá was here too, I, I wish she could be here to hold the baby. Why did this happen to *us? Why?* Alejandra, can I use your room, please? I don't want them to see me like this."

"Come here, mi hija. I'll go with you," Alejandra said as they walked up the stairs. Behind them the screen door creaked open and slammed shut again with a whoosh.

The meal had been over for a while. Only an eerie silence hovered above and around the red-smeared dishes on the dining room table, the empty and half-empty glasses of Coke, the coffee cups. In the middle of the table, on a tray, was a heap of discarded cornhusks. Juan Márquez snored softly in the living room. Alejandra was washing the dishes in front of the kitchen sink, as quietly as she could.

La cena seemed to have sunk so quickly into the past, so effortlessly, as if it had always belonged there. Juanito had sat hushed next to his father and opposite Ofelia during the meal, still avoiding his stepmother's eyes as he gobbled up the four tamales Alejandra had

The Last Tortilla

put on his plate. Only Roberto's police stories had really intrigued Juanito. There had been one about chasing a stolen pickup through the Cielo Vista Mall parking lot, into Eastwood, and then ending in a spectacular crash on the fields of Album Park. That had kept Juanito glued to his chair for a while. Ofelia had spent the meal preoccupied with what her husband needed next—another tamale, a cup of coffee, more Spanish rice—offering to bring him each in a creaky tone that had secretly unnerved Rosanna and interrupted her thoughts. As soon as the meal was over, Roberto and his father-in-law had switched on another football game in the living room, quite happy, or so they said, with how everything had turned out. Teresa had never even called to wish them a "Merry Christmas."

But that was fine with Alejandra. She tried to remember only how beautiful her sister Rosanna looked, how much they laughed at each other's jokes, how they would always be friends, no matter what. When they had finally said goodbye, Alejandra remembered thinking only that she knew they would never really be far apart. It was all they could do now.

It was only after she had been washing the dishes for a while, completely alone, that Alejandra sensed a strange but powerful urge to get out of the house. Luckily, she had already promised to bring some of her tamales to Carmen's tonight. Carmen had just called to remind her. The Priegos had already started the rancheras on the stereo, and Leonardo had asked about Alejandra with an eager look in his eyes, or so said Carmen. Alejandra picked up the remaining dishes and glasses on the table, brought them to the sink, and scrubbed them clean. Finally, she wiped the table and straightened out the chairs. She ran upstairs for a quick shower.

Distant and hidden noises echoed, for a while, in this utter stillness. Ofelia, hovering like a ghost in the living room, stopped to watch Alejandra exit through the kitchen door. Ofelia quickly glanced at the kitchen and saw that all the dishes were clean and drying on the rack. The pots and pans had probably been stacked inside the cabinets already, for they were nowhere to be seen. The kitchen and the dining room were in good order. She heard Alejandra's car pulling out the driveway. Her husband was still asleep, so Ofelia carefully picked up the different sections of the newspaper on the sofa, walked silently into their bedroom, and shut the door.

¡Ay, qué horror! I can't believe this woman can sue her husband for adultery in Texas, and *win!* What's this world coming to? It's her own fault, that's what it is. She should've done whatever was necessary to keep him. It's no one's fault but her own. I have always done the special things Juan has wanted. I even enjoy some of them now. My body's never been completely useless, especially when it comes to *that.* I do what a good wife must. What Adela would never do. It was her own fault he would come to me when he needed what he needed. It was simply her own fault. I never tricked him into anything. He came because he wanted to come to me. What an *actress* she was, getting so hysterical when she found out the truth! I only know that God answered our prayers, in His own way. It truly was fortunate in many ways. It's strange how the world comes together sometimes. How it comes together, and how it falls apart.

Ofelia heard a loud clang from the kitchen. She slowly rose from the bed and walked into the hallway. The refrigerator door was wide open. The cabinet doors were also open. Juanito picked up a plastic Taco Cabana mug from the floor and poured milk into it. Two tortillas, on the placa on the stove, were warming up. She saw the little boy rummage through the refrigerator shelves until he found a small chunk of butter on a dish on the bottom shelf. He took out a dinner plate from the cabinet and finally turned around and found Ofelia staring at him from the bluish shadows in the hallway.

"Niño, are you going to eat again?"

"I was just hungry."

The Last Tortilla

"Didn't you have enough this evening?"

"Yes."

"Well, then, you know you should only have a certain amount of food each day. Everything in proper proportion. From now on, I'm going to start counting how many tortillas you eat. Three a day, and no more. After you eat those two, you'll have one last tortilla today. Is that clear, niño?"

Juanito stood agape and said nothing. Ofelia poured herself a glass of water and walked back into the hallway and into her bedroom. Behind him the tortillas blackened and burned on the stove.

Note

[1] *This is the translation of the posada in the story. A posada is a traditional Mexican song that varies by city and town and that forms part of the nine-day Christmas festivity. In these reenactments, the song describes the efforts of the pilgrims María and José, who seek a place to stay in Bethlehem the night before Christmas. This particular posada was written by Rodolfo and Bertha Troncoso.*

> *In the name of mercy*
> *I ask for lodging,*
> *For my beloved wife*
> *Is greatly suffering.*

> > *This house is not an inn.*
> > *Give me peace of mind.*
> > *If I open I fear*
> > *You may rob me blind.*

> *Do not act cruelly*
> *But have more love and care,*
> *For God in Heaven*
> *Will give you your share.*

You can move on now
and do not bother me,
For I will hit you
If I become angry.

We are so tired.
From Nazareth we came.
I am a carpenter.
My name is José.

I want to rest tonight.
I do not want your name.
You cannot enter here,
I repeat, just the same.

Gentle, kind owner,
She who seeks sanctuary
For only one night
Is the Virgin Mary.

If she is the Virgin
Who asks for one night,
She looks like an orphan
In this gloomy half-light.

The Last Tortilla

I remember the chickens. I also remember how scared I was. At about five in the morning, on a Saturday too, my mother woke me up. She had told me the day before that I would have a job this summer, one way or another. I remember how she said it too. Her large brown eyes glared at me, as if she knew a secret I didn't, and then she smiled. This was after I told her I needed money to go to the movies with my friends. I already had a ride to Cielo Vista. I just needed the three dollars to get in. But I should've kept my mouth shut. I should've asked Jaime for the money. I should've stolen it. "No," she said quietly, "that's not how we're going to do it from now on. Vas a trabajar. Como cualquier otro. A trabajar y

Punching Chickens

ahorrar." She told me she had already spoken to Pepe's mother about it. All of *those* boys did it every summer. One way or another. If I didn't want to help my father load bricks in our truck, then she would find something for me to do before I started high school. "Be ready tomorrow morning, en la madrugada. I'll pack you lunch," she said with her slight smile.

Pepe and his cousin Carlos were already waiting for the truck at the corner. They just sat on the curb of San Lorenzo and San Simon and smiled at me as I sat next to them. I noticed they had bad teeth. Chipped and yellowish. I had played football with them a few times, but I didn't really know them. They lived in front of our house, and in a poor neighborhood they were the poorest of the lot. They were much tougher than I was, however. I had once seen Pepe in a fight with a cholo who shouted "¡Chinga tu madre!" about something or other, and Pepe immediately stiffened like a statue. I thought I saw the short black hair on the back of his neck stand up, like black bristles. He jumped on the cholo, slammed his head against the rock wall behind our house, and choked him until the guy turned blue. I tell you, Pepe and his whole family were tougher than me. Real trabajadores. Me? My brother said I looked like a real ugly girl.

Strange as it may seem, I think Pepe and Carlos were a little shy around me. I mean, we didn't hang around the same group at South Loop School. I was with the brainy group, more or less. But I didn't kiss any teacher's ass. I didn't get my grades the way Nancy Montes did. I just liked to read, and I liked to get things right. Sometimes I did do things that were sort of stupid too. During track season in P.E., I had hurled the shot put right onto Mauricio Pacheco's fat foot. It wasn't my fault, really. I told him to move. He just laughed at me and dared me to come close, like the pendejo that he is. You should've heard his awful scream when that iron ball caught his big toe. The coach was all excited and angry and made *me* run ten laps after school. I tell you, they talked about it at South Loop for days.

Suddenly even the potheads were smiling at me. So I got good grades, but in a way I didn't really belong with the brains. I knew what my brother meant too. It was my face and my hair. I couldn't do much about my face, but I should've shaved my head years ago. Maybe that would've helped.

Pepe, and sometimes Carlos, hung out by the fence on Gonzalez Street. I never saw them in school much. But when I did, it was there, just outside school property, maybe one of them leaning against a low rider, not theirs, a friend's maybe, never smoking pot but with a cigarette. I would always say hello, and Pepe would push his chin out with an "ese vato" nod, and sometimes smile a little, cool yet definitely friendly. Doña María and my mother were best friends, so in a way we were connected. But really, we were from two different worlds. My older brother Jaime was more like them, and I usually just stayed away from him.

The farm truck stopped at the corner at exactly 6:15 A.M. We had barely jumped on the back bumper when it lurched forward into the darkness again. I just made it over the high wooden slats around the truck bed. A few hands helped me over, pulling on my T-shirt and even my pants. Maybe it had been Pepe and Carlos. But I didn't really know. I couldn't see anybody's face in this dark and sweaty pit I was now in, this pit that was rattling wildly toward the cotton fields beyond my house, deep into Ysleta or Socorro or God-knows-where. I think there were nine or ten of us in there, bouncing around like loose haystacks every time the truck hit a bump. We were on a dirt road for a while, that I do remember. I think animals had been transported on this truck, because I thought I smelled animal shit, and I did smell hay. I mean, it could've been human shit I was smelling, but I just didn't want to think about that possibility then. I'm sure it was animal. Don't ask me how I know. My chest was scratched and bleeding. I had caught a pencil-like splinter on one of the slats when I had been pulled into the truck. I was looking at the streak of the Milky Way high above the desert sky. I started praying for a quick sundown.

After a while—it seemed like forever to me then—I began to see their faces. The bright orange rays of the sun punched through the horizon like a gigantic crown of thorns on fire. It was already hot, and some of them were sweating, their skin almost maroon, leathery, and old looking, even if they weren't very old. In fact, I think I was the youngest one there. There was one other "kid" who was not as fat as I was, about the same height, with dusty black hair, and baby fat on his cheeks. He could've been younger than me. But even then I could tell from the start that Rueben could've eaten me alive if he wanted to. His arms rippled with blotchy little biceps. His legs were always in a boxer's stand, ready for a fight. He usually scowled when he was by himself, yet later, much later, I did see him smile once. I still remember those big perfect teeth, like a hyena's.

No one smiled now. A few brief conversations came and went, all in Spanish. But no one smiled, much less laughed, on the way to the farm. El rancho del señor Young, I heard someone say. There were a few old men who looked like my abuelito, maybe slightly younger, but just as crappy-looking. Most of the men were in their thirties or forties, my father's age. But they were different from him. Their jeans were frayed and ripped. Their skin stony and lean. They were, for the most part, thin. Only their hands looked like my father's hands: calloused, thick, and strong. Sure, my father had never been rich. In fact, I remember when we had an outhouse in the backyard, and awful kerosene lamps that released a quivery jet of the blackest, most acrid smoke. But now my father had men like these working for him, even if only a handful. My father's construction business even turned down a few jobs once in a while. Now, my father really smiled when he ate breakfast with my mother.

Just about the time I was thinking we'd be in this shitty truck all day, we turned off the dirt road. We drove toward a faraway complex of huge buildings in the middle of a flat plain of perfectly straight, planted rows. I really didn't know exactly where we were, but I did know we were miles from home. Somehow I immediately felt like a prisoner here. There was not another building for miles. No stores. No cars. Not even a highway. Just a few farm trucks now and then. Already two more trucks like ours had arrived, and their men milled around impatiently near the machines that had brought them here, anxious like hungry cats. We jumped out of our truck as soon as it stopped and waited too.

"What now?" I asked Pepe, who had sat down against one of the truck's wheels. These were my first words to him since we had left San Lorenzo and San Simon. Pepe was as big as my brother, and probably stronger. He had beefy arms, a kind round face, and huge feet. He'd always been a power hitter in our softball games, an enforcer in football. Yet I had never seen him get angry. I remember now that we hadn't played together for a while, ever since he had gone to Ysleta High School. Was he even in high school anymore? Jaime had never mentioned him as one of his buddies there. I really didn't know Pepe at all. It occurred to me that it was strange to live so close to someone for years, see him grow up—from trips to the canal to look for cangrejos, to driving around in a Chevy Impala with a smiling girl—and not really know him at all. Carlos I knew even less. He apparently only stayed with the Quinteros during the summer. He was a good football receiver, furtive and quick like a weasel. That day he just seemed like a gangly mute.

"Ahorita viene el patrón," Pepe said quietly, in an Indian squat, just staring at the dirt. For a second, he looked like a big kid again. "There's probably nothing ready yet, para pizcar. But they'll have something for us. They always do. They'll need us later in the summer for all sorts of things. He'll come out and tell us what we're going to do and what we're going to make."

"How much is it usually?"

Punching Chickens

"Well, I don't know. It depends what they have. If it's cotton or chile, then they do it by the twenty-pound bag. The more you pick, the more you earn. But I don't think anything's ready, ése. One summer I shook pecans off the trees. The machines were broken. So it could be anything, Manny. Sometimes they do it by the day."

"By the day?"

"Sí, by the day. You work until it's dark."

"All day?"

"All day."

"¡Ay, cabrón! I thought we'd be home early, *before* it was dark."

"Este güey," Carlos sneered. "No seas huevón, Padilla! What do you think this is, Disneyland?" I ignored him. He was just an idiot. Pepe didn't even look up from staring at his hands. He didn't seem to give a shit what his cousin said either. Carlos scowled at both of us and stomped away to the other side of the truck.

"Don't worry. You'll get home. One way or another."

"Ése, Pepe. What if it's not enough, what they pay?"

"Not enough?"

"I mean, what if you want more money?"

Pepe looked at me and with his beady brown eyes basically said, "What the fuck are you talking about? I thought you were the *smart* one in that family." He was exasperated with me, but something kept him from dumping me in that heap piled high with all the idiots of the world. Maybe my mother had said something to his mother, and his mother had said something to him. Maybe I was being babysat. *Right.* What did they know anyway? I didn't need anyone. I just wanted to be left alone. Pepe finally shifted his big body, stood up, brushed off his butt, and stretched his arms skyward in a big yawn. His muscles were definitely bigger than my brother's. Suddenly Pepe reminded me of Lennie in Steinbeck's *Of Mice and Men*, except, of course, Pepe wasn't retarded. "That's just not the way it is," he finally said. "They pay you what they pay you."

"And you have no choice at all?"

"Pues, you don't have to work. Nobody does." There was a brief silence between us. I must've looked alarmed. Either that, or maybe I looked like I was capable of anything. Capable of embarrassing the shit out of him in front of these men who didn't talk to each other, who didn't know each other, who just seemed *there,* like the trees. Because he immediately added, "But the pay's not bad. Not bad at all," although I knew, from his forced little smile, that he had never given much thought to the pay being good, or bad, or shit. It was *there.* That was enough for him.

A large güero walked from one of the smaller buildings, the only one with windows. He was wearing a cowboy hat and looked chunky, an overweight Marlboro Man. He talked to the three drivers of the trucks, who were sitting apart from us, and apparently waiting for further instructions. El güero walked back into the building. Each driver talked to a group of us, told us what the job was, how much they would pay. I heard something about chickens but didn't really pay attention after I heard what I wanted to hear: $1.50 an hour, about eight to ten hours of work more or less, in any case, most of the day.

Fifteen dollars for the day! My mind reeled with images. I could go to the movies for almost an entire week with this money! I could go three times a week and buy as much popcorn as I wanted! I had never actually *seen* fifteen dollars in my hand. My mother gave me only a dollar or two at a time. Three if I begged her and agreed to scrub the trash bins, wash Elmo with the black disinfectant soap from Juárez, clean out her flower beds, and pull out the weeds from the front and back yards. It usually took most of the day, and she inspected everything I did. If I complained, she'd tell me that at her father's ranch in Babonoyaba they had suffered and worked, and suffered and worked, from dawn until midnight. She'd tell me about milking the cows and feeding the pigs and cleaning the barn and

Punching Chickens

cooking and cleaning and not having shoes in grade school and walking five miles to school every day . . . and . . . and . . . . ¡YA! I should feel *lucky,* she'd say, to have only these little chores to do. I should feel lucky. Well, with fifteen dollars in my hand every once in a while, I'd definitely feel lucky from now on.

I remember that I never figured out who got to unload and who got to carry. I'm not sure it would've mattered anyway; I got to carry and at least saw the light of the sun for a few seconds at a time. The other thing about carrying was that you could take your time, especially when your hands and arms and shoulders started to twitch and then simply disobeyed your brain's commands. When I wanted to faint, just about an hour before we finished, these few seconds of daylight, precious seconds when I suddenly remembered that I was hungry or out of breath or so god-awful sore I almost cried, these seconds were my only life. My real life.

There were three eighteen-wheelers backed up against a huge warehouse. Three metal ramps dropped from the back of these trucks more or less in the direction of the warehouse. The warehouse itself was like a cavern: dark, eerily quiet, and spooky. The air was thick inside, as if the shadows were somewhere between being nothing and becoming black gelatin. The cages and the smell. That's what I noticed first. Hundreds and hundreds of small cages. All in neat rows. Planks on the floor separating each row of cages. And a horrible smell of feathers and chicken shit and dust everywhere, this impossibly *thick* air! A stench that made me gag at first. Yet, after the first hour, I didn't smell it anymore. I also remember that, before we started, when the warehouse was quiet, the feathers and pieces of feathers dangling from the wire mesh seemed even delicate.

We were to unload the semis and carry the chickens to the warehouse and put them into cages, two in each cage. We were to unload and carry chickens. A few men climbed into a truck; I stood with Pepe and Carlos and a few others outside. Then we started to work. The warehouse was gloomy and quiet, but the inside of the truck, this long and suffocating tunnel, was a riotous chaos of flying feathers. The chickens were inside wire-mesh racks. Those unloading flung open a door, grabbed whatever chicken legs were nearby, and yanked the shrieking animals out, a pair at a time, and handed them to us, upside down. We took a pair with one hand, waited in this wretched din and half-light, grabbed another pair with the other hand, and carried them out.

It was a damn good thing that Pepe was in front of me. At least I could see what to do a few seconds before I descended into this madness. The claws! My God, I saw them! These ugly, yellow, scaly claws and legs! You had to grab them, keep them from tearing at your hands. Why didn't we have gloves? Why? Some of these guys were wearing gloves! When you were carrying them, the first time I carried them, you focused on these powerful claws and legs, how they kicked away from you, how they'd scratch and rip your flesh if you didn't grab them just right. It was all a matter of half inches, of keeping these little evil, manic claws from reaching a finger or the fleshy part between your thumb and your index finger. I got careless only once, when I was so tired I didn't care anymore. This yellow claw from the depths of hell curled itself around my thumb and squeezed it until I thought it would snap off. After that, the shock of this awful pain flushed out just enough energy and will to carry me through the final hour.

Down the ramp we went, two dangerous, screeching chickens in each hand, their heads, these quavery masses of eyes and red flesh and beaks, pecking away at our knees and thighs whenever we dared to drop our outstretched arms. I think it might've been easier to carry snakes for a living. I hated seeing these spasmodic upside-down chicken heads stretching to puncture my flesh. I imagined once that they reached my groin and pecked out my penis and my huevos and kept pecking until they got to my gut and my eyes and my brain, until I was just a pecked-out piece of human meat surrounded by thousands of nervous, dirty white chickens. I think that was about the time I fucked up a pair of chicken heads against a warehouse wall when no one was looking. Well, almost no one. Rueben was right behind me, and that's when he grinned his stupid grin. Maybe he hated the chickens as much as I did. Maybe he just knew que ya me iba también a la chingada. Maybe I was going on my first joy ride to hell and back, and it was fun to watch.

My first four chickens in hand, I followed Pepe to the cages. The birds squawked and tried to yank free. Their heads swiveled wildly. Their bodies, grayish and yellowy underneath their legs, lurched up in spasms, like the bad end of shredded electric wire. I could see their butts. I realized I'd be looking at chicken butts the whole day. Some of these fucking chickens were shitting in midair. Maybe I'd lose a little control too if some giant bastard grabbed me by my ankles and hoisted me upside down to God-knows-where. Maybe I'd smell the barbecue sauce too. A drop of chicken shit had already smeared one of my sneakers.

¡Ay, chingada! I couldn't get the damn chickens into these cages! They squawked even louder as I lifted them up to the open mesh door and contorted their feathery bodies, swiping at my stomach in a crazed fury. It was awful. That first time, when I felt I was gripping my way up one cliff of shit after another, was the most awful. How was I going to do this for hour after hour? I almost dropped my four chickens right there. I almost dropped them and walked home. Fortunately, Pepe was right next to me and probably noticed the terror and anger in my eyes. Without saying a word, he took the two chickens from my right hand, found an open cage door next to him, and *punched* the fuckers home. Their little bodies twisted horribly, unbelievably, through the door. Yet, like old tires, they popped back up and ran circles inside the cage. My first "punch" almost made me feel good again. Pepe winked at me, and I almost smiled back.

It took me about half a dozen trips back to the semi before I started to look around again, before I started to ignore what the chickens did in their panic. They became simply pieces of dangerous meat I had to deal with, for a few long minutes at a time. I didn't give a damn about the chickens, and I'm sure they weren't in love with me either. My arms were already becoming sore. My hands were turning yellow! The scaly skin on these chicken feet was rubbing itself into my own flesh. This yellow slime mixed with dirt. ¡Híjola! My hands stunk! It was horrible, like the smell of a rusty open can of tuna abandoned in the refrigerator for years. A tide of vomit surged up my throat but splashed back into my stomach. I kept my hands away from my mouth and my nose. I would never eat chicken again.

I remember that, after three hours, my arms suddenly started dropping immediately to my sides whenever I punched in another two pairs of chickens. My arms and my shoulders. I couldn't control them completely anymore. For a few minutes right before lunch, my right shoulder became numb, and I had the sensation that it glowed brightly, as if some madman had jabbed a blowtorch into my muscles and revved up the heat for good measure. I shook it back to life. Time after time my arms and shoulders would drop listlessly next to me, exhausted and inert. Yet, just as I left the sun behind and entered this loud cramped tunnel of flying feathers, I forced my hands and arms to reach up again, to grab on to these animals as if they were saving me from a fall into a bed of razors. I fought back a blinding pain.

Why did I do it? Why did I keep doing it? The whole thing seems crazy to me now. I wasn't thinking then. I *couldn't* think. I remember that I felt ashamed of my weakness. I remember that I stared at these old men, these viejitos, and they were going back and forth, up the ramp, into the truck, and back to the cages. Like machines. Four chickens at a time. Their faces were stoic and hard. Their pace was sometimes even faster than mine. Their muscles— old, decrepit, sinewy muscles—seemed oiled with sweat, stronger at each turn, packed with a deep reservoir of power that I didn't have. Work begat power, which begat more work. Four fucking chickens at a time. I wasn't about to quit. Not now. Just one more time, dear God. Just one more time! But I would not quit *now*.

As soon as someone said it was lunchtime, as soon as this chain of chickens and men stopped just as suddenly as it had started, I deflated like a punctured inner tube. I could barely move my arms, and even squeezing my hands into fists seemed painful. I wanted simply to chop my arms off. When I carried my bag lunch to the trees where some of us were sitting, my fingers quivered and would not close tightly around the paper bag. I was afraid I would drop it. I was afraid they would know I couldn't do it. More than anything else, I was ashamed of this weakness inside of me that screamed to burst into the empty cotton fields. But I did not do anything. I did not show them any pain. When they smiled and asked where I was from, only then did my heart begin to break away from the agony of my body.

It was strange, but they were very friendly to me, friendlier than they were to Pepe or Carlos. My two friends seemed to slip into the background. The older men, especially the ones that looked like my grandfather, they wanted to know about my father and mother, whether I had ever worked on a farm before, what school I was at, and so on. One of them had a grandchild who went to South Loop School too, but only a third-grader. Another said he thought he had met my father at a boda last year. These viejitos, with their dirty jokes and banter, made me forget my pain. I remember their smiles too. Really nice smiles. Wide open, toothy, and mischievous. Secret smiles only for those who belonged underneath the trees. Wonderful smiles for me. I also remember how they laughed and how much they made me laugh. I think that's the first time I laughed from my gut. I couldn't move my arms, but I could still laugh from my gut.

One of them mentioned something about the pace of our work. It was much too fast, he said. We were already done with over half the semi. He motioned to two of the "younger" men leaning against a tree, and they seemed to agree. Much too fast, they also said, these two who were my father's age. So it was settled. Just like that. After lunch, we'd each carry only two chickens at a time, one in each hand. Slow the pace down. If we needed to, some of us would pick up the pace toward the end of the day to make sure we finished our work. There was no need to cut short our own time, someone else said. "Shit yeah," one of the "younger" ones said. "I heard one of the drivers say they'd be back around six or so, after they finished some errands for el güero." We just needed to look busy and keep an eye out for the big guy, in case he came around to see how we were doing. The other two semis would do the same. Get the work done, but slow the pace down. That's what we would do after lunch. Shit yeah, I said too, without uttering a sound.

I remember that the first hour after we ate our lunch, that first hour back to work, was brutal. My muscles would not work. I could not move my arms. I felt that God Himself had severed the connection between my brain and my arms. We were walking back to the semi, and I was panicking. My God! Just one chicken in each hand! That's all I had to do! Just one horrible little chicken! What's wrong with me? My arms! I needed new arms! There was also, all too suddenly, this piercing pain across my lower back. I had just been sitting down, eating my lunch. I should've felt better now. I should've been ready. But my body! Now, as I walked back, I couldn't even stand straight, or so I thought. My spine seemed about to snap. One wrong step and this delicate balance between my back and my hips and my legs would implode like a termite-eaten shack collapsing onto itself.

I remember that when I grabbed my first two chickens after lunch, the guy unloading handed them to me around my thighs. I simply could not lift my arms. He said nothing, quickly grabbed another pair for the next guy, and I walked down the ramp, the chicken heads going to town on my knees. I didn't care. I just didn't want to collapse. I just wanted to get it done. I remember that each step of my sneakers, each step into the soft chicken shit on the floor, seemed a glorious victory. I was a tank trampling through chicken mud. I would not quit now. I found an open cage and swung my arms over, in a clumsy arc, it seemed, and smashed the chickens through the hole. After every trip, for a while at least, my arms felt better and returned to me. For a while at least, until the end.

I did finish, and I did not faint. In many ways, the claw that nearly tore my thumb in half, that greedy yellow claw, saved me. I woke up. I went back. And again. Until the semi was empty, and they were turning us away. The sun had already set. At first I couldn't believe there were no more chickens. I had this wild desire to rush into the truck and see for myself that it was absolutely quiet. But I didn't. As soon as my mind realized that we had stopped, as soon as I knew it was over, I needed to focus on standing up. I think my legs were shaking, but I'm not sure. I tried to be calm, and I waited quietly next to the truck, unsure about what my body would do next. I imagined that I suddenly found myself in this dark haunted house which threatened, among other things, simply to disappear in the cold empty space. But nobody paid any attention to me, and I was grateful for that. Pepe sat next to me, leaned against the truck tire just as he had when we first arrived, and closed his eyes. He seemed peacefully asleep. I didn't see Carlos again until we were inside the truck, on our way home.

One of the last things I remember about that day, my first day of work, was that when el güero handed me my fifteen dollars, I didn't even look at it. I stuffed the crisp new bills into my jeans and walked away and tried not to fall flat on my face. The crisp green paper crinkled in my hands for a moment, like the wax paper around candy bars, and I really did not want to touch it. I didn't know why. My hands were smeared with chicken slime, my sneakers were caked with chicken shit, and I wanted desperately to go to the restroom. I had only one thought in my mind: how was I going to climb into the truck again if I couldn't lift my legs or move my arms? I still don't know how I did it. I guess I did lift myself to the bumper, I guess I did lift my arms over the wooden slats, and I guess someone did push me from behind and someone else pulled me in. But I don't remember any of that. I remember only that the money in my pocket crinkled again as I went over the slats and that I was relieved to be in this dark pit again, alone with my pain.

At San Lorenzo and San Simon, I walked up our driveway and around to the back door. I pushed off my sneakers before I stepped inside the house. Elmo immediately took an interest in them but then just as quickly walked away into the darkness. My mother, who hears everything, heard the screen door slam shut and said, "Manny, is that you? Dinner's ready." From the hallway, without ever seeing her big brown eyes, I said that I was taking a shower, that I was really tired, and closed the bathroom door behind me. I could hear her walk up to the bathroom door and stop in the hallway, waiting, before she asked, "So, how was it? What did you do?" I had already taken my T-shirt off, and I was sitting on the toilet slowly removing my dusty, shit-splattered jeans from my legs, which were dotted with welts around my thighs and knees. Finally, I was naked, and my entire body throbbed with pain. "Nada. No hicimos nada.

Punching Chickens

Cargamos gallinas." There was a silence on the other side of the door, at least I think there was a silence, because I don't remember that I said anything else to her. I don't remember that I responded to anything else anymore. I stared at my swollen thumb; I couldn't move it. Finally, after a while, the hot water seemed to wash the crap away. But really, it didn't. I could smell the chicken shit for days.

Doña Rosita took the small ax, raised it, and severed the hind leg from the trunk of the pig on her counter. A clear liquid dripped over the side and onto the floor. Thick blood filled the empty socket and crept over the bone. She took the leg and rinsed it underneath the faucet with cold water, then threw it in the battered tin pot full of boiling water on the stove. Pieces of two onions floated on top of the bubbles of water. Chopped up garlic swirled at the bottom. She lifted the cover of another pot on the kerosene stove. With a fork she pinched off a strand of white meat from the cheek of the pighead, whose snout stuck out above the water line. The meat was still tough. She added more salt. Outside the hens clucked away from the rooster, run-

Day of the Dead

ning underneath and into the rusted frame of the Ford Fairlane that was still on cinderblocks, right where Joaquín Pérez had left it eleven years ago. He had worked on a shrimp boat in Yucatán before his brother had told him about the money to be made working in the maquilas on the American border. Cochinita pibíl had been his favorite dish. Rosita knew just the right amount of achiote, lime, and orange juice in which to marinate the pork meat overnight after boiling it first for a few minutes. Doña Rosita and Lupe would eat most of the cochinita pibíl by next week. Just a small bowl of it, with a smattering of red onion rinds, would be left at the altar for Don Joaquín today, on Día de los Muertos.

"Mi hija, wake up," Doña Rosita called from the kitchen, stirring the pighead so that the scalding water would lap up around the snout. "Get up, niña! El rutero will be here in an hour."

"What? ¡Ay Dios!" Lupe said weakly, still half asleep, lying on a foam mattress on the living-room floor. A Pemex diesel truck slowly creaked to a halt in front of the twisted "Alto" sign outside. A cloud of white dust rolled against the front wall of the shack, which had been painted aqua. The other three walls were covered with a raggedy blanket of white plaster that exposed patches of sandy brown adobe underneath.

"You're going to miss it."

"No, I'm up already."

"I made you some sandwiches, with cajeta and cheese."

"Ay, Mamá. I told you: la familia Rogers feeds me. Why don't you just eat them yourself?"

"Take them. What if you get hungry after they feed you? Then you'll have enough to eat. Take them. I'm making cochinita. I'll have enough to eat for a while."

"It's just more for me to carry, but ándale pues. Are you going to save me some of this?"

"Sí. I'll put some of it in the freezer."

180

"I hope you don't poison me. I don't trust that freezer. Maybe la señora Rogers will give me the same Christmas bonus as last year. Then I'll have enough for a new refrigerator at Aurrerá. I saw one for 1.25 million pesos. I can give a down of 200,000 with my Christmas and what I have now."

"But what about you, mi hija? You're always paying for this or that, and you still don't have anything but rags for dresses."

"I don't need a dress. What for?"

"I don't want to argue about this now."

"Neither do I. I'm getting ready."

"Aren't you taking a shower? What are those Americanos going to say about you? 'Phew! All those people from Juárez stink up la frontera.'"

"I took a shower last night. Just leave me alone. I'm already tired and I haven't even started the week. Por favor, Mamá."

"I was just trying to help."

"I don't need it."

Lupe took a washcloth that was hanging over the sink in the bathroom, soaked it with cold water, and scrubbed each underarm until a red patch of warmth shined through her chestnut skin. She soaked the washcloth again and wrung it free of cold water. Holding on to the edge of the sink, she scrubbed hard against her vulva, between her thighs, and over her legs, which she splayed out over the cement floor. She scrubbed until she was free of the grimy deadness in her pores, until she reached a place beyond the impurity of her skin. She hung the washcloth on the shower curtain rod and splashed water on her face and black hair until all of it was dripping wet.

"¡Mamá!"

"What?"

"Didn't I tell you to plug up the hole in the wall underneath the sink! Spiders are crawling all over the bathroom floor!"

Day of the Dead

"Oh, I forgot. I'll do it, don't worry. Those spiders are harmless anyway."

"¡Mamá! I can't do everything! You have to help me. We have to get things done around here. It's disgusting! I can't live like this. We live like animals!"

"Don't get so excited. Stop yelling, mi hija. What are you talking about?"

"We live like animals!"

"What? What are you talking about?"

"Just look at this place! I hate it here!"

"Cálmate. Why are you screaming?"

"We live like pigs here! We live like pigs, and you're cooking pigs for a dead man!"

"What? ¡Dios te disculpe! You're talking about your father."

"Look at what he left us. ¡Nada! Spiders are running all over the floor! We barely have enough money to eat! We live in this barraca!"

"We do what we can. We're not rich."

"We live like pigs. I don't want to live like this anymore."

"What are you saying, mi hija?"

"I don't know. I just don't want to live like this."

"Please, look. I have the spiders here on this towel. There are no more spiders, mi hija."

"Ay, Mamá. That's not it. I'm tired of all of this. I'm tired and I just got up."

"Son nervios. Just relax. Please, mi hija. What's wrong?"

"I want to throw up. My head hurts. I have blisters on my feet. My back feels as if someone has been sticking needles in my spine all night. I can't even sleep when I have the time."

"Maybe you could call la señora Rogers and tell her you're sick. Tell her you can't go until Tuesday or Wednesday."

"I'm not going to tell her anything. I'm getting dressed."

Joaquín will love this, Doña Rosita thought, admiring her handi-
work. Atop two milk crates she stacked the small shoebox carefully
wrapped in gold foil paper. The crates themselves, also encased in
gold, sat on a rickety wooden table by the front door. She had
already wedged a folded piece of cardboard under the short leg of
the table. Over the warped tabletop planks Doña Rosita had
smoothed a white tablecloth embroidered with tiny yellow and red
roses. In her bedroom she unhooked a picture in a black frame from
a thick, rusted nail by her dresser and, gently, arranged the picture
upright inside one of the crates. The crate started to tip over, but she
caught it with one hand before it crashed onto the cement floor.

She placed the picture flat on the table and hurried to the
kitchen, where she found, on a topmost shelf, a large clay bowl with
"Mariscos de Yucatán" etched in white on the side. She gingerly
leaned the picture against the back wall of the milk crate again and
set the heavy bowl inside too. The crate was finally steady. Back in
the kitchen, Doña Rosita busily prepared the rest of what would
adorn the pyramidical altar of the table and the milk crates and the
shoebox. From the picture inside the crate, the faded image of a man
with a vaquero hat—green eyes dancing above parched, sunburnt
skin—gazed out the window. His smile was easy and kind. His ears
flapped out from under his hat. His brown flannel shirt seemed old
and comfortable. An image of life frozen beyond time.

Just before Lupe waved goodbye, the streetlights flickered and
then went out in Colonia Loma Linda again. Plan de Ayala Street
was absolutely black except for the soft glow of kerosene lamps
inside a few of the shacks on the street. Whenever a car zoomed
through the street on its way to Calzada Tampiqueña, the bright
flash of headlights would sweep across a flat and dusty bleakness.
The broken pavement of the curbless street. The earth, scarred and

beaten down, and forsaken. A terrible starkness that seemed almost to engulf even the aqua and oyster white splashed onto these adobe walls. But, indeed, it did not.

Doña Rosita lit her own kerosene lamp and moved hurriedly about her altar for Don Joaquín. The awful silence around her seemed shut out as she attended to her task. She filled a bowl with bizcochos and arranged it just at the corner of the small table near the door. Whoever might stop for a visit today would see them and feel free to sample a few on a napkin. On the altar table itself she created simple flower patterns with sweet orange skull candy. At the top of the pyramid, inside the shoe box, she delicately placed a surprisingly vivid picture of Nuestra Señora de Guadalupe that she had purchased at the basilica in Mexico City years ago. She kissed her fingertips, pressed the kiss onto the Virgin's tiny feet, and prayed for a moment. Then she laid a fresh rose in front of Her. Inside a straw basket in the other crate Doña Rosita carefully arranged clumps of white bread glazed to a crispy golden brown and shaped like bones. From a cup containing a few morsels of cochinita pibíl, she spooned the pork meat into the large clay bowl in front of Don Joaquín. She decorated the top of this red heap with five rinds of red onion that interlocked like the Olympic rings.

She slowly lowered the wick until the flame sputtered and died. She peeked through the window into the dark, empty street. Lupita was long gone. Nothing else was out there. Doña Rosita walked into her bedroom, Lupe's foam mattress under one arm. She tied it into a neat bundle and pushed it into a low, narrow closet, then jammed the wooden latch back into place. The old woman, whose strong leathery hands suddenly trembled, stared at the bizarre shape of the altar under the persistent moonlight from the window. The altar seemed to sway in the bluish shimmer. She was at once frightened and excited. She believed the spirit of Don Joaquín might already be lurking among the living, here in this room. She thought she heard voices. They seemed to emanate from the walls. She knew that every day and night the world of the living was visited by that of the dead. But today and tonight, in this unique time, the primordial link between the living and the dead would become a highway easily traversed. An open passage in time would erupt to bring together misery and freedom. The trees and the mountains would shiver with what once was, and what would be. Tonight Don Joaquín would be close to her again. She felt it in her bones. Tonight he would lie next to her again, and she would travel to his own nether world and almost not return to her own bed. Tonight she might remember him again, for this was what her heart could do. She might dream of a better time as she lay on her foam mattress on the floor.

Lupe climbed into the white van that stopped at Plan de Ayala Street and Calzada Tampiqueña. The sky over Juárez was still dark. The gasoline fumes rising from the grates of the gutter seemed to thicken the darkness into a saturate smoke. She handed the driver two thousand-peso bills and told him she was going to Avenida Riberena and Epsilon. He nodded his head while staring straight ahead at the red light dangling over the street. From there she would cross the Río Grande on a pasamojado. There were always so many of them near the Chamizal. Some with huge black inner tubes, others in makeshift rafts, and a few oldtimers who still carried people across the river on their shoulders. La migra sometimes rushed in to try to stop them, but someone always saw the pale green trucks coming at full tilt on the Border Highway. The pasamojados had arranged it so that one of them was always on the lookout while the others ferried people across. By the time the mojados were on the other side, it was just a matter of time before they could spring out of the bushes and trees that lined the river. They would dash across the highway and into the Ascarate neighborhood. Then they would be free. A few blocks north, on Alameda

Street, Lupe would take the bus to San Jacinto Plaza in downtown El Paso, transfer to the Mesa Street bus, and take that all the way up to Festival Drive on the west side. Here, in another world, tony houses with whiterock landscapes and yucca plants were quiet and clean in the chill of the morning.

Four other people were riding in the van with her. Two men sat on the wooden bench in front of her and looked as if they were friends, both in jeans splashed with plaster and cement. Their faces were wrinkled red and stiff, and altogether stoic. Another man, in a shiny lavender polyester shirt, sat in the passenger seat next to the driver and yapped about his favorite rancheras, about José Alfredo Jiménez, and about that joto Juanito Rodríguez and the shame he had brought to Juárez with his effeminate incantations of "¡Arriba Juárez!" at his concerts throughout the republic. Another woman, with a cherubic face and stocky legs, sat next to Lupe in the cushioned seat at the back of the van. Lupe had seen her before and presumed she was also a maid who worked in El Paso although they had never said a word to each other. When Lupe had ducked into the van and found a seat in the back, the woman had glanced up from her folded hands on her lap and smiled at her. But that was it. For the rest of the ride, the woman just stared at the calluses on her palms, gazed blankly into the street once in a while, and shut her eyes whenever the van stopped in traffic. In a brown bag between the woman's legs a plastic skeleton mask crinkled whenever the van would halt. Underneath the mask Lupe could also see the chest of greenish fluorescent bones of a garish Grim Reaper outfit.

The van stopped at 16 de Septiembre and López Mateos, in front of the Río Grande Mall. One of the construction workers in the back opened the sliding door with a tug, and his buddy followed him out. Before they could push the door closed again, another man climbed in from the street and handed the driver two folded bills. Wearing a cowboy hat, black boots, and a large silvery belt buckle

with a rider atop a bronco, the new man sat down on the empty
wooden bench and shut the door behind him. He turned to Lupe
and the woman sitting next to her and stared at Lupe's legs and at
her crotch and at the tightness of Lupe's dress around her breasts.
Lupe turned away and focused on the traffic outside: a policeman
was ticketing a motorist in front of the Plaza Monumental while the
driver held out a wad of bills to the cop and seemed to plead for him
to look up from his busywork. She turned again to the mustachioed
vaquero with the bronco belt. He was still looking her over. She
glanced at his face, but just as a smile seemed to form on his lips, she
closed her eyes and tried to shut him away. Still she imagined his
eyes roaming up and down her body like the tiny black legs of a
thousand spiders pattering over her flesh. After a while, in the
reddish darkness behind her eyelids, she began to daydream about
the eyes of Roberto Carlos. The bold and intelligent eyes that sprang
out from her album cover at home. His curly brown hair that just
grazed his shoulders. His lips and his mouth. He holding her hand
and walking with her on the beach. His caress behind her back, his
body tightly against hers. His hand slowly tracing the outline of her
face. Her lips reaching out to kiss his fingers. Their kisses and their
passion, uninhibited and profound and free.

"Señorita, Avenida Riberena."

Lupe opened her eyes and stepped out of the van, which
resumed its course toward downtown Juárez. She walked across an
empty field, in the direction of a clump of trees on the river's
embankment. The sky was still mostly a purplish blue, but in the
horizon toward Van Horn a reddish glow already crept up from the
ground. The line of amber streetlights along the Border Highway on
the other side of the river also shimmered. The desert air was cold
and stiffened Lupe's ankles, calves, and thighs so that her hurried
steps thumped hard against the dirt. She stepped over a knee-high
metal rail about twenty meters from the river. Its coldness against

the inside of her knee zapped a shiver up her spine and across her back. Now able to look down the embankment, she scanned the edges of the river. About a half kilometer to the west of her she saw a group of five or six persons waiting on the river's edge. One raft, with a man astride on it, waited on the Mexican side while a man in another raft was just pushing off the American side with a long pole. Three people were scurrying up the embankment on the other side. They stepped through a perfectly square hole in a chainlink fence that was welded atop a guardrail and curved toward Mexico like an upright hand with an infinite number of fingers bent at the knuckle. Lupe walked quickly toward the pasamojados.

She glanced up and down the highway just beyond the chainlink fence and spotted only one pair of headlights slowly descending from the overpass to the east. Far away and apparently not in too much of a hurry. Lupe had never been arrested crossing the river, but she had heard stories about what they would do to you if they did catch you. They might rape you in the back of the INS truck. They might rape you for a few hours and then let you go. Who would believe a poor Mexicana anyway? They'd ship you back to Mexico before you had a chance to tell your story. They'd say somebody at the detention center raped you, but *they* surely didn't. Or they might just beat you up because they're angry and frustrated that hundreds and hundreds of Mexicanos cross everyday. They might kill you. Lupe did read in *El Fronterizo* how a man from la migra had shot and killed a pasamojado last month. Self-defense, he claimed. Self-defense when there were no other witnesses. When the poor bastard only had a stick. A stick against a gun.

The blister on her little toe on her right foot rubbed against her flat shoes. Rubbed until the pain seemed to throb through the bone where she planted her weight. Rubbed and hurt so much that she limped as a matter of course, not noticing that her every step forward was more of a sway and a lurch than a smooth walk. By the time she reached the group, another raft had already drifted across the Río Grande and was on its way back. A couple waited anxiously together, holding hands and looking around and stamping their feet to ward off the coldness of this morning air. With great care Lupe slid and stepped down the crumbly dirt bank. A few rocks of dried mud tumbled almost to the feet of the couple at the river's edge. The man, wearing a Dodgers baseball cap, turned toward Lupe and offered his hand so that she could steady herself once she jerked to a stop at the bottom of the embankment. They smiled at each other quickly, and Lupe said gracias, and together they peered at the pole and the raft creeping over the sheet of still blackness toward them. The river Styx of the Americas. The pasamojado took their money as they climbed onto the raft, waiting patiently, his pole stuck deep into the river's mud. Only after the other pasamojado had reached their embankment did Lupe's raft begin to push over the murky current.

Underneath their raft the water gurgled against the rotting timbers. Once in a while black water splashed over the side and trickled across the top plank and disappeared into a bead of water. The raft itself rocked gently from side to side, but Lupe kept her balance. Her feet apart, she would drop to one knee if she felt unsteady and wait out the rough rocking motion. For the most part the river's current was lazy and smooth. The pasamojado pushed the raft diagonally across the river, getting the water to help him and not worrying about the aesthetics of his own haphazard effort to drag the raft across the water. Lupe could smell the earthy sweat of the young man struggling with the pole. She could see that his feet were anchored inside two slots that had been carved into the wood. As soon as the raft jammed against the weeds and grass on the other side, the couple jumped out and ran up the embankment. Lupe jumped out too, but she slipped on the loose sand and almost fell back into the water. She steadied herself before standing up and

Day of the Dead

trudged up the dirt toward the hole in the chainlink fence. She looked up, but the couple on her raft had disappeared.

"¡Allá viene la migra! ¡La migra!"

A shot of fear from her innards almost choked her. Lupe peered back at the pasamojado on the other side of the river. He was pointing to the west. Lupe began to run. Trying to leap through the hole between the guardrail below and the chainlink netting above, Lupe smacked her left shin against the rail's metal edge. The utter sharpness of the pain exploded in her head like a bomb of white light. She stumbled over the guardrail and onto the ground, her purse flying in front of her and embedding itself in a tumbleweed. She pushed herself up and ran toward the freeway in front of her, turning her head toward the Franklin Mountains. Instead of headlights she found only the glint of amber streetlights reflecting off a darkened windshield still so far away that the truck would disappear now and then in the dips in the pavement. Her heart almost burst inside of her chest. Her legs were numb with pain. She couldn't breathe. She was gasping for air, she was running with everything she had, she was running and gasping and falling forward. In front of her, across the westbound lanes, a few seconds away, Lupe saw an opening, an irrigation ditch that separated two backyard rock walls abutting the freeway. Just a dilapidated chainlink fence stretched across the ditch. The fence's metal mesh had a hole the size of a refrigerator. On the other side she would be in Ascarate, safe. Her eyes were transfixed on the hole in the fence. She ran across the freeway. Her eyes were dilated and shimmering in amber. She turned her head to find the truck in the distance again. Her eyes were wild. She was dead.

The tires of a gray Camry screeched and slid on the black pavement and finally settled to a stop on the red gravel of the right shoulder of the westbound lanes. A man in a white oxford shirt and a red tie leaned over the empty passenger seat and peered out the window. He seemed terrified at what he saw: the twisted body of a woman lying just beyond the shoulder. Her legs were bloodied over the thighs. The skirt she had been wearing was pushed up to her chest. Her head was swollen and crushed on one side such that it seemed just a distorted black mass above her torso. She wasn't wearing any shoes. She didn't move. He looked through his rearview mirror and saw a pair of headlights miles away, like two tiny jewels floating in empty space. In front of him, and also in the distance, he saw only the faint outline of an INS truck, with its siren and search-lights perched atop the cab. The truck veered off the highway and onto a dirt road in a cloud of dust, apparently on its way to the river. The gravel suddenly spun out from the Camry's rear wheels. Soon it was cruising west again at exactly fifty-five miles per hour. The face of the driver was angular and pale. The small blue eyes stared blankly at the road in front of him. He took his right hand and wiped the thick sweat off his forehead, held his throat for a moment, and then vomited a spurt of yellowish bile on the passenger seat. Switching hands on the steering wheel, the man shoved his left hand into his back pants pocket and yanked out a billowy cotton hand-kerchief with his fingertips. He wiped his mouth clean, collected the viscous liquid on the seat, and wrapped it up in a neat little ball of white that he tucked into the leather pocket of his car door. The gray Camry bounced over the pavement dip just before the Paisano exit. Even the trees and the mountains now seemed suddenly inert.

Helen Rogers hoisted her son onto the changing table and pulled off his pajamas. Her brow was sweaty while her blue eyes darted around his bedroom. The sheets had been thrown on the rug, the large plastic fire engine was upended, and a brownish red mark had been smeared across the closet door.

"Brett, if you kick me one more time, I'm throwing Mr. Frumble into the trashcan," she said, an edge in her voice. This morning she was just one more spark from a catastrophic explosion. She was doing her best to check her temper. Where the *hell* was she? At least Sarah was asleep. Or maybe the baby was screaming her head off and she couldn't hear her. Last night Helen had dreamed that Sarah couldn't breathe, that she was suffocating quietly in her crib, that somehow, inexplicably, her tiny little chest had stopped rising and falling in that slow and precious rhythm. Helen had jumped out of bed. She had peered at the baby and looked and listened and even gently placed her palm on that tiny chest. And everything had been fine.

"I don't want that one! I *hate* that one! Mama!" The muscular little legs kicked at the navy blue shorts and sent them flying against the wall. The three-year-old flailed and squirmed and rolled on the changing table like a tuna on the dock.

"That's it! No more videos for you tonight, young man! I'm calling Aaron and giving him all your videos!" Helen said, one hand on his chest, the other gripping the shorts tightly. "*He* never kicks his mother!"

"No! Please! No!" Brett squealed, suddenly still. He sucked his thumb pensively and stared at his mother and knew that was it. Her eyes glared at him in that especially ferocious way.

"Are you going to stop kicking me?"

"Yes."

"Are you sure about that?"

"Yes, Mom."

"Okay," she said, choosing the faded blue denim shorts instead. "You have to listen to me, honey. I'm just trying to get you dressed. Okay, up you go. When Lupe gets here, you'll help her do the laundry. She'll let you turn the knob on the machine. And if you find any quarters, you can get ice cream at Big Boy's."

"Nieve."

"That's right."

"Nieve de chocolate."

"Is that what Lupe likes?"

"No. She likes 'ganilla.' I like nieve de chocolate."

"Chocolate ice cream for my very good boy," Helen said and kissed her son.

"Nieve de chocolate."

"Okay. But no more yelling or kicking. I want you to behave yourself. Today Mommy's taking little Sarah to see the doctor."

"Does, does, does, Mom, does Sarah have an ouchie?"

"No. It's just a checkup. To see how much she weighs. To get her first shots. It's just a checkup. Not an ouchie. Don't worry. Little Sarah's okay. We'll only be gone for a few hours," Helen said, stroking his cheek as he climbed onto the sofa and lay down. He sucked his thumb quietly again. The phone rang. Helen stared at her watch. It was almost ten o'clock. What now?

"Yes, this is she."

"Yes, what about her?"

"*What? Where?* My God! Yes, yes. Lupe Pérez works for me. I was expecting her about an hour ago. What? I just can't believe what you're telling me!"

"Mama! Mama! *Mom!* Look! I found an hormiga! A big one! Mom!"

"Please, Brett. Officer, please. I have to sit down."

"Mom! Mom! Look over here!"

"Brett, something's happened. *Please,* honey. She was in an accident on the freeway? Oh, God! That's horrible! My phone number was in her purse? Yes, that's right. I always told her to keep it there in case she forgot. No, no. I don't know about her family. Yes, in Juárez. No, no address. No, she didn't have one. Are you sure it's her? Are you absolutely sure?"

"Mom! Mom! What is it? What did you say?"

"Brett, please. Here, honey. You can watch Mr. Frumble now. It's okay." The little boy rushed to the rocking chair and jumped into it. His face was beaming. He waited rapturously for his mother to start the VCR. "Officer, please, just one minute," she said, wiping away a tear, her back to her son. Suddenly she was having trouble breathing. She thought she heard a soft whimper from her bedroom. Maybe Sarah was waking up.

"Officer, can you please give me your number? Okay, go ahead. I've got it. Tony Hernández. Okay. If you need someone to go to the station, my husband will go. I'll tell him to call you right away. We knew her for almost three years. My kids loved her. I don't know, I just, I don't know what I'll tell them. We trusted her completely. She was a part of the family."

"Okay. Anything you need. Yes. He'll call you in a few minutes. Listen, Officer Hernández. Please, I can't help it. Yes, I'll be okay. It's just so horrible. It's, it's, I don't know," Helen said, sobbing, holding Sarah in her arms now. The baby was still asleep, but she held her close anyway. Tears rolled down her cheeks and blinded her. "Listen, Officer. Just a second. Okay. I want you to take care of her. Please. I want you to make sure you take care of her. We'll be responsible for her. Okay? I want you to take care of her. She was a part of this family."

"Goodbye."

"Mom, Mom. What, Mom?" Brett said from the doorway, the TV showing the "Play It Safe!" interlude between stories. The little boy stared at his mother, who was crying with the baby in her arms. He started to suck his thumb again. "Mom, what Mom?"

"It's okay, honey. Something's happened. I have to call your father now. Please, Brett. Go watch Mr. Frumble. It's okay. Mommy's just a little sad. But she'll be okay. I'll tell you later. It's okay, honey. I love you, you know. Do you know Mommy loves you?"

"Yes."

"Does she love you a little bit or a whole lot?"

"A lot!"

"That's right. I'll be there in a few minutes. Run quickly! It's Captain Willy and the Pirates!" Helen walked to the bedroom doorway and watched him climb into the rocking chair again. She tried to smile when he glanced back, but her head was spinning. She stared at the red and blue clown whose floppy feet you pulled to start a gentle Brahms lullaby. The dinosaur printouts on the butcher block by the kitchen. The door where Lupe always walked in with a half-smile. There seemed a new and awful space between these things. A very cold and frightening space. Quietly she pushed the bedroom door and left it ajar a few inches, just enough to hear what happened on the other side. So many parts of this world seemed important and irrelevant at the same time, in a sudden, almost nauseous flux.

He kept thinking of her face. He kept thinking of her eyes. They had been wide open, almost welcoming. They had been surprised. If she had smiled the slightest of smiles just then, it would have been a look he had seen dozens of times. That look a woman gave you when she suddenly detected that she was being appreciated from afar, not in a lustful way but aesthetically, as the beauty she secretly wanted to be. But, of course, she had not smiled at all. Hers had simply been a look of utter astonishment. Now it was a picture in Michael Ochoa's mind.

He tried at least to remember this picture instead of the image of the bloody mass atop a torso. He tried to focus on certain things that he knew to be true. He had not seen this woman run in front of his car. Yes, he had been trying to shove the change tray back into place after it stubbornly refused to click shut. His eyes had momentarily left the road. But in those two or three seconds when he stared at the metal clip to figure out how it worked, she appeared in front of him, with that look. It was an instant he would never forget.

What was she doing in the middle of the freeway? Why was she running in front of his car? The early morning road had been practically empty. Why the hell did she run in front of *his* car? How could he have stopped in time? How? Please, dear God, why did these things happen? Nothing made sense anymore. It was simply the bad luck of having been in that awful moment. She had stepped into it and dragged him inside. He had been as utterly shocked as she had. Why did this happen? Why? His stomach churned again.

Michael felt a little dizzy. He stared at the construction schedule he had to complete today. Dozens and dozens of rows of numbers that signaled when the grading for the Rosa Linda project would be finished, the plumbing, the foundations, the frames, the electricity, the masonry, even the landscaping. Everything for nearly one thousand "housing units" of the federal government. Sometimes he had imagined the armies of plumbers and electricians and bricklayers who would follow each other from one house to the next. As soon as one T-joint was dry, the sawdust would fly from a two-by-six. After the nickel-like outlet covers clanged to the floor, the sheetrock arrived in massive stacks. Hundreds and hundreds of times, until a small town, with streets and trees and sidewalks, arose from the desert. But now he couldn't imagine anything beyond these rows of numbers. He could only see that startled face. Her brown eyes.

The entire morning Michael Ochoa had been sick to his stomach. It was the thick red blood that made him sick. It was the worry. He had killed a human being. *He* had killed her, and then escaped without anyone's noticing his crime. Had it been a crime? It was certainly a crime now, he told himself. Maybe if he had stayed and notified the police and explained how *she* had come out of the

196

bushes, like a frightened rabbit, maybe they would not have blamed him for this accident. Maybe. But he panicked. He saw no one there, no other witnesses, and he panicked. It was a breathless leap into nothingness, into a world of your very own making, into a world where you were the only witness. He really felt sick to his stomach. What the hell had he done?

He remembered the woman's face again. Her smock of a dress. The darkness of her skin. The whitish spots on her thighs. Her jet black hair. The thin ankles. His mother would have probably called her "just a poor Mexican woman." He had never liked her way of saying things, especially *those* things. It was really distasteful in a way. But that was what came to mind just now. Just a poor Mexican woman. That was the way his mother would have dismissed the tragedy and defended him. She would have said his life was at stake now. His accomplishments. His marriage. His children. Why would he throw it all away because a poor Mexican woman had sprinted in front of his car on the Border Freeway?

His father would have laughed at him for being so weak. His father, Mr. Chicano. In many ways the old man had been worse than his mother on those things. At least his mother had had an excuse. She had not known any better. But Juan Ochoa, the *great* Juan Ochoa, had always known what to say in public about Mexico and illegal immigrants and la raza. That's how he had gotten elected so many times in El Paso County, from the school board to the city council to the county commission. But Michael had also remembered what his dad had said at dinnertime, when he had been there. "¡Qué se vayan a la chingada! ¡Pinchi Juarileños! Who the fuck do they think they are?"

It killed his father that the Mexican politicos saw him as an inferior Mexican, that somehow they felt *sorry* for him. Michael also remembered how ashamed his father had been when once, at a big picnic at the Chamizal, one of them had asked Michael a question in Spanish, and he had not quite understood. Mr. Chicano turned beet red, and the veins in his neck almost erupted. Michael immediately recognized the glare; he understood *that* quite clearly. It meant "pendejo."

That, and many moments like that, had convinced Michael Ochoa of certain things. He did not want to be a politician, and he did not want to be a lawyer. He would not hate Chicanos or things Mexican, but he would try to discover his own way to this part of his heritage. Maybe it wouldn't be outright love, but it certainly wouldn't be outright hate either. He would also try to get his pride out of the way of the most important decisions in his life, and he would never be a social climber. He wanted to learn better Spanish.

His head ached, but he finished the project schedule and handed it to John Cooper just before 3:00 P.M. He had felt weak all day, and as soon as nothing was immediately hanging over his head, Michael Ochoa shut his office and came out only to throw up in one of the private executive bathrooms on the first floor. He was shaky and faint. He kept imagining that sickening thump against his car. The flash of her body flying through the air. That thick red blood. In an hour or so, it would finally be time to go home.

Little Sarah burped sitting up on her mother's lap, and her small white head lolled to one side. The baby was finally asleep. The house was finally quiet. Helen thought about removing the three small bandages on the baby's plump thighs but then just carefully lowered the child into her crib. Helen needed the peace; she needed to sort out the storm inside her head; she wanted to cry. It had been hellish taking Brett to Sarah's checkup. He had sprinted from the doctor's waiting room into the hallway at every turn. He had refused to listen to her, and even screamed when she had tried to talk to him. Her attention had been on Sarah. They had been in a public place. And Helen had been busy listening to the doctor's explanation of the

DPT shots and how much infant Tylenol she could give Sarah in case she reacted badly to the vaccinations. Brett had probably *smelled* his mother's weak position. It had simply been a miracle that Sarah had gotten her shots, that Helen had paid the bill on her way out, that Brett had not been lost or had not killed himself. Strapping him into the stroller, *restraining* him, had felt absolutely wonderful. That had been, until now, the best moment of this terrible day.

Helen snapped her bra shut and peered into the crib again and listened. The house remained dead silent. With any luck, Brett would nap for another hour and a half. With any luck, she could start to put all of these shattered pieces in her mind together. With just the tiniest bit of luck, she might think about Lupe Pérez for a few seconds before the rush of life swept this poor young woman into oblivion. It all seemed so brutal. The way Lupe died. The way she could hardly be remembered. Maybe even the way she lived. This last fact at once terrorized Helen Rogers, and she hid her face in her pillow and sobbed. She had never known *where* Lupe had lived. She had never known her address. There was nowhere, yet, to send the body. Lupe's place now was a dark vault in a funeral home. It was simply too much to bear.

It was so hard to remove yourself from this world. It was just so hard to think about who you were, and who were the people you saw almost every day. There was no time to think about anything. There was no time to react thoughtfully, to arrive at grand conclusions, to find the truth before it slipped away forever. Helen could barely wipe the slobber off the baby's onesie before she heard a loud crash or a squeal or that dreadful, unexplained silence. This world, my God! It twisted this way and that, and threw everyone about, and left those who still possessed a bit of sense to organize the chaos into, into . . . what? A dream better than this reality? A hope more attractive than this brutality? It was better just to keep living and not think too much. It was better to keep your fingers crossed and pray that this brutality would never visit you or your family. It was better, then, simply to cry.

After a while she called her husband's office again. The police had found Lupe's address through a government health card that was also found in her purse. The Juárez authorities were probably on their way there right now; it was somewhere called Colonia Loma Linda. Her husband had the exact address. He had told the police that as far they knew, Lupe had lived with her mother.

"I'm going there tonight," Helen said immediately. "I need to be with her. Her daughter has just died." Her husband almost protested aloud, but in the end said nothing. Helen knew she was pushing him, especially after she had insisted that they pay for the funeral and whatever else was needed. Yet she also knew her husband. He would do the right thing whenever she demanded it, and there would be no negotiation over this today. "I'll call my mother and she'll help you with the kids. I need to see her. It's really the least I can do. As it is, it's hardly enough. I just can't believe our Lupe's gone."

The car was clean. That was the important part. The car was clean, and nobody had seen him. No one knew. He was the only person who knew. That was the fact he focused on as he drove home on I-10. Michael Ochoa had finally inspected his car just before he left for home. It had not occurred to him before, and he had been lucky. He had found only a small dent next to the left front headlight. He had found no blood. It was simply a small dent that happened at a gas station while he was pulling in, a bump against the metal rail protecting the pumps, a careless mistake. . . . Just the slightest of dents. It was amazing that a human body could do so little damage to a car.

Michael drove slower than usual and stayed to the right. It would all get easier after a while. Occasionally he'd glance at that left front corner when no cars were directly in front of him. He once imagined her eyes in front of him for a split second again. He raced right through her again. Behind him, the diesel trucks and motorcycles and sedans also punched through this selfsame freeway roar. She was just the whirling air now, the backwash of traffic. There really was no use torturing himself anymore. Anything he did now could only hurt him. Nothing could be done about what happened, about her. Wasn't that the truth?

What would Mr. Chicano do here, eh? He'd laugh it off. He'd go fuck one of his bitches and laugh it off. He'd think about it, maybe, and he'd be happy to be alive. He'd have a beer and piss off the back porch. He'd comb his hair, and look so pretty, and tell his reyna he'd be back in a while. Another meeting. Another rally. A strategy session. One of those goddamn fundraisers, you know? And he'd be gone, happy, oh-so-happy he was the one who lived and not the one who died.

It'd be a victory for him. That's how he'd see it. He'd see it as *not* being him. Another narrow escape. The luck of the gods who walked the earth. The gods who didn't fail. The gods who didn't die until *they* wanted to die. A fucking poor Mexican woman wouldn't bring Him down! Not one of those goddamn Juarileños! They'd never touch Him. They couldn't touch Him. Mr. Chicano wouldn't let them. It'd be His secret victory over them. It'd be what made Him smile confidently when they laughed in His face again, when they wouldn't give Him the goddamn *respect* He deserved. Sure, esta pobrecita had died, an innocent. She had really nothing to do with His fight against those cabrones. That was true. But she stepped into it and made herself a symbol. She had simply become a symbol of La Chingada. We were all fucked, weren't we? Mr. Chicano would just be the one doing the fucking this time. Those were the breaks, he'd say.

Again, a certain thing became clear in Michael Ochoa's mind.

Day of the Dead

He suddenly took the next exit off I-10, at Yarbrough. His small
blue eyes stared at the road in front of him, and his stomach at once
felt better. He first stopped at a Dunkin' Donuts and called his wife
and talked to her for a while. It was a good conversation, he
thought, and he was glad that she was always practical and supportive, even if she did cry now and then. She was a very good woman,
and he was damn lucky. Michael Ochoa got into his car and drove
north on Yarbrough, to where he thought he had seen it once before.
Yes, there it was. For the first time in a long time, in what had
seemed a day composed of years of childhood and years of lonely
struggle and years of this cursed history all around him, he felt good
again. Before he opened the door to the Eastwood police substation,
his eyes caught a glimpse of a billboard for Spanish lessons at night
at El Paso Community College. It was time to start again, even if
some of his friends might laugh at his accent.

It was now dark outside, and Helen Rogers was a little frightened.
No stores were open on this dusty two-lane highway anymore. There
were no streetlights, no sidewalks, and hardly any street signs. Just
the highway between downtown Juárez and Zaragoza, an occasional
car or truck, and half-dirt roads snaking into neighborhoods that
also seemed dark and desolate. She had sometimes driven into
downtown Juárez, usually with visitors who wanted to go shopping
at the Mercado Juárez or to a fancy dinner in Mexico. She had not
been the stereotypical jittery gringa who never crossed the border.
But she really didn't know this part of town. She didn't know these
poor hamlets that dotted la frontera between the big city and the
next port of entry on the Río Grande. She was lost.

Helen pulled off the highway and slowly drove to a street corner
that seemed one of the entrances to this neighborhood. She knew
she wasn't far away, but Colonia Loma Linda could be anywhere

within the next two or three miles of road. As her car stopped, the wheels crunched the gravel and chunks of dirt underneath. She was looking for Calle Venustiano Carranza, which according to her map would go from the Zaragoza highway to Colonia Loma Linda and eventually to Plan de Ayala, Lupe's street. The small blue metal sign on the grocery store's wall was hard to read. Part of it was bent, and a slash of rust obscured the lettering. She clicked on her brights for a better look. Aha! It wasn't the right street, but it was on her map, not too far away from where she wanted to be. Soon she found Carranza and slowly eased into what seemed a pitch-black cave with distant yellowish lights, like candles, and an unpredictable, even ominous terrain.

The house at the end of Plan de Ayala didn't seem like a house. It was impossibly small, the size of a garage, and the roof seemed oddly tilted, as if it had caved in or was about to cave in at any moment. There was an abandoned car on cinderblocks next to it. Helen could smell chickens and hear them clucking, but in this darkness she could not see them. It was also one of the last houses in this neighborhood, on its outskirts, and almost not a part of it. This house was at the edge of what seemed a vast plain of nothingness. Only a faint aura glowed in the horizon, probably El Paso. But this was where the old woman had pointed when Helen asked, in her broken Spanish, for "la casa Pérez." When the old woman had opened her door, she seemed to have been expecting Helen. "Es la casa del color del mar." It is the house the color of the sea.

"Me llamo Helen Rogers," she said to the dark figure in the shadows behind the door. "Busco a la señora Pérez." He was an old man, an ancient man, who waved her inside. Helen could hear faint murmurs just in front of her. A candle flickered in one corner, but it was too dark to see their faces very well. Somebody gently led her by the arm to the threshold of another room. Here she could distinctly hear three or four women's voices. She could see a bed. They were huddled around a bed. A crucifix was on a box or a crate next to the bed, and candles had been placed around it in a semicircle. They did not know she was there, and she did not yet make a sound. The bed was a foam mattress on a bare concrete floor. Helen could smell the heavy burning wax of the candles, the wetness of the earth, these adobe walls, old wood. She heard heavy sobs coming from the bed, and these voices that responded and chanted and seemed to surround this black grief with beckoning little angels.

As Helen stepped forward to the bed, she was overwhelmed by the sense that she was passing through a wall in the darkness. She felt as if she had stopped breathing, as if time had been suspended within this thickness. One of the women noticed her and stared at her as if Helen had been a shocking apparition but finally ceded her place slowly in this human circle around the bed. Helen kneeled and found Doña Rosita's anguished face and unrelenting tears, and a pain so powerful that Helen almost gasped. In a very raspy voice that turned every head in that room and reached deep inside the pit of grief, she said in her Spanish, "I am Helen Rogers, and we loved Lupe very much. She will always be a part of our family." Then Helen Rogers grasped the old woman's trembling hand, and her own tears gushed out, and they held each other in a moment beyond this world.

I almost left the City because I could not find myself there anymore. I found many desires in the City. My gaze would never settle on one thing. It would jump from face to face to face. I enjoyed watching the many beautiful women in the City. Yes, I would study their faces and bodies. I would imagine making love to them. I would imagine their touch on my own body. Sometimes they would smile in return. Sometimes I would talk to them, and their eyes would sparkle. Often they would turn away. A few seemed angry at my open look. But I never meant any harm. I simply wanted to find myself there, to find some-one, and I wanted to reach out. But there was nothing there. Or else, it was simply

My Life in the City

too far away. They were too far away. I was not there. I did not know where I was.

Cars always sped a few inches past me whenever I crossed the street to buy groceries. It was this near danger that one day prompted me to think about the lack of God here. One wrong moment, a misstep, and you die a chance death. A beautiful woman with dark brown curly hair, deep brown eyes, and a friendly, casual air about her stopped a few inches from me on the curb. We waited for the light to change to cross the street. There were others too, in heavy coats, with briefcases or shopping bags, all waiting. She stepped off the curb, ready to jump into the road as soon as the danger was gone. Her face turned toward me as she drifted farther into the street, almost swaying with readiness. Behind her, I saw first the bright lights, then heard the roar of the engine, and before I could say anything—would I have said anything or would I simply have watched the spectacle if given another moment?—a speeding blue and white bus brushed against her hair just as she turned to face it. She fell back as if into an abyss, her face white and blank. Her knees buckled. She smiled nervously, took a deep breath, and watched the bus zoom across the intersection. She seemed stunned, and I wanted to hold her, at least to say something, but I didn't. I was afraid too. I felt lost.

I took my groceries up to my apartment on 86th Street and Broadway. I shop when I don't want to be alone in my apartment, when the silence seems too loud. I also shop when I don't have food. Often, these two things coincide. Shopping is about walking in the street. Walking on Broadway is about getting away from yourself and apparently going somewhere. Apparently. But now, as I put away my orange juice and seltzer, I thought about the dark-haired woman who had almost died a few minutes before, and about the lack of God in the City. It was something palpable here. There was a certain meaninglessness to what happened on these streets. A wrong step and you might be crushed. And then your family would spend days, and then years, adding meaning to what happened to you, adding religion, adding morality.

But really, there was nothing there to begin with, just that wrong step, just her slight smile before the headlights flashed against her face, just *us*. Some of you might think that this meaninglessness I sense on the streets of the City, like a thick cloud, is reason for despair. I don't think so. Or you might think that this lack of meaning is the reason for my thinking about leaving the City. But again you would be wrong. I just find the lack of meaning on Broadway to be the present state of things. The way things are. There is only the urgency to do something about this present, to create what might be a passing fancy into, well, an idea. I feel the need to take out my hammer and *work,* but not the swoon of not finding a grand blueprint in front of me. As for leaving the City, I will tell you about that later.

I needed butter and bagels, so I went out again, toward H & H Bagels. I mean, I didn't *need* them, what I needed was to think, and I did my best thinking on the move. Walking is almost synonymous with thinking in the City, with an added numbness that prevents you from going too far. Walking almost teases you to think, and yet it's just a tease. You have to enjoy it for what it is, or you'll be disappointed once you stop. There will be no grand revelation at the end of it, just your body warm and sweaty, maybe your mind at ease. I wanted to think about the dark-haired woman again. Maybe I'd run into her again. Maybe I just wanted to immerse myself in that meaningless present on the street again. I wasn't sure what I wanted.

I didn't meet her, but I did meet someone else. Maybe I exuded the scent of wanting to meet someone. Maybe I had a certain kind of look, I don't know. I bought a poppy, a sesame, and two sour-dough bagels, and then I walked across the street for the ninety-nine-cent toilet paper. Might as well, I thought, I'm already here.

My Life in the City

In the drug store I was looking at sport bandages. My left ankle was still tender from veering off the pathway to the boardwalk on 79th Street to avoid a pit bull off its leash. I had twisted my foot on a rock, but I had escaped the savage animal, which hadn't been very savage then, just savage looking. I also dropped a box of Equal into my red basket. A woman next to me, with blond, slightly disheveled, shoulder-length hair, said, "That stuff will kill ya." She smiled at me, and I liked the way she looked—slim, not deformed in any observable way, possibly intelligent, big blue-gray eyes—so I asked her how, exactly, I was poisoning myself with this sugar substitute.

She said it contained "chemicals" and that something like honey would probably be better. I said I'd try honey in my coffee, but that I also thought the caffeine would kill me first—or at least scramble up my neurons to leave me permanently damaged—before anything I added to make it sweet. "Going herbal" was best, she said, which made me immediately suspicious of her. Maybe she was a radical tree-hugger type, in which case I wasn't sure why she was talking to me except to save my body and tell me what to do. I asked her if she was a vegetarian too. Vegetables had chemicals sprayed on them, didn't they? She said she occasionally ate meat, which made me like her again. At least she wasn't a wild-eyed fanatic. I said I would buy the Equal and take my chances. Live free or die, I thought. She smiled at me and asked me what I did for a living.

I told her I was independently rich, which was a lie, and which she knew was a lie because I was grinning too much. We walked to the checkout counter of the drug store. Really, I said, I was an architect. I especially liked doing bridges I told her, which wasn't a lie. She was in front of me in line, and I noticed again that she was pretty, a little funky in dress—jeans, boots, sweater, a big loose jacket, a red scarf around her neck, like the pit bull, and big triangular earrings—and about my age. Young, but not stupidly young. She was a "performance artist," which I thought meant she was unemployed. But I was wrong. She had had shows at Dia and a few other places I recognized, although she said things were kind of slow now. She was working on music for a new show, and writing. Maybe she was making it in the City, I thought, which was good. Or maybe she was independently wealthy and talented, which was even better for her. In any case, I still liked her, and she was still being friendly. On Broadway she gave me her phone number, and I gave her my e-mail address, and we agreed to have lunch or something someday. We said goodbye, and just as she walked toward Zabar's, she turned her blond head and smiled again. I was feeling pretty good myself. I bought a bar of chocolate on the way home.

As soon as I walked into my apartment, I washed my dishes from last night and picked up the few things that shouldn't be on the floor but were. It was Sunday, and I almost called my parents in Texas—it was cheaper on Sundays—but then I decided to wait until night. I'd have that little something to end my weekend, and calling them usually made me happy because they were in love with each other and never really bothered me about my life in the City. I did some push-ups because I sensed the atrophy in my arms. Sometimes my brain felt like that too, and having a good conversation with a friend usually remedied that terrible encroaching weakness. I suited up for running, which meant black shorts and a thick, oversized navy blue sweatshirt that I loved because it was comfortable. I was ready to kick some pit bull ass.

As I worked up to my pace on Riverside Drive, I first thought about the dark-haired woman who had almost died. Well, not about her exactly, but about what she had taught me about living in the City. I saved performance-artist Becky for the end of my run. It was okay not to have God here. In fact, it was better than okay. It was liberating. I didn't mean it in a drunken sort of way. It was pleasantly free. I could understand that some people needed the Godhead, needed the structure provided by knowing what would happen to them once they died, or needed reasons for the evil acts or accidents that befell them. God was reason and order for many, even though God was often inscrutable. That heavenly world, that world in the beyond, gave meaning to that Ford Explorer's crushing you at the 96th entrance to the Henry Hudson.

But what if you didn't need God anymore? What if you could deal with your attempts to make the world a secure and happy place for you, alongside the unpredictability and chaos and vulnerability of life? I guess if you were hooked on the ultimate meaning of the holy world, this rip-roaring view of life would mean everything you do is okay. Let's start slashing each other with knives, raping your neighbor if you can get away with it, and stealing whatever your arms can carry home. But we have this extreme reaction to the lack of God simply because our minds are accustomed to giving so much power to God in the first place. Without Him, we're lost, but only because we expect so little from us in this world. Get used to a godless world and you depend on yourself more, and you expect more of yourself, and you still know that shit can happen. That way of looking at things seemed to me like a great and dormant freedom coming from my bones, but also like a call to get to work. Time's a wastin'!

I didn't see any pit bulls on the way up to Columbia, and the air seemed suddenly cleaner and crisp. I was having a damn good run. My head seemed clearer too. Okay, so God was outta' here. Where did that leave me? I wasn't panicking, and I wasn't feeling high. I was excited, and yet I was also a little mad at myself. I felt like I had suddenly found myself in the middle of a construction site with my people asleep on the job and the deadline looming. Okay, so I wasn't going to be a great poet or a legendary writer. I wouldn't lead revolutions, and I wouldn't compose extraordinary music. I was only a guy who had just found the world as it was, after throwing out thousands of years of dreams and nightmares to secure my fragile existence. Maybe I was just playing catch-up, and everybody else was already there. Nobody had mentioned it to me. Still, the fresh air stung my cheeks. It was good to feel the pain a bit. It was good to want to turn the page to the next part of your story. Let's pick up the pace and get a move on. That girl who whizzed by me in black spandex had such a nice ass.

Immediately I started thinking about Becky the blond. Enough of this God-business. I'd sort it out one burst at a time. Sure, I wanted to sleep with her. If it didn't happen, it didn't happen. But I would give it a shot. I wasn't looking for a one-night stand, but I was lonely. I was open to a sexual friendship, and maybe more. We would just have to see what happened. Maybe she had just been friendly for its own sake, and yet she had flirted too. It was tough to tell this early in the thing, and I'd call her tomorrow to push it further along. It was never good to wait. She'd become another unfulfilled dream, perfect because it's far away. She'd get mad at you and move on. She, or you, might disappear into thin air, just like that. Anything could happen in the City.

After playing phone tag for a few days, we agreed to have dinner on Friday. Dinner and maybe a movie. Becky sounded happy to have heard from me so soon, and our conversation gave me the impression that she was pretty busy for not being busy at all. I liked that. She was negotiating a contract for something or other, she had a rehearsal, and she was also traveling upstate to participate in a workshop and seminar. More than anything else, I got the impression that she was smart and active. I really liked that. I thought that maybe my initial suspicion of her being a fruitcake was way off, and probably a defensive maneuver on my part. There *were* plenty of fruities in the City, committed souls hell-bent on ideas and causes rather than on just living a life, making a few good friends, tasting that perfectly toasted sesame bagel. An obsession with ideas had often fucked us up, and the God-idea was only the first among many such disasters. It was better to keep an idea at bay, to use it as a tool, to criticize it and laugh at it once in a while. What was the point of substituting your mind for the real world? So Becky seemed scrappy and practical, and had already taught me a lesson about not jumping to conclusions. I had my own idea prejudices to fight against after all.

The other thing I liked about our phone conversation was her voice. She really had a sexy voice. I hadn't noticed it in the drugstore, probably because my eyes had taken over my mind's focus then. But on the phone I had just her voice in front of me, as it were. It was first an absolutely clear voice. I'm a little hard of hearing, especially the lower tones, so it's kind of important to me. I had already had a girlfriend in college who mumbled just the slightest bit, and in a low voice. I'd spend half the day asking her to repeat herself and feeling like a stupid invalid. Even when I asked her to speak up because of my hearing problem, she wouldn't really. She always thought I was admonishing her or something. We lasted just short of three semesters, and then she flew off to San Francisco to become a mumbling oncologist.

Not only was Becky's voice clear, but it was also the slightest bit squeaky, in a singsong way. I knew some girls created this affected, come-hither squeak to sound pretty for the guys. That sorority squeak. But Becky's squeak was nothing like that at all. It was sort of a natural squeak, if that makes any sense. It was a soft squeak at the end of a sentence, a squeak and a pause and a rhythm that seemed unique to her and also perfect. We could've easily gone for another hour about her rehearsal or my latest project in Philadelphia, but it was already ten o'clock. I hadn't eaten dinner yet. And yet her words and cadence had mesmerized me after a long day at work. It was a good feeling.

I was feeling a little lonely again Thursday night, so I took another walk around the Upper Westside. Walking at night is nothing like walking during the day. I feel excited when I see all the life on the street at night. During the day, the crowd in front of me just walks too slowly. At night, there is time to kill, time to think, a possibly adventurous and even dangerous time. In the morning or when I come home from work, my mind focuses on tasks-to-be-done. Nighttimes and weekends—there really should be more of them.

I've been in the City for years, and I still love seeing the lights at night. They don't even have to be lights from a skyscraper or anything. Brownstone lights are just as good, or even better. The lights of grocery stores or cafés. The lights in pre-war buildings that seem more yellowish and soft. In fact, one of my favorite lights is from an old block-long apartment building on Broadway. The apartment's on the first floor, and all the windows are covered with old newspapers and magazines. Real newsprint light. It's been that way for years, ever since I first saw it. Someone does live there. I have occasionally seen a shadow gently walk across the yellowish light and sit down—maybe an old New Yorker who knows she can do whatever the hell she wants with her windows. I don't know if I'll be here that long.

On Amsterdam, I started thinking about God again. Or the lack of God. What kind of life was left here on the street, in my home, without the meaningfulness of the Holy, or its counterparts like Linear Progress, Eternal Life, and Ultimate Victory? I had my life here, with its fragility up front, its occasional power, random possibilities around it like flies circling shit, and this vessel of desires and thoughts that was my self. A sort of self, who's here and not here, who stood apart from this beautiful woman strolling with her little white dog, who was made by her when she offered me the slightest of smiles. I felt like dancing, but I didn't know why. Maybe

Fred Astaire was left, or the *desire* to be Fred Astaire. But I really wasn't that good of a dancer.

No, I thought, what was left after God was something else. At least for me. It could, and probably would, be different for each person. You'd have to take that road and understand yourself in the way that you would, that certain coldness in the air that was beyond the work of winter. What was left for me was first a little fear that I was walking without any protection anymore, that I was walking without a net under me. I really did feel like a reckless trapeze artist. I still *hoped* I wouldn't be hit by lightning or run over by those god-awful cabbies. But I knew this hope was my doing, and only my own. It was like a beer for my mind to make me brave about walking naked outside. I really was naked in a way now.

But the next thing that occurred to me, as I crossed over to Broadway on 79th Street, was that nothing terrible had yet happened. I mean, I did stop at the stoplights, even though the goddamn cabbies didn't. I had some time here. Sure, anything *could* happen now. I might feel pain at any moment, and it'd just be what happened to me. I wouldn't moralize my suffering anymore. But if I watched my back and looked where the hell I was going, probably nothing painful would happen. It could, but it probably wouldn't. With just a bit of luck, there was this time to do something. My brief, or not-so-brief, life. No heaven afterward. No becoming a giant panda later. No starship to take me away. My life, period.

So I thought, what was left after God were the days of my life. A few days, many days, let's keep our fingers crossed and say many years. My life would end, and that would be that. And yet I still had my days, and nights. I'd be remembered, or not, by what I did during my days. I might be remembered for what I did, my work. Maybe my family would remember me, my kids. Maybe my friends. If I had been a shit during most of my days, that's probably what I would pass on: life is shit, and some people crack quickly and give out as much shit as they get. Look, I didn't resolve then and there to be a saint. Why create another stupid ideal that's unnatural, unattainable, and self-destructive? But I knew I could be much better. That's when I started thinking that maybe I shouldn't be in the City.

You see, I have a temper. Everybody's different and responds to different environments differently. I'm the type who gets a little too worked up when the delivery guy on a bike, swinging a monstrous chain around his neck, just misses my liver by a few inches as he weaves up the sidewalk with his dumplings. Actually, that kind of stuff used to bother me much more, and now I just get out of his way and wish the marauder a slow and painful death. In New York, you yell at someone, and you're liable to be shot. *Everybody* here will call your bluff. So it's better to move along and live for another day.

So I thought that maybe I shouldn't be in the City. This environment aggravated a character like mine, or at least it forced me to use a lot of energy to counteract myself in the desire to function well in the battle zone. But change the environment, and maybe I could do something more fulfilling than getting by during my days. Yes, these days. Now, in my mind, they were all I had. Really, I don't blame New York at all. It is what it is. Too many rats in too small a box. Some of these rats really liked it that way. Maybe this rat wanted to try something else.

Becky. Becky. Becky. It was Friday, and I was meeting her at Isabella's. It was a little fancy for a first date, but what the hell. I was feeling pretty good about my days. I hadn't done anything about my future yet, but I did feel good. Becky was right on time, and we got a small table by the windows. I could see the castle-like red stone facade of the American Natural History Museum and decided then and there to check out the dinosaur exhibit that weekend. I had really liked Pteranodon and Deinonychus in Texas, as a kid. Becky was being super-nice, and she was wearing a long wool skirt that was sexy because it tugged at her hips in just the right way. Under her black leather jacket, she had on this vest and crisp white shirt that kind of lured me in by showing enough, but not too much. Where the hell did I ever get the impression she was a fruitcake? I can be an idiot sometimes.

She told me she lived a few blocks away. Actually, she lived in that big apartment building with the newspapers on the first-floor windows. She was a born New Yorker and had lived her entire life on the Upper Westside, except of course during college, when she had lived in Boston. She had inherited her rent-controlled two-bedroom (with twelve-foot ceilings and a marble fireplace!) from her mother, who had moved to Sanibel, Florida, years ago. Becky wasn't rich or anything, but I got the sense that she had a modest income from a trust fund or the like. I told her about growing up in the desert of West Texas, around cotton fields and combines and cattle guards. I told her about going to school in Austin and swimming naked in the Brazos River. I didn't mention my obsessive love of genuine pit barbecue because I didn't want to provoke her if she didn't like meat that much. Hey, if I had been born and raised in New York City, I probably wouldn't like barbecue either. It was generous to call the stuff they served here "meat." I also told her how a chance glance at a recruitment letter on a bulletin board had metamorphosed into the better part of a decade in the City.

Becky really had a sweet laugh. When she laughed, her blond hair would dance around her head. It was very festive looking. When I told her some of the stupid things I'd done as a kid, and the more recent stupid things I'd done as an adult, her laugh would tumble out, and she would smile this tight little smile, as if catching herself from going too far. Yet her eyes would shine mischievously, as if the laughter continued inside her head, rolling and rolling. The room started to get quiet even though it was packed, she started to tease me just a bit and one-up me with horror tales from her past, and time slipped away into the cold night outside like the steam heat from the street gutters. We had both stumbled onto a really good time.

We were nearing the end of our main course, and I was imagining dessert, when I did something a little rash. We had been thinking of a movie, but the night had only gotten colder outside. I could feel the chilly breeze whip around my ankles as it slipped through the cracks of the white window doors next to us. Really, I thought, I'd rather spend more time with her than simply looking at a movie screen in adjacent seats in the dark. I really wanted to hold her, that's all. Strangely enough, it wasn't a horny feeling. I was cold, and I wanted to hold her, and I thought she might share the thought. It wasn't yet love, I knew that. It was more like wanting warmth and a little attention, and finding someone across the table who got along with you and who was pretty good-looking. I thought about my days too. So I reached across the table, and told her I really appreciated her company, and kissed her hand.

At first, for a second or two, Becky seemed stunned, and she blushed just the slightest bit. Then, immediately, her blue-gray eyes searched my own like lasers seeking the truth, whatever this obscure thing was. I was trying to look harmless, just trying to communicate that I simply liked being with her, which was exactly what I meant—nothing more, nothing less. Then, after what seemed centuries gone by, she squeezed my hand and said she enjoyed being with me too. I really didn't know where we were anymore. It seemed as if we had suddenly gotten lost together.

She asked me if I was cold too. I said that I was. I said I liked holding her hands because they were so warm, and they were. It was as if she had a little heater inside her body. Dessert came, and we were drinking hot coffee. She asked if I still wanted to see a movie. "Still" was exactly the word she used too. She wasn't exactly smiling, and yet her eyes gleamed. I was really lost now, and for some reason

I felt a fluttering in my chest, as if a sparrow had gotten stuck in my chest cavity. Maybe I was having a heart attack, I thought. It was cold and also suddenly hot in that restaurant. I told her I'd be open to her suggestions. I really couldn't think of anything else to say, and I thought I stammered. How about renting a video and going back to her place and starting up her fireplace? That sounded like a really good idea, I said. The sparrow seemed stuck in my throat now, but I did manage a smile. My mind was blank, and I at once thought I was a passenger on a boat mysteriously guiding itself through a dense and dark jungle.

We rented the video, but I don't really remember what it was anymore. Most movies are not that memorable. They're meant to waste your time, and that's not a bad thing to do once in a while. But it'd be better if you had just a few movies every year that would really challenge the culture instead of just reciting acceptable platitudes under the guise of being serious. I guess they have to sell whatever they make, and therein lies the problem. The other reason I didn't focus on the video was that I was listening to a really good story Becky was telling me about her most recent performance. It was a piece that included her own music, a poem by Li-Young Lee, and some "interpretive movement" about the destruction and creation of life between men and women. To tell you the truth, I didn't understand everything she said. I don't think she was making it up. I think she knew what she was talking about, and was earnest about it. It just wasn't my language yet. I'd have to read the poem and see her performance and think about it, and then I might understand what she was trying to do. Anyway, her talk about her work was better than any goddamn movie, and it almost prompted me to ask her what she thought about a godless world, and your days in it, but I didn't. We were soon at her apartment.

The tiny black elevator with the accordion door creaked and groaned as it jiggled upward to the sixth floor. The hallways were long and spooky even though bright brass lamps glowed every few feet. This building was old and, I guess, had once been luxurious. My own building really had a completely different feel. Modern, yuppie, clean. I sometimes found it charmless. No dead souls behind its walls. Becky's building, however, teemed with ghosts, it seemed. I immediately thought of "The Cask of Amontillado," and the body or bodies I might find behind this white plaster. Poe had actually lived not far from here, on 84th Street. Maybe if I hung around the hallway for a while, I might spot an old woman, one eye askew, clutching a butcher knife, a trowel, and half-smiling at me.

Inside Becky's apartment, I was surprised again. My bit of excitement at the hallway gloom transformed into a feeling of comfort at the quiet inside. It was quiet and warm. I hardly felt like I was in the City anymore. On one wall of her living room were these old wooden shelves with glass doors and shiny brass locks. Behind the glass were dozens of books, odd figurines, the foot-long jaw of an animal, ornate metal and wooden boxes, and a squat, bejeweled vase that probably housed an evil genie. I felt like quizzing her about the origin of each of these items, like an anthropologist, but left that for another day. I sat on one side of an L-shaped sofa, a beige brocade from another time and place too, and tried to take in more of this musty, odd labyrinth I had stepped into. Amid this museum were things like a digital answering machine and a monstrous color TV buffeted by minispeakers. Becky said she'd make popcorn and hot chocolate. In the kitchen, too, I noticed this old-new coexistence. An old-fashioned milk pail sprouting tiny purple flowers. Shiny copper vats hanging from a grid in the ceiling. A pristine white microwave, its clock glowing a soft neon green. I helped her bring the hot chocolate to the living room, and we settled into her couch, next to each other, in front of the humongous tube.

It was right at the beginning of the movie, when we stopped chatting about the actors in it, when Becky gave me another mischievous smile. Her mind was rolling again, but we hadn't been talking about anything funny. I reached out and held her hand. She put her hand around my waist and kissed me. And I kissed her. It was really the most delicious of kisses. Wet, but not slimy. Our lips playing off each other so easily. A sort of rhythm building up, like a crescendo, and dropping off to stoke our desire. Becky became much more beautiful to me when I kissed her. What she could do and what I felt seemed to flash over me like a new kind of light that transformed what I saw in front of me. I touched her face and stroked her shoulders and gently rubbed her legs as if to confirm this strange and wonderful metamorphosis. This was the same face, and yet it wasn't. Her body had been pretty, but now when I touched it, when she let me touch it, it seemed I was touching a star exploding alone in the abyss of the universe. I was short of breath, and it wasn't simply because I was excited to be with her. The hard reality of this City, this black pavement, seemed suddenly alive like skin. I was crashing through this surface into—what?—the vibration of life. It was better than walking down Broadway at night, the cold on your cheeks. It was like walking, and then levitating into the lights.

I am grateful to the following publications for publishing my stories first. "Remembering Possibilities" originally appeared in *Other Voices*; "Angie Luna" in *New World: Young Latino Writers* (Dell Publishing, 1997) and *Electric Mercado*; "A Rock Trying to Be a Stone" in *Blue Mesa Review* and *Electric Mercado*; "The Snake" in *Blue Mesa Review* and *Electric Mercado*; "The Abuelita" in *Río Grande Review*; "The Gardener" in *American Way*; and "Espíritu Santo" in *Electric Mercado* and *T-Zero Writers' Annual*.

Acknowledgments

Sergio Troncoso, the son of Mexican immigrants, was born in El Paso, Texas, and now lives in New York City. After graduating from Harvard, he was a Fulbright Scholar to Mexico and studied international relations and philosophy at Yale, where he now teaches during the summer. His work has appeared in *Hadassah Magazine, Other Voices, T-Zero Writers' Annual, New World: Young Latino Writers* (Dell), *Electric Mercado, American Way, Blue Mesa Review,* and *Río Grande Review.* His e-mail address is STroncoso@aol.com.

About the Author